RUSHED

Gina Robinson

Gina Robinson
SEATTLE, WASHINGTON

www.ginarobinson.com

Publisher's Note: This is a work of fiction. Names, characters, places, and incidents are a product of the author's imagination. Locales and public names are sometimes used for atmospheric purposes. Any resemblance to actual people, living or dead, or to businesses, companies, events, institutions, or locales is completely coincidental.

Book Layout ©2014 BookDesignTemplates.com

Rushed/ Gina Robinson. — 2nd ed.
ISBN 978-0692237960

For my very own live-in houseboy

Alexis

My mom called it rushing. The university called it recruitment. I just called it hell. Dressed in a short, bright sundress and ridiculously high platform pumps, I stood in the hot August sunshine in front of the Delta Delta Psi house. I was surrounded by my Rho Gam group of nervous, excited girls all hoping for the chance at instant popularity. Was I the only one who wished she were anyplace but here? And not out of fear, but genuine desire not to become a Double Deltsie?

The Greek system was supposed to be about finding a house where you fit in. About choice. About joining a group of likeminded girls who would become your sisters. Not about being forced into a certain house because of family pressure. A house where you were sure you would feel like a misfit.

Delta Delta Psi, with its tall, stately, columned white house and manicured lawn, was the top sorority on campus and ridiculously crazy hard to get into. The Double Deltsies, as they were popularly known, were the hottest, richest, blondest, hardest-partying house on campus. They led the Greek system with the most homecoming queens, cheerleaders, and heiresses. They got astronomically top scores on GreekRank.com. So high, even sniping trolls from lesser houses couldn't bring it down.

Get into the Double Deltsies, and not only did you have drop-dead gorgeous sisters for life, you had connections that could not be bought. And access to the hottest frat guys at the university. The guys who would inherit their parents' fortunes and businesses. Guys who, if my dad's friends were any indication, would become the fat old dipshits of the future.

I was blond enough, skinny enough, dressed well enough in the right designer brand of clothes, and passably well off enough to be a Double Deltsie. I certainly didn't feel gorgeous enough. But that didn't matter. Because I held the trump card. I was a third-generation legacy. The only way I had a prayer of *not* getting into the house was if I intentionally blew the recruitment process or didn't preference their house.

Tempting. Very tempting. And a totally stupid, futile show of defiance. My parents held the purse strings and were paying for college. Which meant I toed the line. Even if I sabotaged my interviews and the Delta

Delta Psis didn't invite me back after the first round, my parents would raise hell and get me in. They had the connections to do it.

I would be a Double Deltsie even if I dropped out of recruitment week. Probably even if I dropped out of college. That's how serious my parents were about this "opportunity of a lifetime," as they called it. And upholding the family Double Deltsie tradition.

The morning sun was parching. It was already past eighty in the shade. The breeze did little except feebly rattle the leaves overhead, like the heat had exhausted it, too. Our Rho Gamma, Molly, the sorority girl assigned to shepherd my group around, looked uncomfortable as we waited for our appointment. We weren't supposed to know which house she was from. But we'd pretty much figured out she was from one of the lowliest houses on campus. The misfit house, the house that took anyone. No one wanted to be there except social outcasts desperate to be Greek at any cost.

I felt for Molly. She was tall and big-boned with fine, mousy brown hair and eyes that were set too close together. Soft at the middle. Dressed in the obligatory Rho Gam T-shirt for the first day of house visits. And awkwardly sweet and conscientious to the point of trying too hard. At least she attempted to coach us and give us good advice and encouragement. Some of the snootier Rho Gams didn't.

But she was out of her element here and a liability as far as getting into the Double Deltsie house. Or any good house, really. She'd tried to take me on as someone she wanted to impress. So she hung by my side as often as possible, trying to be my friend in a way that reeked of desperation.

The house she was rumored to be from was trying to up its prestige by getting a higher caliber of pledges. They needed a good pledge class or they would fall further in the rankings. Their alums would cut off their support, and without them, the house would close. I was apparently in their crosshairs.

I'd heard some of the girls make unkind comments about Molly. Most of them were unhappy about being assigned to her group.

I was already tainted with the scent of Double Deltsie-ness as far as Molly was concerned. That's why she was after me for her house. At the same time, she was skittish and wary when I was pleasant to her, doubting my motives and wondering if I was just trying to make fun of her. And ridiculously pleased with herself at the same time.

The door to the house opened and the homecoming queen from last fall, now the chapter president, opened the door to welcome us in. Looking at her, and how perfect and pretty she was, I thought that if it wasn't for being a legacy, there was no way I had a prayer at this house. I had to fight my insecurities.

A line from my AP Lit class, from Dante's *Inferno*, came to me: "*Lasciate ogne speranza, voi ch'intrate*" or "Abandon all hope, ye who enter here."

Yes, I was in the ninth circle of hell, trapped by my parents' vision of what was right for me.

I walked in the middle of my recruitment group into the house that was decorated with banners and balloons. Past the cheering, chanting Double Deltsies as they showed their exuberance for our visit.

Next to me, my new friend Emily gave me a small smile. Emily was the right kind of girl to get into a decent sorority—friendly, smart, pretty, knew how to dress. She was a brunette, which counted against her as far as being a Double Deltsie. But that was easily remedied. I gave her a shot at getting a bid from the Double Deltsies, but it was a long one. More likely she'd end up at a comfortably middle-of-the-road house. Which was where I wanted to be.

I envied her. She was going to have the right kind of Greek experience and probably make real friends for life.

"What do you think of your future home?" Em whispered to me as we looked around. She knew about my legacy status.

The formal sitting and living rooms were the nicest and best kept of any of the houses we'd visited. Everything was immaculate and smelled of perfume and flowers. Bouquets of dahlias and late summer blooms sat on the console table and end tables. Unlike the other houses, it was air-conditioned and welcomingly cool.

I rolled my eyes. "I don't belong here."

Emily laughed. "Sure you do. Keep your chin up."

Then we were paired off for our interviews with a girl from the house. Emily got her partner first and disappeared into the study room. I was the last girl left standing when my name was finally called. Maybe it was my imagination, but I felt the chapter president staring at me and taking my measure as the crowd thinned.

Generally, it was a good thing to catch the attention of the president. It meant you were under serious consideration, that the house loved you. I had the feeling this winnowing from the herd was intentional. That the president wanted to see the legacy that was being forced on her. Was I worthy? Or would she have to find a way to neutralize my stench on the house reputation?

I smiled at her with the smile I'd been coached by my mom to use during rush. I pretended to be pleased and flattered by her attention. Confident and shy at the same time. Reverent. Respectful. Excited. It was a good thing I was a good actress. I had a moment of panic that she would be interviewing me. But at the last minute, she waved a hand and a girl named Morgan stepped up to lead me away.

"You have a beautiful house," I said to Morgan just loud enough for the president to hear, too. Always lead with flattery.

"We like it." Morgan led me to the living room and a comfortable sofa. Clearly, I was being given VIP treatment. "How has your experience been so far?"

"Awesome!" I smiled back at her, hoping it didn't look forced. "I love the campus and the feeling of camaraderie among the girls I've met." At other houses.

Morgan smiled back at me and listened with what looked like rapt attention. But I knew her kind of girl—confident to the point of stuck-up. A total viper. I had been paired with the premier house interrogator. The snake sent to swallow potential pledges whole.

Lucky me.

I was parched. I had to clear my throat several times as I gushed about recruitment. My dress stuck to my damp back and thighs as I sat straight and poised on the sofa with perfect posture. I suppressed a shiver as the air conditioner kicked on.

Some of the houses served refreshments and had a casual, friendly vibe. Not this house. A pitcher of ice water, beading with condensation, sat on the coffee table in front of us. Morgan made no move to offer me any. And I was too stubborn to ask for some. Something told me that if I poured myself a glass I would fail an important test. So, of course, I was tempted. I wanted water and I wanted to fail. But I resisted.

Morgan was totally pleasant and kept the conversation going almost effortlessly. Which made me wary—when would she strike? Yes, we were supposed to like our interviewers. For now. Until they axed us after acting like our best friend for half an hour.

I did think that we connected. I tried, anyway.

We chatted about almost nothing at all, just made small talk about home and majors and family. This is the way recruitment went. You talked and talked so the house could get to know you. But really, it was just one person's opinion that was going to make or break you in the first round. Just this one girl I had to impress.

She would act like all the rest—friendly, like she could be my new best friend. And then she'd use subterfuge and innocuous questions to find out whether I was Double Deltsie material or not.

"Why do you want to be part of the Greek system?" Morgan leaned forward like she really wanted to know.

"The sense of community! I love the sense of community." I repeated what my mom had told me to say. "Not just for now, but for life. I'm an only child. The idea of a sisterhood is simply thrilling. Sisters I've never had, hundreds of them!" My voice was full of exclamation points, my mother's exclamation points and inflection.

Morgan's smile grew more real as she listened.

"I also love the commitment to philanthropy and community service that the Greek system embodies. In high school I was president of the Key Club..." I went through my practiced talking points, saying all the right things like the good girl I was. Like the girl who would not disappoint her overly proud parents, no matter how much she wanted to.

I had just finished my get-into-the-best-sorority dissertation when a movement near the entrance to the living room caught my attention. I looked up. My breath caught and I had to fight to keep my mouth from popping open into an open gape of lust. The most gorgeous guy I had ever seen stood in the doorway, carrying a tray of tiny cupcakes. He was over six feet and broad shouldered, with dark, wavy hair and snapping blue eyes. He wore black slacks, dress shoes, and a white dress shirt with a bowtie at the collar. His sleeves were rolled up, revealing perfectly sculpted forearms and the hint of a tattoo on the inside of his arm. He was dressed, I realized, like a waiter. Or a piece of beefcake.

"Like what you see?" Morgan asked.

The real test had begun.

"What is a guy doing here?" During recruitment, the girls were forbidden from talking to a guy at all— no phoning or texting or IMing or Instagramming or emailing. No contact. You could get kicked out of recruitment for violating the rule.

What was this, a trick?

"That's just Zach," she whispered to me. There was an undertone to her voice I couldn't quite put my finger on. "He's just one of our live-in houseboys." The way she said it could have been a put-down, but wasn't. It was more like pride. "There are three more like him. Equally hot."

Definitely pride. She was bragging now. "We're the only house on campus with live-in houseboys." Her smile grew from devious to wicked. "They serve our *every* need." The innuendo in her voice was thick. And, if it wasn't my imagination, filled with longing.

Morgan waved Zach over with a flick of her wrist. "I bet you're thirsty." She picked up the pitcher of water and a clear plastic cup from a stack next to it. "And hungry."

I was keenly aware of Zach as he crossed the room and stopped in front of me with his tray of pink cupcakes. Up close, I got a whiff of his cologne. He evidently knew the rules about the girls being unable to speak to guys during recruitment. He didn't utter a word, but he was clearly studying me beneath the mask he put on. His eyes were sharp and intelligent and sparkled with a trace of rebellion and protest that was hinted at by the way he'd rolled up his sleeves.

A kindred spirit, I thought as my awareness of him only heightened. *He doesn't want to be here any more than I do. He's trapped, too.*

I don't know why I found that so exciting, but I did. Since I'd arrived on campus, it had been a constant feast for the eyes—I'd never seen so many totally hot guys in one place before. But what I felt now was something different than mere appreciation. This was that feeling you get only a handful of times, if you're lucky. That adrenaline rush of attraction that is inexplicable, unexpected, and so thrilling it makes you jittery and nervous. Like you don't want to blow it. It's that feeling you get when you read a book you can't put down.

There are a lot of good-looking men around. But only so many that totally thrill you with just a look. My head warned me to proceed cautiously. My heart pounded out of control. This was attraction at first sight at its finest.

I hoped Morgan misread the goosebumps on my arms as the result of the overactive air-conditioning, not a reaction to Zach. It took all my willpower, but I resisted anything but a benign smile.

I was dying to hear his voice. My skin prickled with awareness of him. If that voice matched the rest of him, I would have to melt into the sofa right there.

Morgan snapped her fingers. The rebellious look in his eye intensified. I wondered if Morgan knew how much he resented her. From the hungry way she looked at him, I guessed not.

He offered me a tea napkin and held the tray out for me to pick a cupcake, holding my gaze with his just long enough to be indecent and just short enough to avoid detection by Morgan. His reaction to me confused me. I felt misjudged by him and wanted to correct him. *I'm not like them! I wouldn't act like a princess to your servant.*

I would have screamed it if I could.

I had the strong feeling that if I refused this cupcake offering, I would be snubbing the house. And most particularly, Morgan. I had the feeling she would be a formidable enemy, one I had no desire to make.

I took a napkin embossed with the Delta Delta Psi logo, narrowly avoiding a brush with his fingers. Even still I felt the heat radiating from him. I could have sat there all day deciding between chocolate and pink lemonade cupcakes just so he wouldn't leave. But I also didn't want him to think I was lording his servitude over him. I grabbed a cupcake with a swirl of pink frosting and a gorgeous gum paste pink rose, the house flower, on top, looking into his eyes as I did.

And then the real dilemma set in. I had to show him I wasn't a stuck-up bitch. But if I even said something as benignly polite as thank you, I was in violation of the rules. If I said nothing, I was rude to this enigma of a guy.

Something about him made me fight to come up with a solution. Beneath his calm exterior pulsed a strong sense of pride. The look in his eyes challenged me to either defy Morgan or snub him. The last thing I wanted to do was insult this guy. Suddenly, the Double Deltsie house was looking a lot better than it had five minutes ago. All because of him.

What did the Double Deltsies expect? When presented with the unwinnable scenario, stretch the rules. That's my motto. The smart thing to do might have been to ask Morgan to pass along my thanks. But I wasn't the type to beg for favors.

I set the cupcake on the coffee table in front of me and signed the word for thank you to him. Nothing in the rules said you couldn't sign. Or send smoke signals. Or use semaphore code. Or Morse code, for that matter. Frankly, if he didn't know sign language, it wouldn't be communication at all.

He simply stared back at me with a blank, uninterested look. Not a crack of a smile. Almost like I was beneath his notice. But his eyes sparkled with admiration for my guts.

Call me crazy, but I was both intrigued and angered by him. He turned and held the tray out for Morgan.

She took her time choosing. When she finally made her choice, she intentionally brushed his hand with hers. "Thank you, Zach."

He nodded and walked off without saying anything, even to her.

I sensed her seething at him. Longing for him.

But as soon as he disappeared from sight, Morgan smiled like I'd passed some kind of test. "How many years of sign language did you take?"

"Three."

"Excellent! We do some work with a deaf class at the local elementary school. Your skills will come in handy."

I couldn't tell what she was so happy about, but she kept smiling. I got the feeling that I was going to get top marks when she reported to the president and the selection committee. I'd passed the philanthropy test and it wasn't even philanthropy day yet.

Morgan leaned in and whispered to me, "You'll be making a suicide bid for us, I hope." Her eyes danced with amused malice and the excitement of putting a prospective pledge on the hot seat.

"If that's what it takes to get into the house, absolutely." I kept my game face on, but beneath it, I was seething now, too. I picked my cupcake up and casually pulled the paper back from it.

Asking for a suicide bid was supremely arrogant. And against the rules. The girls at the houses weren't allowed to talk about bids, not even to hint about them. Saying something as innocuous as "I'll see you later" was a violation. Morgan knew there was no way I could rat on her. Who would believe my word against hers, anyway?

A suicide bid meant that when it came time to select a house, I would put in that I would only accept an offer from the Double Deltsies. And take the chance they'd screw me over and not offer back. She thought she was scaring me. But she wasn't. For me, a suicide bid could be the perfect out.

I took a bite of my cupcake. "Delicious!"

When the interview was finally over, Morgan led me to the lobby and made a point of introducing me to Kelly, the house president. I had been anointed.

After my quick interview with Kelly, I met up with Emily and the rest of my group. Molly was scowling at Kelly like she was poaching in her territory.

The Double Deltsies ended our visit with their house chant. "Delta Delta Psi, my, oh, my! Delta Delta Psi!"

Molly led us into the heat of the day to the front walk of the house that ambled past a row of basement windows on its way to the main sidewalk. As we walked away, I caught a glimpse of a guy in the basement window. *Zach.* Watching us. Watching me with a look that me made me hot and flushed all over.

I looked away from him, feeling exposed and elated, hoping he couldn't get a glimpse up my skirt and wondering if he sat there because of the view during rush. Or had he been watching for me?

"There's a guy in the house!" A girl named Caitlin giggled and pointed. The surprise was evident in her voice—she had no idea there were men in there.

The entire group, except for me, came to a halt and looked. From the corner of my eye, I caught the movement of Zach looking away. Conversation and speculation about guys living in sorority houses, particularly the Delta Delta Psi house, erupted around us.

Molly grimaced and hurried us along. "The Double Deltsies are the only house that has live-in houseboys. The others have houseboys that come in for the day."

She nodded toward the house we were walking away from. "They choose theirs based on looks, not skills. Any girl in that house should be warned to stay away from them. Those houseboys have a bad reputation and are beneath a girl in the Greek system."

Molly's sense of class entitlement shocked me. A guy as hot as Zach would never notice her, but he was beneath her because he was working as a houseboy? In her dreams.

I realized something else, too—not every girl had gotten the cupcake treatment, or they would have known about Zach or one of the other houseboys.

I turned to Em. "Did they offer you a cupcake?"

"Cupcake? Are you joking?" She rolled her eyes in a way that made me laugh. "Feed the masses? Let them eat cake? Ha-ha!

"I barely got water. And they withheld that until my throat was so dry I could barely talk. It's like they were torturing us in there."

"You got water?" someone else asked Em with admiration in her voice. "Lucky! You must have had one of the nice interviewers."

I had gotten special treatment, then. Very special treatment. And Em had gotten semi-special treatment. Maybe she had a chance after all.

I linked my arm with hers.

"Did they actually give you a cupcake?" she whispered in my ear.

"No," I lied. "Just wondering if they gave refreshments to anyone or if I had the least pleasant interrogator in the house."

She gave me a puzzled frown. "Did you even get water?"

"At the very end." That much was true.

"Hey, maybe they like us!" Em squeezed my arm, but she didn't seem particularly impressed.

"Let's pledge the same house!" I said on impulse. "A house with lots of cake." I figured she had at least a ghost of a chance of getting into the Double Deltsie sorority with me. They'd offered her water, hadn't they?

CHAPTER TWO

Zach

"There's a guy in the house!" The group of girls going through recruitment stopped outside our basement room window and pointed down at me. My view was mostly of them from the waist down, legs and ankles made slender by incredibly tall heels.

Shit, their surprise never got old. It was damned hilarious. We lived for this view. Give me a girl with long, sleek legs any day.

"Seth, get your lazy ass over here before you miss the latest view," I said to my roommate.

I looked for a particular pair of shoes in the tangle of legs passing by my window. Wondering if her ankles were as slender and fine as I remembered. I got lucky.

She stood far enough away at just the right angle so I could see her stunning face.

I was looking at her, the girl Morgan had been interrogating. And trying to get her out of my mind as our eyes met and she caught me. She glanced away quickly. I'd caught her looking back.

Dwelling on her was fucking stupid. My head warned me against her. My mission here was to be a big brother to the girls in the house, not a lover or boyfriend. I was doing penance for not being the big brother I should have been to my real sister. I would be atoning for that for the rest of my life.

If I were smart, I would be hoping she wouldn't get into the house. But I knew she would. Morgan had been giving her special treatment. For some reason, this girl was a VIP PNM—potential new member.

Across our room, lounging on his twin bed, my roommate Seth laughed as he pulled his bowtie off and flung it on his desk next to the bed. "Shit! It never gets old hearing their surprise."

"My thoughts exactly."

Seth was the heartbreaker of the four of us, the guy who cared least about being in the servant class.

The pudgy Rho Gam in charge of the group issued a command to move on with enough disgust and volume in it to let us know how she felt about us. Can't be late for the next appointment. She was probably a Siggy Piggy Up, as the frats and the girls unkindly called them.

"Too late," I said. "They're moving on."

"What did you think of this last group of girls?"
Seth asked.

I spun around in my desk chair to face him.
"They're interested in one, at least. Morgan made me
drag out the cupcakes."

Seth made a downturned-mouth, raised-eyebrows
face of surprise. "You had one. Lucky you. None this
batch for me. It was a damn waste of a bowtie."

I grinned at him. "Better luck next time."

"What did you think of her?" Seth unbuttoned the
collar of his shirt. Perspiration pooled beneath his
armpits. He took the shirt off and hung it over his desk
chair to dry out.

I weighed my answer carefully. "The recruit in the
living room with Morgan this morning surprised me."

Seth raised one eyebrow in question. "Yeah?"

"She looks the part of a Double Deltsie, right down
to her blond hair and makeup. She was hot, just as
smoking as any girl currently in the house. She'll be
getting a bid, I'm sure of it." Which meant more temptation, surprisingly for me. Usually Seth was the guy
who was tempted.

To date, no girl had broken through the wall of my
big-brotherly feelings. Damn if I would let this one. As
gorgeous as the girls of the house were, I'd never been
hot enough for one to jeopardize my position here. I
told myself it was because I saw them the way most
guys didn't. Not the guys they were trying to impress,
anyway.

I saw them hung over and pale, puffy-eyed from
crying their eyes out over some douchebag, without

makeup, in their ratty pajamas with their hair at odd angles, bent over with menstrual cramps. I cleaned their toilets, emptied their trashcans, and set their tables. Listened to their problems, inner turmoil, and insecurities. Kept their secrets.

The veil was lifted for me, their illusion of perfection shattered. If this girl, the PNM, joined the house, she would be the same, just another little sister. I hoped.

Seth sat up straighter. "Then what's the surprise?"

"This one was different. She said all the right things to Morgan. Had the perfect smile on her face. Looked just right in just the right brand of dress. But she put Morgan in her place. Subtly, but she did it."

Seth gave a low whistle. "A girl with spunk. I like her already. She defied Morgan." He nodded like he applauded the effort. "Why are you so sure she's getting in?"

I didn't feel like explaining. "She did it so subtly, I'm not sure Morgan even realized." That was what I admired about her.

That and, in the unguarded moments when Morgan wasn't looking, the look in the girl's eyes that said she would rather be anywhere but here. In the two years I'd been a houseboy, I'd never seen a girl as unimpressed with the Double Deltsies as she'd been. Or a PNM as creative and thoughtful.

The way she signed thank you to me had been sweet and defiant with that little flourish she put in it. In two years, no PNM had thanked me for anything during rush. Most of them were too damned afraid to speak and be kicked out.

I'd worked in the house since my freshman year, when a friend got me in. Shit, I would rather have been an RA in the dorms. I could make amends in a coed dorm as well as here. But this job gave me room and board *and* a small salary. The dorms only gave room and board. I needed every dime.

So I stuck it out with Paul, Seth, and Dillon as breakfast cooks, handymen, waiters, and shoulders to cry on. And developed some genuine affection for most of the girls, despised a few as shallow and vain, and made a few true friends with both the girls and the houseboys. At least I had a sense of community and be-longing. Something I never had at home.

I unbuttoned my shirt and pulled it off. Seth and I both sat in our room naked-chested, trying to cool off. It was hard to believe, but the basement wasn't air-conditioned. It was hotter than the main floors this time of year. We had an hour to relax until the next group of recruitment girls came by. We were going to stay as cool as we could.

"Think they'll make their quota?" Seth got up and pulled an energy drink from our mini fridge. He grabbed a second one and tossed it to me.

"They always make their quota."

"Girl on the floor!" The happy singsong tone reached us about half a second before its owner did. "Boys!" Morgan appeared in our doorway and shook her finger at us, playfully. "You're out of uniform."

Her gaze slid over our naked chests, lingering on mine with hunger in her eyes, like she wanted to give me a lap dance then and there.

She'd changed, too, into cutoffs so short her butt cheeks hung out, and a crop top so thin her dark, round nipples poked through even in the heat. She was tan and toned and wore a bellybutton ring with crystals dangling.

She was into me and mostly ignored Seth's charms. Yeah, she flirted with him. All the Double Deltsies were unrepentant flirts. But it was purely playful. For some unfathomable reason of her own, Morgan wanted me. Maybe because I remained unobtainable. Or because I was forbidden fruit. Or she was rebelling against authority. Who the hell knew her thought process?

I wasn't about to risk my job for a girl as changeable and vindictive as Morgan.

"You're out of uniform, too, Morgan, babe." Seth winked at her.

She took that as invitation, strutted into our room with hips swaying, and sat cross-legged in Seth's desk chair.

"What brings you to our lair?" Seth pointed to the mini-fridge. "Help yourself."

"No thanks." She rolled her eyes. "I had to escape for a minute and relax. Kelly is on everyone's case about recruitment."

"Not going well?" Seth kicked off his dress shoes and put his legs on the bed, lounging against his pillows as he sipped his drink.

"Not many good candidates this year. Bad crop. Kelly's on our case to up our game. Like we can magically produce girls who meet our standards." She swung her gaze back to me. "Only one or two we're even mildly interested in. Zach, you met one of them last hour. What did you think?"

Shit. I'd guessed Morgan had an agenda in coming to see us. Agenda revealed. She wasn't dragging me into this. The way Morgan watched me, I sensed my opinion mattered more than it should. Like whether that girl got into the house or not hinged on me. I could have gotten the girl axed right then if I let any hint I found her the least bit attractive show. With the way my body reacted to her, maybe I should have. My sense of fairness stopped me. That and my raging desire to see her again.

I shrugged like I'd hardly noticed her. "What do I know? I just handed her a cupcake. You're the one who interviewed her."

Morgan wouldn't let it drop. "You don't have an opinion?"

"She looks like a Double Deltsie. Talks like a Double Deltsie. Dresses like one." I set my can on my desk.

"If she looks like one, talks like one, and dresses like one, what's the big deal, Morgan?" Seth held his hands up like he really didn't understand the fuss. "Make her your rush crush. Get her into the house and get Kelly off your back. Problem solved."

Morgan's eyes lit up at the thought. "Good idea, Seth. I will. I definitely will. It will save me a whole lot of trouble. The girl's a third-generation legacy.

There's practically no way we can get rid of her anyway. If she turns out to be a disappointment, there's no
way I can be blamed." She smiled at me as she watched
my reaction.

"Congrats, Morgs. I hope you and your rush crush
will be very happy together." I picked up my energy
drink and downed the rest as if I didn't care about seeing the girl again.

In reality, my heart was racing. But my head was
saying *slow down*. A third-generation legacy? The girl
had Double Deltsie blood running through her veins.
And I was nothing but a houseboy. Fuck it.

Alexis

As we walked down Greek Row past the frats back
to the dorm where we were staying, we got hoots and
whistles. Some of the frat houses were just animals.
They were easy to ignore. But as we walked past Tau
Psi, the top frat on campus, three gorgeous frat guys
lounged on the stone steps that led up from the sidewalk to the walkway of their house. They were shirtless
and in cutoffs. Ripped abs slathered with suntan oil and
glistening in the sunlight. And they were holding and
playing with one of the cutest tiny puppies in the
world.

My Rho Gam group slowed to a halt and let out a
collective sigh. "A puppy!"

The guys got up and came toward us.

Em's eyes went wide. "A Pomsky puppy!" She took a
step toward the guys and the puppy.

The hottest guy reached us, grinned, and held the happily barking puppy out to Em like candy.

I grabbed her arm and hissed into her ear as if I was her mom or her conscience, "Are you crazy? That puppy is their version of a siren song. A hot guy with a cute puppy is simply irresistible. They know it. They'll put that puppy in your arms, and the next thing you know, you'll be talking to the guys and get kicked out of rush. Is that what you want?"

Em froze. "You're right! Wow, devious of them."

Molly failed us then, almost falling prey to the puppy trick herself. But then, she wasn't the one who would be kicked out.

"Girls!" I called out to my group. "It's a trap to get you to talk to them. Ignore the puppy and keep walking."

Heads turned to me. Eyes snapped with gratitude. "Crap! She's right," someone said. I had just made fifteen friends for life.

The group surged ahead even as the guys stood and carried the baby Pomsky into the middle of us, nuzzling it, holding it out as they cooed to the puppy and us. Molly finally sprang into action and tried to shoo the boys away.

The ringleader stepped in front of me, blocking my path. "Blondie," he said to me as he cuddled the puppy beneath his chin and grinned. "Future Double Deltsie." He whistled and gave me an up-and-down look full of appreciation and lust. "I'll be seeing you at a function soon."

He pulled his cell phone from his pocket and held it out to me. "You don't have to talk to me. Type in your number so I can call you."

I looked away from him before I gave in to my desire to put him in his place for treating me like a sex object. And yet, at the same time, I enjoyed his attention. I tried to step around him. Much as I hated to admit it, he had charisma.

Em tried to help me. But he blocked my path whichever way I moved, tempting me to ask him to get out of my way.

Finally Molly came to my rescue and pushed her way between him and me. "Get away from my PNMs."

I looked up from beneath my lashes at them to see what was going on.

The frat guy shrugged. "Sure, Rho Gam. Whatever you say." He backed off. As he walked away, he leaned into me and whispered in my ear, "Looking forward to talking with you soon, PNM. Name's Dakota Bradley"—he glanced at my nametag—"Alexis Turner. Pretty name."

The puppy squirmed in his arms. Dakota cuddled the cute little dog to him and walked off, laughing.

That evening we filled out our preference forms. There were fifteen sorority houses on campus. In the first cut, we could only be invited back to a maximum of ten. We had to submit an electronic form with our bottom five choices. I hesitated over my last choice, so tempted to fill in the Double Deltsies. Good sense—and a futile sense of destiny—won out. I didn't enter their name. The truth was I wanted to see Zach again.

I turned to Em, who was sitting next to me in the Student Union Building—SUB—coffee shop as we filled our forms out together. "You're not cutting the Double Deltsies, are you? I can't go to them alone."

She looked across her laptop at me and rolled her eyes. "No. For your sake, legacy girl." Then she laughed and grinned at me, and I knew she was teasing. She wanted the Double Deltsies to invite her back.

"Good." I took a sip of iced mocha.

"Don't look so relieved. They probably won't invite me back for philanthropy day."

I smiled back at her. "You are so totally philanthropic, I bet they will."

The next morning, I woke up early and checked my Group Me app for instructions. Our Rho Gam group was meeting at eight. I logged into my recruitment account and held my breath. I had ten invitations, including from the Double Deltsies and Molly's house, even though I'd cut it.

I texted Em. She replied immediately. "Yep, still under consideration with the Double Deltsies."

During the second day, we no longer traveled as a group. Our individual appointments were at different times. I went to the Double Deltsie house full of anticipation, hoping I would get a glimpse of Zach. I was on my best behavior as Morgan interviewed me a second time, and Kelly stopped by for part of it. This time they offered me sparkling punch instead of water, but no cupcake. Maybe I was out.

That afternoon I met with Em at the SUB again. We now had to preference down to seven for the house visits. Em and I discussed our choices.

"I envy you," I told her as I looked over my list. There were two houses I was absolutely in love with. The girls were fun and friendly and warm. I felt like I really fit in there. Two houses that were almost as good. None of them were the Double Deltsies.

"Why?" Em asked. "I might not even get a bid."

"You'll get a bid. One from the perfect house for you. And you have a choice. You can actually pick the house you want to get into. You'll make friends for life and have more fun than you should be allowed to."

"And you?" she said.

"I'm stuck with the Delta Delta Psis no matter how much of a misfit I'll be there."

"Some girls would kill to have your problem." She sounded genuinely envious.

"Are you going to cut them?" I asked.

"Not this time."

"I'm cutting Molly's house. Again," I said with a grin. "They didn't get the hint last time."

Em laughed with me. "Not from me, either! They want us, girl."

The next morning, we met with our Rho Gam group. As the cuts became more severe and more and more girls weren't being invited back to their favorite houses, I began to dread meeting up. There was too much heartbreak and too many tears.

I joined Em as Molly handed out our invitations. I held my breath as I read my list. My two favorites, my legacy house, and Molly's were still on my list of invites for house visits. "You?" I asked Em.

"Still under consideration at all our favorite places." She flashed her invites at me.

"Okay, then," I said, feeling relieved. "Off to see the wizard!" I linked my arm with hers.

"Let's just avoid little dogs." She squeezed my arm. "How soon after recruitment's over do you think Dakota will call you? You know, he's the Tau Psi president."

I frowned at her, surprised by the news. "Really?" I shook my head. "Then why would he be interested in me? I'm sure he was just teasing."

CHAPTER THREE

Alexis

I was still in love with two of the houses with a desperate kind of longing, the kind you get when you know something is out of your reach. Em and I went to the first two houses together. Then parted ways for separate appointments and ended up at the Double Deltsie house together in the late afternoon in the next-to-last appointment of the day.

As recruitment progressed, everyone got more serious, more tired, more competitive, and more stressed. Both the PNMs and the girls in the houses. The bubbly, perky atmosphere vanished. Tonight we PNMs had to preference down to only three houses. And the houses had to decide whom they were serious enough about to show the inner workings and some of their rituals to tomorrow.

Kelly greeted us again at the door for our tour. This time, there would be no separate appointments. She gave us an introduction and a brief history of the house, which I knew by heart thanks to my mom, and then we were shown the house. It was truly gorgeous, with the nicest sleeping porch, the largest rooms, the most amenities, a large, sunny breakfast nook, a pretty formal dining room, and a comfortable study room. The house itself was wonderful. I just didn't feel I fit with them.

The PNMs, too, had been culled. The group I took the tour with were all Double Deltsie material, or close to it. I kept thinking that a subset of these girls would be my pledge class. And, sad to say, the thought wasn't thrilling.

As Em and I toured the house side by side, I felt Morgan, who was one of the girls helping with the tour, watching me. Which messed with the part of me that wanted to sneak off and "accidentally" run into Zach. Halfway through the tour, my feet were killing me, and I was still under Morgan's tight surveillance. After a day on my feet, I just wanted to sit down.

I flagged one of the girls helping with the tour and asked for directions to the powder room.

She pointed the way. "Down the hall, around the corner, first door on your right."

"Want to come with?" I asked Em.

She shook her head. It was like she was actually into the tour.

"Take notes so you can fill me in later. I'll be right back," I told her, and made my way around the corner. The powder room was easy enough to find, but small— only two stalls—and mercifully empty. I zipped in and closed the door behind me, taking a deep breath as I leaned my head back against it. Free at last! For the moment, anyway.

I was just about to open a stall door when I spotted a pair of bare, muscled male legs sticking out from beneath one of the sinks. I let out an involuntary gasp of surprise.

I must have startled the guy. His legs moved and then his head banged something beneath the sink.

"Fuck!" he said in the smoothest, sexiest voice I could have imagined.

"Sorry!" Even though he couldn't see me, I pointed and looked back to the door like it was to blame. "There was no sign that warned a guy was in here doing repairs." And okay, I had just failed recruitment and spoken to a guy.

He slid out from beneath the sink, holding his head and squinting up at me as he sat up. My heart plummeted to my stomach like I had just gone over the steepest hill of a rollercoaster. *Zach!*

"Crap!" I fell into a crouch beside him and stared at his bloody fingers where he was holding his head. He had an open gash on his gorgeous forehead. "You're bleeding."

I popped back up, grabbed a couple of paper towels from the dispenser, soaked them in cold water in the sink next to the one he'd been working on, and crouched back beside him to press it gently against the gash.

He winced and wiped his fingers on his sweat-soaked T-shirt.

"Don't do that. You'll ruin your shirt. Here. Use this." I kept the pressure on his head while I handed him a spare damp paper towel.

He wiped his fingers. "Why couldn't you just ignore me, pee, wash your hands, and leave like the rest of the girls?"

I stared at him, stunned. "Girls actually do that? Act like you're invisible while they pee?" I made a face to show my disgust.

He grinned at me, making me weak in the knees. "Yeah, PNM, they do. Get used to it."

I didn't think I would ever get used to him and that golden voice of his. I pulled the paper towel away from his head long enough to take a look at the damage. "You're going to have a goose egg. It's already popping up."

He grimaced.

"No, that's good," I reassured him. "It means you probably don't have a concussion or a serious head wound."

"Thanks, Florence Nightingale."

I put the paper towel back against his head and applied pressure, fighting off the tingly way touching him made me feel and trying not to blush. "You should ice that."

I handed him the paper towel and started to rise. "I'll get you some. Keep the pressure on while I'm gone. The bleeding should stop soon. It's just a small gash. But you could use a butterfly bandage, too."

I tried to stand. He caught me by the wrist. I hoped he couldn't feel the way my pulse leaped at his touch.

"No!" He shook his head and squeezed my wrist. "They'll realize you talked to me and kick you out. You'll blow your shot at being a Double Deltsie."

I couldn't help it. I laughed without humor. "You don't know who you're dealing with. I'll be a Double Deltsie no matter how many rules I break." I caught myself too late. That sounded way too arrogant and stuck up. I softened my tone. "Taking care of you is more important than pledging this house. I don't think killing their houseboy is going to win me any bids, either."

He smiled, let go of my wrist, and pulled the paper towel away to see if he was still bleeding. "Stay, please. I'll be okay. I would never forgive myself if I was the reason you didn't get in here."

Something about his teasing tone stopped me and made my heart race. Was he flirting with me? I let out a sigh. "I can't believe this. I've made it past guys carrying adorable Pomsky puppies without breaking my vow of silence toward men, and I blow it in the ladies' room?"

"The Tau Psis are still using the old puppy trick, are they?"

I gave him a hand and helped him to his feet. He didn't let go of mine immediately. We lingered too long holding hands. His was warm and strong. I longed to feel it cupping my head and pulling me into a kiss. But to hang on any longer was almost indecent. "You mean they've used it before?" I slid my hand free from his.

"Every year." He studied me for a minute before turning to squint in the mirror as he examined his head.

"You're a mess!" Over his shoulder, I studied his reflection in the mirror. "Give me your shirt."

"Wow. Subtle come-on." He grinned.

I rolled my eyes. "Take it off and let me rinse it out for you before that blood sets. Stripper moves are optional."

"Anything to get me out of my shirt. I like bold girls." He winked at me. "We houseboys are more than beefcake, you know."

I blushed. "Just trying to help." I held out my hand for it.

He stripped it off over his head, twirled it with a flourish and a sparkle in his yes, and tossed it to me like I was a groupie.

I kind of was. I almost went weak in the knees. The chest beneath that shirt was toned and ripped. I caught the shirt and turned to wash it out. It was filled with his body heat and smelled like him, of cologne and sweat.

I turned the water on and tried not to look at his bare chest as I ran the stained part of the shirt beneath cold water and wrung it out.

He held my gaze as I handed it back to him. Our hands brushed again. I had a crazy urge to grab his and not let go.

"You should get out of here before someone catches us." He took the partially wet shirt from me.

"And you should walk past the PNMs without your shirt on. You're as completely adorable as those puppies." It wasn't like me to be so bold.

He laughed.

I hated to leave, but I couldn't linger much longer without being missed by the all-seeing, all-watching Morgan. "You're right. I have to go."

"Oh, shit, PNM!" He grinned wickedly. "I'd almost forgotten why you came in here. Of course you do. Feel free to use the stall. I'll go back to work."

As if there was any way I'd be able to pee with the thought of him hearing me. I laughed and shook my head. "Not *that* way. I dodged in here to escape the hard sell and get a second of peace and quiet."

"Sorry I ruined it."

"No. You didn't." I smiled like a flirt. "See you around." I turned to leave. At the door, I hesitated and looked over my shoulder at him. "Zach?"

He looked surprised and flattered that I remembered his name.

"Are the girls in this house really as shallow and backbiting as their reputation?"

He looked even more surprised by my question. He shrugged. "They're like any house, a mixture. Some of them are all right."

Not exactly a ringing endorsement. Not a condemnation, either. You could tell a lot about people by the way they treated their help. That's what my grandma always said. Zach had just rendered the Delta Delta Psi as totally neutral.

I nodded and turned to leave.

He stopped me. "Make sure the coast is clear before you slip out, PNM."

I laughed. "Sure thing. Put a *Men at Work* sign up, okay? Unless you're trying to get a rep as a perv."

I caught up with Em and the rest of the PNMs in the dining room as they were eating cookies and drinking iced blended mochas.

"They went all out on refreshments. Wow!" I came up behind Em and grabbed a mocha. We'd been served sweets and sweet drinks at every house we'd visited. What I really wanted was a burger. I settled for a cookie.

Em frowned at me. "You were gone a long time."

"Was I?" I smiled coyly and took a bite of cookie, trying not to give myself away.

After the house visit, Em and I grabbed our laptops and went to sit at the edge of the open green beneath the shade of some tall trees. Guys were tossing footballs and flying discs. Music blasted. The air smelled of suntan lotion and sunscreen as Em and I made one of the most important decisions of our college careers.

Every other time we preferenced houses, we wrote down the houses we wanted to eliminate. This time, we had to enter in the three houses we wanted to keep. The sororities would then match our choices with their preferences and have a big meeting to hash things out. They had a top-secret system for negotiating when two houses wanted the same girl. We could preference three houses, but we could only get one bid. We either accepted that offer tomorrow at the bid meeting at the SUB, or declined to be Greek.

Some girls had only been invited to one house visit. They only had the option of writing that house down. Em and I had been to the maximum five house visits. That meant we could list one, two, or three choices. If we only listed one, that was called a suicide bid. Because if that house didn't want us, we'd just knocked ourselves out of getting into a house at all.

Em stared up at the sky, watching a bird chirp overhead in the branches. "Let's bid the same houses."

"Serious?" I said. "You know I have to put down the Double Deltsies?"

She nodded. "I like them."

I was shocked. If I'd been in her place, I would have chosen one of the other houses, one of two I really loved and felt comfortable in.

"But you could be in..." I named my two favorite houses. "I think you're definitely a rush crush of a recruiter in each house."

Em shrugged and looked away like she didn't want me to see what she was thinking. I hoped I hadn't misjudged her. I had thought she was real, not like the girls who just wanted popularity at any price.

"And you're Morgan's rush crush!" She made a point of watching the guys toss the football.

I rolled my eyes, thinking about how Morgan had told me to suicide bid. "I can't believe you'd sacrifice for me and take the chance of becoming a Double Deltsie."

"You're such a brat, Alexis!" She took a deep breath, turned her head toward me, and frowned. "I would kill to be in your shoes. I'm not doing this for you. I'm doing it for me."

Before I could reply, my cell phone buzzed. "My mom," I said to Em, and took the call. "Mom!"

"Hey, baby kid! How was your last day of rush? What did you think? Aren't the Double Deltsies fabulous!" Mom's voice was full of missing me, mixed with sunshine, hope, and a heavy dose of trying to influence me.

I hesitated. "Everything was great!" I feigned her perkiness and went for broke. "The Double Deltsies were really nice to me. I think I'm still one of their main recruiter's rush crushes."

"Of course you are, baby! Why wouldn't you be? Sorority greatness is in your blood."

It was hard to imagine my aging, graying, slightly plump mom had ever been a partying Double Deltsie. But I suspected, from what she'd told me about her college experiences, that they weren't the top house in her day. And that they were now was part of the reason she pushed me so hard to pledge them. Their prestige impressed her. The college girl she had been showed through in her voice and she sounded almost girlish— the pride, the desire to live through me, her hopes that I would have the excellent college experience that she had had. Her soaring hopes for my future and career.

"There are two other houses that I like a lot, too," I said, testing for wiggle room. "I think I could really fit

in those as well. The girls are fun and friendly, welcoming..."

There was a pregnant pause by my mom that said
just about everything.

"I can make three choices, but we can only get one
offer." I took a deep breath. "Morgan from the Double
Deltsies said I should suicide bid them. She broke the
rules by mentioning bids. There's nothing I can do
about that. But if I do suicide bid, and they don't pick
me..." I paused. "I think I should write all three houses
down."

"Morgan? The girl you've told me about? Their
toughest recruiter?" The pride came through in Mom's
voice. "Against the rules or not, if she told you to suicide bid, you'd better do it!"

"But if they don't pick me, I'll be out! I won't be
Greek. Wouldn't it be better to—"

"No!" I could almost picture Mom shaking her head,
and the wild look she got in her eye when she knew she
was right and worried that I wasn't going to listen to
her. That I was going to do something stupid, like
think for myself. "Do what Morgan says, baby. You
don't want to upset them."

"I could get a call before the bid meeting tomorrow
warning me not to show up. That I'm out and didn't
get a bid." My voice fell to match my heart. "Everyone
would know by my absence that I've been snubbed by
the Double Deltsies."

"No, Alexis! You? Never. I have complete faith in
you!" There was the pride again. And the pressure to
be perfect, just like there had been in high school.

The pressure I had hoped to escape at college. I was my parents' pride and joy. Their only child. Every one of the hopes and dreams rested on my shoulders.

"They won't snub you. They wouldn't *dare*." Her voice was fierce and full of the promise that if they snubbed me, my mama bear was going to come to the rescue. "Suicide bid them." There was that warning in her voice that dared me to defy her on peril of some extreme punishment.

I silently cursed the timing of her call. But I caved. "Okay, Mom."

The smile returned to her voice. "Call me tomorrow the minute you get your bid! This is so exciting. It reminds me of being young and going through rush..."

I ducked as an out-of-control football fell between Em and me, hardly listening as Mom reminisced and Em sized up the guy who came to retrieve his ball. He ignored her and gave me the up-and-down. I ignored him, acting as if I hadn't noticed. "I have to go, Mom. We need to have our preferences turned in by five."

"Oh, yes, yes! Get it done!" I could hear her inhale with excitement. "Call me tomorrow as soon as you get your bid!"

"Yeah, Mom. I will."

The guy left with his football. I hit the disconnect button.

"Well?" Em raised an eyebrow, grinning like she knew what Mom had said.

"Mom wants me to suicide bid. In her opinion, the Double Deltsies are the only house worth belonging to." I frowned.

Em studied me and laughed. "You don't agree?"

I shrugged. "I'm just not sure I fit there."

"What are you going to do?"

"What Mom wants, Mom gets," I said, trying to hide my resignation. "This may be suicide, but I'm going to suicide bid them." I typed them in on my onscreen form. "What are you going to do?"

"I'm not in the great position you are." She sounded almost sad about that. "I'm not committing suicide. I'm going for the Double Deltsies and the other two houses we liked." Then she laughed and turned to her attention to her laptop screen.

As Em typed, on impulse, I did something I rarely did—defied my mother. If the Double Deltsies wanted me badly enough, they could compete with the two houses I really wanted. I hit send with my heart pounding. Morgan wasn't going to tell me what I could do. And I wasn't giving her the chance to double-cross me.

Then, to distract Em from trying to get a glimpse of my screen as it disappeared, I laughed. "At least we can finally get rid of Molly's house."

That got Em to smile as she hit send, too. "Yeah, and I think you were her rush crush. Poor Molly! She'll be so disappointed." She paused and studied me. "No matter what happens tomorrow, let's stay friends, okay?"

I gave her a hug. "Always." But I had my doubts. If we pledged different houses, wouldn't we be competitors?

CHAPTER FOUR

Zach

Seth, Dillon, Paul, and I got up early to make Sunday breakfast for the girls. Betty, the cook, had weekends off. She left casseroles for us to stick in the oven for Saturday, and Sunday dinners and breakfast food for us to fix on Sunday. On Saturday we set out cereal and stuff to make toast and let the girls fend for themselves. On Sunday, we each had a specialty. Mine was scrambled eggs with cheese. Seth was a mean pancake flipper. Dillon was a potato man and Paul was a terrible cook. We usually made him man the toaster.

This was a big day, bid day, and the house hummed with anticipation. The girls had planned a special beach event at the river for their new pledges. The four of us houseboys had to help Kelly and the recruitment committee pack the picnic.

But before I helped Kelly and the rest of the officers haul the pledges' new pledge T-shirts to the SUB and then load the girls' cars with picnic supplies, I had to call my mom. A task that was right up there with scrubbing the toilets on Sunday morning after the girls had had a rough night of partying and drinking.

I went to my room for privacy and called, hoping Mom didn't chew me out for waking her.

"Zach." When she picked up, her voice had that irritated tone that she held in reserve for me alone. Like she barely tolerated me and didn't have the time to deal with my problems. Like I was *the* problem of her life.

"Sorry to bother you, Mom." I was always apologizing to her. In the background, I heard my spoiled twin half brothers roughhousing and screaming at each other as they played a video game.

Mom yelled at the boys to calm down, but her tone was hardly reprimanding. More like amused and thrilled with them. When she turned her attention back to me, her tone hardened. "What do you want?"

"I need you to forward my last paycheck from the summer. I can't pay my credit card bill without it."

"Zach, what have I told you about overspending? Cut down on the partying. Pare back on the social life so you can afford to pay for your responsibilities. Anyway, I thought you had direct deposit?"

Pare back? Like shit! What social life? If I cut down any more, I'd starve. The bitch didn't pay for a thing, but she had the nerve to rag on me about how I spent my money.

Without my job at the house and my scholarships that covered most of my tuition, I couldn't afford to go to college. Neither she nor Dad contributed a dime toward my education. Though both of them were rolling in dough. A half-assed decent mother would have sued my dad for child support and college expenses. Out of revenge, if nothing else.

My bitchy mom hadn't cared enough to fight for me. She claimed Dad had suffered enough. I thought she took perverse pleasure in seeing me struggle. She wanted me punished and in purgatory forever for what I'd done to our family.

I tried to hold my anger and frustration in check. "I did. They screwed up after I quit and cut a check for my last paycheck instead of depositing it. They should have sent the check to the house. Can you look through my mail and make sure it's there?"

She let out an exasperated huff, like I had just asked her for the world's biggest favor. "*Hang* on."

I heard her heavy footsteps. She called out to the boys again. Then I heard her riffling through paperwork. "Found it."

"Will you put it in the mail tomorrow? I need it, badly."

"I have a busy day tomorrow, Zachary. Mondays are always bad. The twins have practice and work is an absolute zoo."

"Mom, please? I wouldn't ask if it wasn't important."

The heavy sigh again. "Okay. I'll *try*."

"Thanks, Mom."

She grunted.

"I have to run." I didn't want to talk to her a minute longer than I had to and waste her precious time. The feeling was mutual. "It's bid day and I have a ton of work to do."

"Work, Zach? Or screwing one of the girls." Her tone was full of disgust and embarrassment. "I can't believe my son lives in a sorority house. Is a servant in a sorority house!"

I cut her off before she could launch into the usual tirade. "It's honest work, Mom. I don't touch the girls. I'm like a big brother to them. That's all."

She snorted, like *right*. "Big brother? I'm glad to hear you're a big brother to *someone*. You could show more attention to your *real* brothers."

There was the accusation again. She was always laying a guilt trip on me. She knew exactly where to place her knife and how to twist it. Like she would ever let me near the twins. She didn't trust me around them. Whenever I was anywhere near them, which was as little as possible, she hovered, acting like I was a bigger threat to their safety than strangers with candy. But she liked to pin shit like that on me. Everything that was wrong, or imperfect, in her life was my fault. She was never going to let me forget what I'd done.

"Thanks, again, Mom. Just mail the check. And say hi to the twins for me. Talk to you later." I hung up, hoping she would follow through on her promise.

Shit, the woman was hard.

I headed upstairs and found Kayla Lucas, my favorite Double Deltsie, trying to lug a heavy box full of T-shirts to Kelly's car. A senior, Kayla was the prettiest, sweetest girl in the sorority. She'd been my first friend at the house when I started as a houseboy my freshman year.

"Hey, what are you doing with that heavy thing?" I grabbed the box from her. "Where are Seth, Dillon, and Paul?"

Kayla relinquished the box without a fight. A cute bead of perspiration was already sparkling on her pert nose. "Out at the car with Kelly. This is the last box."

"Why aren't you using a hand truck?" I headed toward the door.

She held it open for me and followed me to the parking lot. "What's a hand truck? I don't think we have one."

I shook my head and grinned at her. "Sure we do. We used it last year. Remember?"

She followed me to the parking lot, where the rest of the guys and Kelly were loading her car with the picnic coolers and the other box of shirts.

Kelly's eyes lit up when she saw us. "Great! We're running behind. Hey, Zach." She slammed the trunk of her car shut and opened the back door for me to slide the box in. "Coming to the beach with us?"

I cocked an eyebrow. "As your slave?" I looked at the other guys.

Kelly laughed. "Haha! No, as our guest, silly. We'd love to have you join us."

I glanced at the guys as I hesitated and tried to come up with an excuse to bail out of it.

Kelly shook her head. "Come on, Zach. Live a little and have some fun! The rest of the guys are coming."

I hesitated. I was flat broke. Until I got that last paycheck from summer, or the first paycheck from the house, I couldn't afford to waste the gas to go to the river.

"You can drive my car." Kayla jumped in as if she'd read my mind.

"I see. You're looking for a designated driver and someone to set up," I said.

"Maybe." Kayla winked at me. "Or maybe we just want you to have some fun for once."

Kelly was great about inviting us along to house events and parties. Partly it was protection for the girls to have some guys around. Partly they enjoyed our company.

Kelly made a point of batting her eyes at me. "Please, Zach, please? You'll have fun and it will be a great chance for you to meet our new pledges."

"Shit, you too?" My gaze bounced between them. "How can I say no to that?"

Kayla hugged me. "Thanks, Zach." She handed me her car keys. "You can head out now if you guys want. We'll meet you at the river after the bid meeting."

Their trip to the river beach was a big surprise, the important first bonding event meant to impress the new pledges. If most of the girls hadn't been incoming freshmen, the event wouldn't have been a surprise at all. The majority of the frats and sororities took their pledges to River State Park and the cliffs every year after the bid meeting.

The bid meeting made me edgy. The bid list was supposed to be top secret, but I'd overheard Kelly and Morgan and the selection committee—Alexis Turner was getting a bid. But something about it had angered Morgan.

Alexis puzzled me. And the way my body reacted to hers scared me shitless. I was certain the first time I saw her that she would have rather been anywhere but here. But in the powder room, she'd been so sure about her VIP status. And now it was the thought of her that convinced me to swallow my pride and take Kayla's BMW to the river. Even though it was a fucking terrible idea.

Alexis

As I walked into the senior ballroom at the SUB with Em for the bid meeting, I didn't know what scared me more—getting a bid from the Double Deltsies or not. We found an empty spot on the floor in the middle of our Rho Gam group and sat cross-legged next to each other as the houses filed in.

The meeting was simple. The coordinator passed out the bids. Girls who accepted their bids ran to join their houses, where they were each given a house T-shirt. Those who declined, or didn't get a bid, left. From the horror stories I'd heard, generally in tears.

As the bid slips were handed out, Em grabbed my hand. "Friends forever?"

It was becoming our mantra. I nodded. "Friends forever."

I caught Molly's eye and smiled at her. Maybe it was my imagination, but she frosted me out and looked away like I'd betrayed her. They called Em's name before mine. My heart felt like it was going to burst from my chest as she took her bid.

She read her bid aloud. "Delta Delta Psi!" she screamed, and ran to join her new house while I sat, stunned. I had thought her chances of getting a bid from them were only fifty-fifty. No more than mine would have been if I hadn't been a well-coached legacy.

How could Em be so happy about it? She hadn't even hesitated. Within seconds, they had tossed her a shirt and she'd slid it on over her cutoffs and crop top. We had all dressed casually for the occasion, like we'd been instructed.

Girls and girls and girls were called in no particular order. Screams and screams and screams. Tears and tears. The Double Deltsie house was rapidly filling up. Morgan, the girl who'd interviewed me, flashed me an angry, wicked look. I had disobeyed her. I lost my courage. She'd probably tanked me. Mom was going to kill me and then get me into the house under a cloud of shame and suspicion. I should have gone willingly, I realized now.

Finally, as the bids were winding down and it looked like I was going to be among the bid-less girls, I heard my name. I popped up and took my slip with my hands shaking so badly I could barely grab it. My eyes blurred as I read it. *Delta Delta Psi.*

I was grateful and horrified at the same time. Regretful that I couldn't be in a house where I belonged. But I knew better than to show a hint of remorse or disappointment. Or weakness. I squealed and bounced up and down like I was the happiest girl on campus as I ran to join my new house.

The house president handed me the last shirt in their pile and hugged me.

Em grabbed me. We bounced up and down together while I tried to pull my shirt on. Morgan gave me an evil, satisfied look that warned me not to defy her again. It was clear that she had made me sweat on purpose, making it look like I was their absolute last choice. We recited the house motto and ran from the SUB after the members, following them to a group of waiting cars.

"Get in a car! We have a surprise for you!" Kelly pointed to our waiting cavalcade.

Em and I slid into one together, driven by a girl who introduced herself as Leah. She drove us to our dorms. "Get in there. Get into a bikini, grab a beach bag, and get back out here! We're going to a beach party! Keep your shirt with you."

I ran into my room as Leah honked the horn and the other girls leaned out the window screaming at me to hurry. I changed into my pink bikini and grabbed a bag with a towel and sunscreen. As I locked my dorm room, two girls walked by and saw my sorority bid shirt. I heard them sigh heavily and whisper comments about stuck-up Double Deltsies. And so it began—being judged by the house I was in.

We stopped at Em's dorm next. Made two more stops and we were on the road to the river, rocking out to loud music, generally high from bid day.

The drive took over half an hour through wheat fields to barren desert until the road wound along the river. I barely noticed as I tried to fit in with the girls. Everyone was in full makeup with hair styled to perfection. That was a Double Deltsie rule—no going out without full hair and makeup. Leah blasted the air conditioning, when I would have loved to feel the wind from an open window through my hair. We pulled into a parking lot next to another car from the house and tumbled out.

Leah ran a cool eye over us. "Girls!" She sounded like a housemother. "You're Double Deltsies now!" She pulled her T-shirt off and stashed it in a stylish beach bag she pulled from the trunk, revealing a bright yellow bikini and a perfect body. "Follow me. The house guys saved us a spot."

She led the way, walking with the confidence of a model. The park pulsed with music. Smelled like beer, suntan lotion, and hot bodies. And radiated with life.

Off in the distance, people were jumping off the cliffs into the river below.

As we walked through the grass to our party spot, it became clear what being a Double Deltsie meant—total hot-girl status. Dating a Double Deltsie was prestigious. Groups of independent guys, Geeds, and frat parties with their new pledges turned to leer at us. They whistled and called out lewd invitations like construction workers on a job site.

We followed Leah's lead, walking with confidence. Ignoring most of the attention as too far above it. Leah knew her way around the park and the social strata. She also seemed to know someone in every frat group. She called out to some. Flirted with others and ignored the rest.

"The guys from Sigma Upsilon"—she rolled her eyes and made a disgusted face—"animals. All hands. Watch out for them."

She laughed. "The guys over there, the Lambda Rhos?" She nodded toward them. "Totally beneath us. Misfits. Douchebags."

A guy caught her attention. She waved to him with a big smile. "And there are a few, a very few, independents who are hot and worth hanging with. There's one, our student body president."

Another guy waved to her from a sea of Double Deltsie T-shirts. He was tall, blond, and built. With a chiseled jaw and snapping blue eyes. Abs to die for.

She waved back with enthusiasm and a sparkle in her eyes. "There we are! Seth!" She whispered to us as an aside. "One of our houseboys. Seth is simply irresistible. If he wasn't working for us, I would do him repeatedly. Stay away from him. He'll get you in trouble." She spoke like she knew from experience.

"Our houseboys are some of the hottest guys on campus." She sighed. "And off limits to all you pledges. If anyone asks, I warned you. I can't emphasize this enough—they're supposed to be like our brothers. Sleeping with one can get you expelled from the house on moral grounds."

She shook her head. "Yeah. Antiquated crap, but it's in the rules. Pay your dues. Keep your grades up. Participate in house events. Maintain the house image. And, most importantly, don't screw the houseboys. And you'll be golden." She turned her gaze back to Seth.

Seth stood next to two other good-looking guys. But Zach, who was standing a small distance away from them in the shade of a tree, caught my full attention. He was shirtless, with a beach towel draped over his shoulder. His tat was more obvious now, an inscription of some sort, like a date. And maybe a tiny angel and a heart? Hard to tell for sure from this distance. It seemed kind of out of character for a definitely hetero guy like him. He wore baggy swim trunks and flip-flops. Despite Leah's dire warning, it was all I could do not to stare openly at him.

"Paul and Dillon are standing next to Seth," Leah said. "Where's Zach?" She looked around for him. "Oh, there he is! The dark-haired one off by himself." She smiled. "Zach's our superhero guardian. He's always saving someone. Last Halloween, we made him dress as Superman for our house party. He was so adorable!"

He caught me staring at him. There was a hungry look in his eyes. The physical attraction between us rocked through the air, a mini heat wave of our own. He looked away, like he didn't want to face me, and walked off. I had just been snubbed.

Zach
I couldn't get Alexis Turner out of my mind while I waited my turn in the cliff-jumping line. I hadn't been

able to shake her out since we met in the bathroom. I still had the cut on my forehead to prove she messed with my head.

When I saw her get out of the car with Leah, my heart soared and my head warned me I was in deep shit now. Before seeing her, part of me had held the futile, selfish hope that I'd been mistaken and they hadn't offered her a bid. Or that she would turn the Double Deltsies down if they had. Rejecting them would have been gutsy. Being a Double Deltsie guaranteed a girl instant popularity.

Selfishly, I thought about how if Alexis had declined their offer, she would have been out of the Greek system. I could have dated her. I was in that limbo—not Greek, not Geed, independent. As a guy to date, the Geeds accepted me. I was too loyal to the Double Deltsies for most of the other sorority girls' tastes.

My turn finally came. As I stood on the ledge overlooking the river, old, familiar feelings pushed thoughts of Alexis aside. Talking to my mom always made me want to jump off a cliff. I had spent my entire life—that I could remember, anyway—feeling that way, thinking of jumping. Ending it all. Those few seconds of flying and total freedom from earth and then...nothingness. No more pain.

When I was younger, I used to think she'd be sorry if I jumped off the bridge by our house and drowned. Now I knew that wasn't true. She would be relieved. Oh, she would play the part of grieving mom. But she would be reveling in the sympathy the whole time, taking in the love and attention of being the poor, tragic mother whose asshole son killed himself. Thriving on it. Selfish bastard that I was, I refused to give her that.

My life was worth more. I could make a difference to someone. Help as many people as I could. I wasn't sure anymore that nothingness waited at the end. Maybe there was something better. Something I still had to find.

Dad wouldn't be any better, except he doesn't love the spotlight as much as she does. I used to think no one else would miss me. Now I think the girls would. I hope they would. I wasn't going to test it and be re-membered as that tragic houseboy.

As I stood on the edge of the cliff, ready to take my turn and jump, my heart soared. This was the perfect solution—a few seconds of flying, a cold splash of reali-ty, and life. A second chance.

Alexis

I watched Zach walk away and join the line of cliff jumpers. Though I tried to turn away, my gaze kept drifting back to him, watching him as he moved for-ward in line. Morgan showed up and kept her eye on me, my personal hawk.

Em immediately adapted and was in her element as a group of frat guys approached and offered us beer. The party swung into full action. The group ignored the river and the cliffs, partying as if they were back at the frat house.

I wasn't the kind of girl who liked to stay on the beach looking perfect, like the rest of my new sorority sisters. Arching our backs to accentuate our shapes.

Living for attention from guys. None of the frat guys interested me. There was only one guy I wanted to see, and he was about to jump off a cliff to escape me.

After a while, I'd had enough of being hit on and leered at and offered red plastic cups full of beer. I eyed the line of people jumping off the cliffs with longing, watching Zach's broad shoulders and wishing I were next to him. Em was distracted by the attention and headiness of her newfound popularity.

I grabbed her arm. "Let's go cliff jumping!"

She looked at me like I was crazy. "And leave the party? I don't like heights." She turned back to the frat guy she was flirting with, a guy from Tau Psi. A house that was up to our standards.

Paul, one of the houseboys, came up behind me as I stood swirling a head back onto the beer in my hand and dreaming of Zach. "You look like you want to jump."

When he spoke, I did jump, startled that he'd caught me so blatantly staring at Zach.

"I do!" I turned to smile at him, hoping to throw him off from my real motivation. I didn't really want to jump. I just wanted to watch Zach and sneak a chance to talk to him. "No one will go with me. Will you?" I asked on impulse.

"I would." The few words were slurred. "But I know my limits. I've had too much already. Never drink and dive. That's my motto."

I made a face of mock disappointment and laughed. "Very wise of you. You should put that on a bumper sticker."

"Good idea! Maybe I will." When he laughed, he smelled like cheap beer. "You look brave enough. You don't need a partner. Go!"

I hesitated. "I've never jumped off a cliff before." Not a cliff like this, chasing after a guy who'd just dissed me. I glanced at the jumpers. "We're under orders to stay here and party."

Paul got a devilish look in his eyes. "Is that right?" He grabbed my arm. "In that case, I'll cover for you while you sneak off." He tugged me toward the edge of our party.

"And how am I supposed to explain coming back with wet hair?"

He shrugged. "There are plenty of frat rats who will happily toss you into the river on your way back from the bathroom. Oops! Pranks will happen."

"You *are* good." I warmed to him.

"Zach's up there in line," Paul said. "Have you met him?"

My heart suddenly raced. I nodded and tried to play it cool. "Yeah. He served me cake."

Paul laughed nervously, like I'd said something wrong. He was still friendly, but from a distance. "Think you could recognize him?" Paul's tone led me to believe that no girl forgot Zach once they'd met him.

"Possibly." I had to agree with him—how could I miss Zach?

"What are you waiting for?" Paul gave me a gentle shove toward the cliffs. "I have your back. Go! Before the next wave of frat boys shows up."

CHAPTER FIVE

Zach

I hit the cold water and gasped as I sank into the darkness of the river toward the mud of the river bottom. As many times as I've jumped, there's still that moment when I panic. I can't breathe, and death seems like a reasonable escape. When I think, *Shit, it could end here and maybe that's better.* Then my feet touched bottom. I pushed up with a reassuring will to live. Damn it all, I was a fighter.

I broke through the surface and inhaled, exhilarated to be alive. Adrenaline stoked my strokes. I swam toward the rocky shore at the bottom of the cliffs and began the climb to get in line again.

If I had to be at the dunes, this was the way to spend the time, jumping again and again until I didn't have the strength for one more time. Proving to myself over and over that life was worth struggling through.

I pulled myself up over the last ledge of the cliff at the top. The line had grown and wandered down the hill that rose to the cliffs from the dunes and meandered along the river.

I sprinted toward the end of the line, high on life. As I neared the line's end, I spotted Alexis in the arms of a frat pledge, screaming and fighting to get away as he carried her toward the river to dunk her in. A buddy of his egged him on. I fought a surge of anger.

Some girls put up a fight as a way of flirting. Playfully pushing and screaming for attention. Most girls, if they're really into the guy, will wrap their arms around his neck and hang onto him as if their life and their hairstyle depend on it. Pressing tightly against him so he gets a good feel of soft, warm breasts and naked skin, and a hard-on, pleading with him not to let her go.

Alexis' screams were angry. She was pushing him away for real as she tried to squirm free. Fuck. Stupid drunk pledges. I dashed to them and stepped between the pledge and the river. "Dude, she's clearly not into this. Put her down."

Alexis' eyes lit up as she spotted me. She gave me that hero look. "Zach!"

The pledge carrying her stopped. The other one took a step toward me. "How are you going to stop us, *houseboy?*"

I stared them down. *Cocky, stupid freshmen.* "*Pledges,*" I said with the same sneer.

They hadn't realized yet how much pull I had at the house with the girls. I could blacklist these two douchebags if I wanted to. Make sure they had no chance with our girls.

I didn't blink. I was energized and high on adrenaline. Pulsing with anger and jealousy at seeing Alexis in the douchebag's arms. Unafraid to take them on.

The dickhead carrying Alexis tried to step around me. I dove for the douchebag, ramming my shoulder into his back.

He dropped Alexis. I caught her fall as she stumbled and pushed her behind me.

I caught a movement from the corner of my eye as a fist slammed toward my back. I turned just enough to avoid a direct punch to the kidney. I grabbed the pledge's arm and swung him around, wrenching it behind his back. Shit, I was going to make him cry uncle.

The first pledge, the one I had stripped of Alexis, came at me, throwing a punch aimed at my jaw. I leaned back out of the way. The pledge I held tried to squirm free.

I had tunnel vision. I didn't see anything but the two douchebags I was trying to subdue. I didn't want to fight them and beat the crap out of them. Out of nowhere, two other pledges jumped on my back. I took a blow to the back of my knees and nearly went down, taking the pledge I held with me.

"Get off him!" Alexis screamed from behind me as she pulled at one of the guys on my back.

"Listen to her. Get off him!" The commanding voice was calm, firm, and amused. And that of my ex-best friend Dakota.

Alexis

I brushed my hair out of my eyes as Dakota pulled me off the douches that had attacked Zack, breathing hard and struggling to keep up the fight.

The Tau Psi pledges moved away from Zach. Before I could go to him, Dakota Bradley, the frat guy who'd tried to tempt me with the Pomsky puppy, let go of me and stepped between us.

Zach was breathing as hard as the look in his eyes as he stared at Dakota. "QB2."

It might have been my imagination, but the way he said it sounded like a putdown.

Dakota held Zach's gaze without flinching. "Houseboy, are you hassling my pledges?"

"Your pledges were carting off one of ours." As Zach straightened, a bruise appeared on his back.

"Boys!" Dakota snapped his fingers and pointed a thumb back toward the partying masses. "Get back to the party." He turned his back on Zach and smiled at me, running his gaze over me, lingering on my breasts with a lusty look glittering in his eyes. "Alexis," he said, finally dragging his eyes to my face. "Are you okay?"

I nodded, too furious to speak.

He tucked a lock of hair behind my ear. "Good. The guys get a little wild on bid day. You can't blame them.

Sunshine. Beer. Hot girls." His gaze slid down me again.

Zach came up beside me and took my arm. I would have been aware of him even if he hadn't touched me. "We should get back." He was clearly dismissing Dakota.

Dakota ignored Zach and spoke to me. "You pledged the Double Deltsies?"

I nodded again.

"I had you pegged." Dakota's smile was almost a gloat. "I knew you would. You know, you can talk to me now. The recruitment ban is lifted."

I didn't want to talk to him. I just nodded again.

He winked at me and leaned in to whisper in my ear, "I'll be seeing you, Alexis. Real soon." He walked away without looking at Zach.

I waited until he was out of earshot before I took Zach's arm and whispered, "That was stupidly brave of you. I have experience with drunk guys at lake parties. I could have handled them myself."

He winced as he tried to grin. "Yeah, you were really handling them. Don't flatter yourself. I didn't do it for you. I just felt like getting my ass kicked."

"Is that so?" I smiled back at him. "FYI, I was completely safe. There's no way they would have taken a swing at me."

He stared at me like I was naïve. "No, but they would have taken your bikini top, made you beg to get it back, groped you. Any number of things." He frowned at Dakota's retreating back. "It's a good thing your boyfriend came to the rescue." There was a tease in his voice, but something serious, hard, and unhappy beneath it, too.

"He's *not* my boyfriend." I gently touched Zach's back. "I've never even spoken to him."

Zach tried to hide it, but even my whisper of a touch hurt. He winced again.

"That's too bad for you. QB2 is house president of the most powerful frat on campus. He's destined for greatness in his dad's law firm." He laughed, but it held little humor.

"QB2?" I asked.

"Second-string quarterback. In high school." He grinned.

"Who was QB1?" I asked.

Zach kept grinning. "Who do you think? Why do you think he called me houseboy? It sure as hell wasn't to lift me up." He laughed. "Yeah, I was starting quarterback. Drove Dak crazy. He still believes he was better than me. Thinks Coach was biased." Zach shrugged.

"Was he?"

Zach stared at me like he was trying to judge how serious I was. "Dak has delusions of fame and overrates his abilities, on and off the field."

I took that as a warning. "How good was your team, QB1? Did you lead them to victory?"

"We took state in 4A. Enough about me." His teasing grin held, but there was an edge to his voice, like he was being almost sarcastic. "You could do worse than Dak. He was the second most popular guy in my class."

Zach was almost daring me to go for Dakota, yet warning me off him at the same time.

I didn't know why he was acting like this. I didn't want Dakota. I ignored the suggestion and played along with Zach's game. "Who was the most popular guy?"

"Again, who do you think?" He grinned and inhaled deeply, like he was trying to breathe through the pain.

I put my hand on his arm, worried, and caught a glimpse of his tattoo on the underside of his arm. It was definitely a date. "Mr. Popular, you're hurt. That pledge hit you with a literal low blow. Did they get you in the kidney?" I cursed beneath my breath, worried. A guy from my class got punched in the kidney once and had to be taken to the hospital.

"No, they missed me by that much." He laughed like it didn't matter. Like he'd been taught to suck it up and wasn't used to people caring.

"Let me take a look." I grabbed his shoulders to turn him around so I could inspect his injury, letting my hands rest longer on his rapidly drying skin than I should have. He smelled like the river and sunshine, everything wet and wild.

He presented his back to me, lifting his arms so every muscle on his back rippled into definition. An ugly black bruise the size of a fist showed through his tan, just to the right of his spine, too high to have hit any vital organs.

I let out a sigh of relief. "It's nasty looking and going to get worse. Big, too." I outlined it with my fingertip to emphasize my point.

Goosebumps rose on his skin in the heat, like he enjoyed my touch. He held very still.

I leaned up and whispered in his ear. "You should ice this." I left unsaid the promise that I would happily help him.

Being so near him took my breath away. I had this crazy desire to kiss his back all the way up his spine until I nibbled on his ear. To hold him in my arms and take away the pain that I sensed went way deeper than anything physical.

"I'm sorry," I said.

He looked at me over his shoulder. "For what?"

"Causing you to get hurt a second time."

The bump on his forehead was turning greenish yellow. I touched it gently. His hair was still wet from the river and pressed back flat against his head. I itched to run my fingers through it and fluff it. His face was flushed, but his skin was cool from the river.

I stared up at him with hero worship in my eyes, practically begging for a kiss. All I had to do was go up on my toes and brush my lips against his.

He looked away. "We'd better get back."

He started walking so suddenly, I nearly toppled over.

I had to nearly run to keep up with him. "Zach?"

"Yeah?"

"Thanks for back there."

He nodded. "Don't underestimate the Tau Psis. They take advantage of girls. What were you doing out at the cliffs alone?"

I couldn't tell him I was watching him jump. "Getting in line to jump."

He shook his head. "Wise up, pledge. Double Deltsies don't do shit like jump off cliffs. Not unless they have an adoring audience of frat boys egging them on."

I couldn't believe he was warning me. "What *do* they do?"

He made an exaggerated point of rolling his eyes, like, duh, you have to ask? "Flirt with frat guys, party, and look hot."

I couldn't tell if he was teasing or not. Just then, he looked up overhead. I followed the direction of his gaze. Two parasailers were floating down from the cliffs on the opposite side of the river on brightly colored sails.

"Shit!" Zach grabbed me and covered my eyes, playfully. "Don't look, baby pledge."

"What?" I flirted back, pulling his hands away with halfhearted effort and pressing against him and his hard chest.

"Don't say I didn't warn you." He dropped his hands. "Stupid Zeta Nus trying to show off. You have to be better hung than that to actually show off."

I looked up just as they floated overhead, getting a look of two naked butts and dangling dicks. "Ugh." I made a face of disgust.

Zach laughed. "Don't let those tiny dicks scare you off real men."

"That's going to be burned into my brain."

"Yeah, and I packed hotdogs for lunch. Yum." He turned and took my arm, propelling me away as the parasailers landed and ran through the crowd.

We reached our group too soon. As soon as we did, any intimacy between us vanished. Zach morphed into houseboy mode, cold and aloof like a disapproving older brother.

Morgan spotted us and ran to us, suspicion glittering in her eyes. "Where have you two been?" Her voice was almost venom.

Zach shook his head like he was disgusted, and nodded toward me. "The Tau Psis separated one of your pledges from the herd."

His disinterested tone seemed to satisfy Morgan. "And you saved her?"

"They were about to throw her in the river," he said.

Morgan laughed. "The douches. Did they try to untie your bikini top, too?"

Paul came up and gave Zach a playful shove. "Our hero."

Zach was caught off guard and winced.

Morgan's eyes went wide as she saw the bruise on his back. "You're hurt." She glared at me like I was the one who'd hit him. She took his arm, caressing his hard bicep. "Let's get you some ice for that." She put a purr in her voice as she led him away.

I tried to ignore Morgan. She fawned over Zach and held a plastic bag full of ice against his back, laughing when he pulled away because it was so cold. But it was like a traffic accident on the freeway. Morbid curiosity took over. My gaze seemed to wander back to them against my will.

The afternoon passed slowly, even with the house guys barbecuing hotdogs and hamburgers for us. It was torture not to talk to him and watch him while he laughed and talked with the older girls who were already members. Some of the girls were friendly. Others treated the house guys as if they could snap their fingers and the guys should do their bidding. Even though Kelly made it clear that guys were off duty and our guests.

When it was my turn, Zach handed me a hotdog with a straight face. "Perfectly charred. Just for you."

Going along with his kidding, I took it from him, slathered it with mustard and took a big bite, licking the mustard off my lip suggestively. "Delicious!"

Unfortunately, I couldn't linger and spar with him.

After lunch, Kelly called us all together. "Time to pack up! Classes begin tomorrow. Scholarship is important to us."

There was a general round of laughter like everyone knew this was tongue-in-cheek. My new house wasn't known for its high GPA.

"But before we go, we have an important announcement." She bounced on her toes like the former cheerleader she was. "Exciting news! For the first time in years, we actually have spots open in the house for five lucky pledges to move in immediately!"

A momentary, stunned hush fell over the girls. This was unprecedented. No one got to move into the house until second semester. At the *earliest*. I had been counting on that.

Then someone whistled and everyone started cheering. I cheered with the rest of the pledges, trying not to stand out. Girls whispered to each other, speculating. I crossed my fingers, hoping that I wouldn't get one of the spots.

Kelly whistled to quiet us. "The recruitment committee, along with the officers, spent hours coming up with the fairest way to fill these spots. We voted on which girls we thought would be the future leaders of the house, which would represent us best, and whom we thought would fit in the most. We've been watching you today to confirm we'd made the right choice.

"It was a tough decision. We would love for all of you to be able to move in immediately. We're so excited about getting to know all of you and know you'll all be fantastic assets to the house. Remember—we hand-picked each of you!

"But we voted, taking into consideration rush crushes and recommendations. One girl stood out as the leader."

I relaxed. There was no way that girl was me.

"Alexis Turner, you're our top pick!"

My mouth fell open. Either I was a better faker than I thought, or someone had set me up. My mouth went completely sandpaper on me. I panicked. Live in the house so soon? It was terrifying.

The entire house was looking at me, the pledges with a mixture of envy and disgust. Kelly had just drawn a target on my back. I was public enemy number one. The girl to take down.

I stuttered. "I don't know what to say. I'm overwhelmed." I blinked back tears that they all mistook for joy. "Thank you."

Kelly beamed. "Alexis, as our top pick, you get to pick your roommate. Pick a pledge, any pledge."

Every girl in my pledge class turned to me. Morgan was wearing a smug look and I got the feeling she was behind this. Whoever I picked would be loyal for life and everyone else would hate me until I could prove myself to them.

The house leadership was watching to see to see what my strategy was. I could have done something democratic, like had the others vote. Or something random like draw names. I knew very few of the others and none of them well enough to make an informed decision.

I simply blurted out a name. "Emily! I pick Emily."

I don't know what I did right, but Kelly smiled broadly and nodded subtly to the other officers. They approved of my choice. All I knew was that if I hadn't picked her, Emily would have hated me. I would have lost the only friend I had. I still might. Emily grabbed me and squealed in my ear as she hugged me. As I bounced up and down with her, acting excited, I worried that living in the house would go to her head and separate us in the end.

"Great!" Kelly beamed. "We'll get your things and move you in tonight. Now for the other three..."

She called out three more names, but they meant nothing to me. I kept thinking this was like some kind of survivor reality show and I had just shown my strategy to the opposition. Next time someone took a vote, I was off the island.

CHAPTER SIX

Alexis

It was a good thing I hadn't settled into my dorm room yet. I'd barely even seen my randomly assigned roommate. Both of us had been too busy with recruitment. She had pledged another house. When she saw my Double Deltsie shirt, I think she was glad to see me move out. She'd pledged a less prestigious house. Her envy was palpable.

My new sisters packed me up and moved me into my room in the house in less than an hour. They dumped all my stuff into a tiny cubicle of a room with two dressers, two desks, and one twin bed, leaving it up to Em and me to sort out the space. Mom had gone crazy and bought me every matching accessory imaginable for my dorm room, thinking I could bring back the extra when it was time to move into the house. There was no way it would all fit with Emily's in our tiny shared room that was less than half the size of my dorm room.

We flipped a coin to see whose sheets and comforters to put on the bed. I won. Then we crammed as much stuff into the closets and dressers as we could and called the houseboys to help us haul the rest to the attic for storage. I felt like a prima donna or something for asking the guys to haul my junk around. I didn't want them to think I thought of them as my own personal slaves. But I wanted to see Zach so much it was worth the risk.

Unfortunately, Paul showed up. While Em was preoccupied, he whispered to me, "Zach gave me hell for telling you to go to the cliffs."

I was secretly pleased. "I didn't give you up."

Paul didn't seem impressed. "I made the mistake of outing myself and teasing him about his overprotective nature." He paused and not quite scowled, but something close to it. "Be careful, Alexis. Don't lead him on."

There was an undertone of dislike in his voice, like he didn't trust the girls in the house. Like we were nothing more than cock teases to the house guys. Ways to get them in trouble.

"I like Zach," he said. "Girls think he's a charming guy. I would go to the mats for him. But he's been through a lot of crap. He has a dark side and he keeps to himself."

I didn't reply.

"If you're trying to sleep with him, you're going to be disappointed. Zach doesn't mess with the girls in the house." He grabbed my disc chair and an armful of framed posters and headed up the stairs to the attic. He didn't speak to me again.

I spent a fitful night on the sleeping porch. I was a light sleeper. Every cough and movement woke me up. In the morning, the houseboys set out breakfast. I looked for Zach. Someone said he had an early class and was already gone. Carol, our housemother, welcomed Em and me as we ate breakfast.

All the girls in the house dressed in their pledge T-shirts and skirts for the first day of class. Most of the girls wore flip-flops. I wore a pair of wedge sandals, which turned out to be a mistake as I trudged up the hill to campus.

The entire Greek system was out in their house shirts. Walking up Greek Row toward campus with some girls from the house, through the shade-lined streets, the mood was happy and hung over in equal measure. The pledges like me were excited. Em bubbled over with pride.

Em and I didn't have class together. We split in different directions when we got onto campus proper. I hoped I didn't have class with any of my sorority sisters. If I did, I was expected to sit with them. I had three classes on Mondays, Wednesdays, and Fridays. I had sisters in the first two and sat in a clump with them, wishing for the freedom to choose my friends for myself. Resenting my mom and her insistence that I pledge the Double Deltsies.

I ate lunch at the house and headed out to my two o'clock class with fingers crossed. I was looking forward to The History of Rock and Roll as my skate class to fill one of my general education requirements, GERs. The classroom was easy to find—Led Zeppelin's "Fool in the Rain" was blasting from the inside. I loved that song. Classic rock was one of the few joys I shared with my dad.

I breathed a sigh of relief when I walked in and didn't see another Delta Delta Psi T-shirt in the room. Then I saw Zach sitting in the back by himself, wearing a Modest Mouse T-shirt, and my heart raced.

A Double Deltsie I actually wanted to sit by! Ignoring Paul's warning, and Zach's obvious signals that he wanted to be alone, I walked right up to him. "Is this seat taken?" I sat without waiting for an answer.

Zach

Getting out of the house and going to class was the freest time of my days. When I was on campus, I wasn't a servant. I wasn't beneath anyone. I was just me. I was looking forward to The History of Rock and Roll as a break from my science-heavy schedule of the past few years. And time away from the girls and their drama. I'd been lucky and had had only a couple of classes with any of them over the years. When I did, it was always awkward.

I settled in the back of the classroom. When I looked up, I caught a glimpse of a Double Deltsie light blue pledge T-shirt, nicely filled out by a pair of perfect breasts. *Shit.* Then I lifted my gaze, saw Alexis' face, and cursed my odd combination of good and bad luck.

I hoped she didn't see me, afraid if she did, she would diss and ignore me. And even more worried she wouldn't.

I don't know why I cared what the girls thought. In high school, being the star jock had been enough to impress any girl I wanted. But being the houseboy was enough to make me beneath the Double Deltsies. As I began my third year in the house, I still had my pride. Though I didn't know how I'd managed to hang on to it. Seth, Paul, and Dillon helped.

I didn't miss the way the other guys in the class watched Alexis as she strode to the back of the class-room and took the seat next to me. Double Deltsies stood out wherever they went. She'd already mastered their confident walk. She probably came prepro-grammed with it.

"Is this seat taken?" She slid into it without waiting for an answer.

"You're supposed to sit with the Double Deltsies." I wasn't about to encourage her. She made my pulse race too damn fast.

When she smiled, her eyes danced. "I am."

"Do I look like one of your sisters?" I said.

Her gaze slid over me like she was taking full meas-ure of me, letting it linger on my shoulders and chest. "In that Modest Mouse T-shirt? No." She grinned. "I like Modest Mouse."

"Shit." I couldn't resist teasing her. I reached for the hem of my shirt.

"What are you doing?" She laughed.

"I can't wear this now. It's tainted. I'll to have to burn it when I get back to the house." I pulled it over my head and dropped it on my desk, waiting for her reaction.

Her mouth fell open as she stared at my naked chest. "Why?"

"By the time one of the girls from the house likes a band, they've gotten way too popular. They're tainted with the stench of pop and mainstream music."

She grabbed my shirt and stuffed it in my hands, smiling appreciatively. "Stop showing off and put that back on before the prof shows up. No shoes, no shirt, no class."

I'd gotten the reaction I wanted. "This is the history of rock and roll. Which is notorious for shirtless guys. There's a better than fifty-fifty chance the prof shows up shirtless."

She laughed again and made a disgusted face. "I hope not!"

I shrugged and pulled the shirt back on.

She shook her head at me. "You've got me all wrong, Zach. How do you know I'm one of those pop music girls? You don't even know me."

I raised one eyebrow. "Yeah, you really look indie. You're a Double Deltsie. They don't get into the indie music scene."

She shrugged. "Stereotyper. I guess I won't show you my signed Thermals event poster, then. I was at their August fifth concert on Capital Hill."

"You listen to The Thermals?"

She'd surprised me, pleasantly. Listening to The Thermals was about as Seattle indie street cred as you could get. I had been dying to go to that concert, but I'd had to work. And I needed every penny I could earn.

She shrugged. "Don't judge a book by its cover."

The prof walked in, interrupting our conversation. He was a graying, aging rocker with long hair, a beard, and a love for music. And, yeah, he was wearing a shirt—a well-worn, classic Pink Floyd *Dark Side of the Moon* T-shirt that looked like it had been around since the seventies.

He turned off Led Zeppelin just as "Stairway to Heaven" got going. "Welcome to The History of Rock and Roll. This class is going to blow your mind. I'm not here to flunk you out or tank your GPA. My goal is to give you an appreciation for the best music on the planet.

"The term 'rock and roll' emerged from the rhythm and blues fusion music in the nineteen fifties. Most white Americans have no concept of the original meaning of the term. 'Rock and rolling' was originally used in the African American community of the day to mean 'having sex.'

"'Sex, drugs, and rock and roll' is, therefore, a redundant statement." He laughed. "Disc jockey Alan Freed coined the term, naming his radio show, where he played a collection of rhythm and blues albums, 'The Rock and Roll Show' with full knowledge of its sexual connotations. And yes, that will be on the test."

Sitting next to Alexis, the last thing I needed to be reminded of was sex. Like it wasn't on my brain constantly when she was around. Crap. Now I was in a class with her that was essentially named "The History of Sex." It was burned in my brain with the music.

Near the end of the period, the prof sprang a joint assignment on us. "Pair up! I have a playlist I want you to listen to, discuss, and write a joint paper on what you experience when you listen to it."

Alexis turned to me. "I choose you."

Shit. More dangerous territory. There was no way to turn her down. "You sure? You don't even know me. I could be a slacker and not do my part."

"I'll take that chance." She paused. "Besides, I know where you live and how to make you pay."

"You're an evil woman."

She grinned.

The bell rang. The prof dismissed the class.

Alexis grabbed her backpack. "Let's go to the College Grind and get a head start on our assignment."

I froze. Until that check came, I didn't have money for three-dollar cups of coffee. "What kind of a Double Deltsie are you, overachiever?"

"The kind who likes music and good company."

I grabbed my backpack. "I should get back to the house—"

"And what? Study? Isn't that what I'm asking?" She started down the aisle. "My treat. I'm buying. If you can resist free iced coffee, you are not the man I thought you were."

Like I could resist a taunt like that. I swallowed my pride and caught up to her in two steps. I bent and whispered in her ear. "I'm trying to give you an out, pledge. FYI, the girls don't hang with the houseboys outside the house and certain sanctioned frat parties and events. It's not good for your image to be seen with the help."

She shrugged and kept walking. "They can't complain about me doing homework with my partner."

"But somehow they still will. You don't get it—we're from two different worlds."

She raced on, expecting me to follow her like her puppy dog. And damn, but I did.

"I don't think we are, Zach. In case you haven't noticed, we don't have a caste system here."

I followed her into the crowded hall. "We have something worse—peer pressure."

She flashed me a flirty smile. "I handle pressure like a pro. Years of dealing with my mom. Come on, Zach. Chill. It's just a cup of coffee. Do I have to beg? Or are we going to do this assignment at the last minute? In the study room in full view of everyone." She laughed like the thought was delicious.

"Yeah, beg. I like it when girls beg." She had me where she wanted me. I pictured Morgan giving us death looks. The College Grind was safer.

Alexis laughed and grabbed my arm. "Please, please, *please*. Pretty please." She batted her eyes with her ridiculously long lashes, exaggerating comically for effect.

How could any hetero guy resist that? Up close, I could see a faint spray of freckles across her nose. She had a light scar on her chin that she'd tried to hide with makeup. She wasn't perfect. She wasn't even the most gorgeous Double Deltsie in the house. But her face was arresting. Her long blond hair fell around her shoulders, tempting a guy to run his fingers through it. My pulse wouldn't stop racing.

She was damn striking. Imperfect enough to be real. Her personality was magnetic. I liked her way too much.

She wasn't looking where she was going. She tripped on the uneven sidewalk and nearly went down.

I caught her by the arm just in time and pulled her to her feet. "You okay?"

"Besides being embarrassed? Yeah, I'm fine. Just turned my ankle." She tested her weight on it.

"Don't be embarrassed. These sidewalks are killers. You should see people slide onto their butts on them in the winter. Let me take that." I pulled her backpack from her shoulder and slid it over mine. "Can you walk?"

"If I can't, will you carry me?" She batted her lashes again in that ridiculous way.

"Depends on how much you weigh."

She shoved me playfully. "Forget it." She grinned. "Give me your arm."

I held it out to her. "Now you want me to be your crutch?"

"Absolutely." She took my arm and snuggled against me.

She was going to kill me. She couldn't know how hard my heart pounded. We looked too much like a couple as we made our way to the edge of Greek Row.

The College Grind was crowded. It took fifteen minutes to get our iced coffees. I asked for an extra cup of ice. She paid before I could whip out my non-existent money. We found a spot on the grass outside and sat in the shade.

I insisted on inspecting her naked ankle. That was another mistake. When I took it in my hand, I could see up her skirt. Her shapely leg felt too good in my hand. All I could think about was sliding my hand up her leg and beneath that short skirt of hers.

"What do you think, doc?" she asked. "Will I live?"

"Looks like you just twisted it." I put the cup of ice against it and she jumped at the touch of cold, laughing. Her leg was as imperfectly beautiful as the rest of her. "Where did you all these scars?" I slid my hand up her shin and lightly caressed one.

"Just trying to get a feel?" Her eyes sparkled like she was enjoying this. "I thought you were worried about appearances. What do you think my sorority sisters will think if they see you holding my leg in public?" Her eyes danced like she didn't care.

I caressed her ankle and let go slowly. "They know I like to play doctor."

"But not with the girls?"

"You didn't answer my question," I said.

"I took a spill over a hurdle at the state meet in high school."

That took me by surprise. I didn't have her pegged for a sporty girl.

"Freaked my mom out. She thought I had permanently disfigured myself. And she's not good with blood. Speaking of that—am I trusting my leg to someone with medical skills? You aren't a premed major, or maybe physical therapy?"

"Are you fishing for information? If you want to know what I'm majoring in, just ask."

She grinned. "So?"

"Food science. But if it makes you feel better, I've taken anatomy and physiology, organic chem, and biology. I have some experience with injuries from my years of being sacked on the football field."

She tilted her head like she was trying to figure me out. "Food science? What's that? Like, nutrition?"

I stared at her. I got that question a lot. "No, *not* like nutrition. It's pretty self-explanatory—the science of food."

"It's not self-explanatory to me."

"New product development, food packaging and storage methods, food safety. Super tasters for new products. That kind of thing. Food scientists work at all the major food producers, at dairies, wineries, breweries, coffee companies. There's a lot of science involved in developing new products without destroying the nutritional value of the food and still making it tasty. And finding ways to preserve food safely using fewer and fewer chemicals and additives."

"It sounds interesting. And you're a junior?"

"More fishing?"

"Maybe."

"Yeah. Junior. Since we're asking the mundane 'what's your major' question, what's yours?"

She shrugged and smiled brightly. "Business, I think. I haven't really decided for sure."

Typical Double Deltsie answer. Most of them would never have to work. I don't know why that irritated me, but it did.

"I like what you're doing, but you can let go of my leg now. Before people start talking."

I'd been stroking her leg, almost without thinking. Just for fun, I held it more tightly. "Only if you're all better now. Are you sure?"

She smiled and I let go and grabbed my phone. "We have work to do."

The prof had posted the playlist online. We plugged headphones into our phones and sat side by side, listening to the birth pangs of rock and roll. *Sex*, my mind whispered.

Alexis lay on the grass with her blond hair fanning around her. She closed her eyes as she listened to the music, with a rapturous look on her face that matched the way a girl should look after a hot round of lovemaking. A look I would love to put on her face. *Sex*, that's what the music really was about.

I lay back, too, so close to her, our arms brushed. I could barely focus on the music.

"Zach! Did you hear that riff?" Beside me, Alexis suddenly sat up.

"What?" I tried to act casual, like I hadn't been thinking of her.

"That riff. It's like heaven. Like the birth of the whole genre!" She tried to describe it to me.

"Where are you? I don't hear it." I tried to play it back and find the spot she was talking about.

She pulled one earbud out and pulled me close to stick it in my ear. We were so close, cheek to cheek. Her expensive perfume bloomed in the heat, giving off sensual undertones designed to turn guys on. Her lips were moist. Her nose so cute in profile. Everything about her made my heart pound. And then I heard the riff, wrapped in the middle of cheesy fifties music, and knew what she meant.

We turned our heads just enough to face each other. My breath caught as she realized I got it and smiled at me.

Damn, but I wanted to kiss her. All I had to do was cup the back of her head and bring my lips to hers. I came to my senses before I did something stupid that would get me fired and kicked out of the house.

"Awesome." I pulled her earbud out of my ear and handed it back to her. "Where did you learn so much about music?"

Her eyes clouded with disappointment and confusion. Like she'd been trying to trap me in that kiss. She didn't know that I was easy prey and fighting temptation only as a means of self-preservation. If she'd been just another Geed girl...

"My dad," she said. "But he's into classic seventies rock. This fifties stuff is too early for him. What about you?"

I shrugged. "I've always liked music. It's an escape."

"From what?" She seemed genuinely interested.

I wished she wasn't sitting so close to me. It made it hard to think. "Everything."

The tiniest of frowns creased her forehead. "Everything?" Like she couldn't believe anyone would want to escape life.

I changed the subject. "You don't fit the Double Deltsie mold. Why did you pledge them?"

Her frown became a scowl. "I didn't have a choice. You know I'm a legacy? Mom would have *killed* me if I didn't." She rolled her eyes. "My mom is the queen of pressure and expectations."

"You could have defied her." It didn't seem like such a big deal to me.

She shook her head. "You don't know them." She was gorgeously imperfect even when she frowned. "I'm their only child. Their one hope for the future. Failure isn't an option."

I still didn't understand what the problem was. You live your own life. Screw your parents if they don't like it. They'll find something to disapprove of no matter what you do, or how much you succeed.

You make your own way so you don't have to rely on anyone. Prove people wrong about their expectations. And then don't give a shit whether they acknowledge them or not. It's the "not giving a shit" that takes practice. It's one of those simple things that was not at all easy to master. No one had ever expected anything of me.

"What about you?" Her eyes sparkled with curiosity, focused fully on me.

Damn, but I wanted her to look at me like that forever.

She leaned toward me, intimately, like I was the most interesting person on the planet. "Why are you a houseboy, Zach? Give me the inside scoop. What do your parents think about having a *son* who lives in a sorority house? Do their friends tease them? I bet that takes some explaining! 'No, our son is not gay or transgendered. He's just found his calling—living with girls! Yeah, it's a tough job for a guy, but someone has to do it.'"

She put on a low, mock-dad kind of voice that almost made me laugh. And sad at the same time. I could almost hear my dad explaining away my existence.

"'He's going to write a book someday—*The Smart Man's Guide to Living in a Female-Dominated Society*,'" she said. "'As one of the handful of guys in the world who has survived the pressures of living with one hundred menstruating women, his insights are invaluable. It's going to hit number one on the *New York Times* list.'" She paused. "I bet this gig scores points with your buds back home." Her eyes lit up at the thought.

I laughed, but I refused to be drawn out. "It pays the bills."

She missed the cues I was sending her. "You know what you should do?" Her eyes went wide with excitement. "Dress in drag and send them the picture! Tell them you like the house so much, you've decided to join after all!"

"You think the Double Deltsies would take me?" I said.

"If you wore a long blond wig and short skirts. And maybe plucked your brows. They're a little thick." She laughed.

"My parents don't explain anything to anyone. They barely acknowledge I exist. They don't give a shit about me or what I do." The words came out with more force than I intended. As terse as my confession was, I immediately wished I could take it back. I'd shared too much.

She looked startled, like she couldn't comprehend what I'd said. Or what she'd said to upset me.

I felt like a real douchebag.

She hesitated. "They must care at least a little?"

I shook my head. "Just the opposite—they wish I'd never been born."

"That can't be true." She smiled tentatively, like I must be joking or exaggerating. Like every parent wanted the kid they were stuck with.

"It's the absolute truth. Ask them yourself." I held my phone out to her. "Their numbers are programmed in."

Her smile faltered. "Shut up." She pushed the phone away. "You're crazy."

"Certifiable." I laughed to cover the truth and put her at ease. People who haven't fucked up their childhoods and who've grown up with normal parents don't understand how a mother and father can hate their kid. I didn't feel like explaining.

She punched a button on her phone. Mine rang a second later.

"You're calling me?" I stared at my phone. "This better be good. This is an emergency contact number only for girls in the house. If you haven't tripped a circuit breaker, blown out an outlet by plugging in too many flatirons and blow dryers, overflowed a toilet, or locked yourself out, I'm unavailable."

She stared me in the eye as my phone kept ringing. "Shut up, houseboy. I'm calling Zach, my study partner. I want him to have my number."

I answered her call. "Hey, study partner." I couldn't help grinning. If I didn't watch myself, I could fall in love with this girl. If you believe in love at first sight, maybe I already had.

"My number is not for emergencies only," she said. "It's open to friends any time, day or night. Whenever they need to talk. Or want to discuss music. Or just need to hear another person breathing. I'm here and I'll listen."

She hung up. I swallowed hard.

"Away from the house, you aren't a houseboy to me, Zach. And you're never a servant. Or a lower class." Her tone was fierce. "You're just Zach and I'm just Alexis, and all those other trappings don't matter."

"You really think that will work?" I wished I were as innocent as she was.

She was so naïve.

She shrugged. "I don't care if it works for anyone but you and me."

"And in the house?" I asked, curious.

"You're my favorite houseboy."

I laughed again, seriously doubtful her plan would work. "Fair enough."

"Zach?"

"Yeah?"

"As my favorite houseboy, I could use your advice about house politics."

"What? I'm the houseboy now? I'm off the clock."

"Please?"

"You know I'm a sucker when you beg. I'll answer as your friend. What's on your mind?"

Her face lit up. "You were there yesterday when Kelly announced I was the top pledge and I got to pick my roommate. When I picked Emily, they seemed to approve. Why? Was Emily their second choice?"

I couldn't tell whether she was just playing naïve now or seriously thought Emily was their second bid pick. If she'd studied her pledge class at all, she would know better. "You and Emily are friends?" I had observed that much. "That's why you picked her?"

She nodded.

I sighed. "You aren't going to like what I'm going to tell you. This stays between you and me, got it?"

"Absolutely."

"Your friend Emily barely made the cut. She was their last pick. They wanted a couple of other girls more. But you know the politics. They have to coordinate with other houses because the Greek system can only offer one bid to each girl. They reluctantly took Emily as a compromise. Even the Double Deltsies don't always get their way.

"When you picked Emily, the other girls approved of your choice of a girl who was no competition to you. Your strategy proved that you really are one of them."

CHAPTER SEVEN

Alexis

Was I really one of them, a Double Deltsie deep down? As I tried to get my mind off Zach and concentrate at study table, I began doubting myself. Was I missing something? Was I really that good a fake? Should I tell my parents I was done living the exact life they wanted for me?

Em sat across from me writing a paper for English 101, freshman composition. I had laughingly asked her if the topic was *What did you do on your summer vacation?* Wasn't that always the subject of the first paper of the year?

I thought about what Zach had told me about her, too. There was no way I would ever mention it. What didn't they see in her? She was puppy-dog enthusiastic about being in the house. And trying so hard to impress and do everything they asked of her.

And Zach, I couldn't figure him out. I had been so certain he was about to kiss me. He was certainly flirting with me. Then he drew back, just like that. I understood I was playing with fire by flirting with him, that we could both be kicked out of the house if we started something. But I had never felt this kind of attraction to a guy before. I couldn't stay away. I had to be near him, even if I could only be his friend.

But I also wanted to know more about him. What drove him? Were his parents really as bad as all that?

Studying made me hungry. Dinner was long past, but the kitchen was always open. Unfortunately, Betty, our cook, was rumored to lock up most of the cupboards when she left for the night.

As soon as study table hours officially ended, I took a chance she had left something edible out. "I'm going to get something to munch on," I whispered to Em. "Want to come with?"

She shook her head. "Not now. I'm on a roll."

Never interrupt a writer in the zone. I left her alone.

I was hoping to find Zach in the kitchen. Instead Kayla was sitting on the counter next to the sink, laughing and talking with Seth.

I walked in. "I'm starving. Did Cook leave anything out? Or have you two scarfed it all up already?"

Kayla swung her legs and laughed. "If there was anything left after dinner, it's long gone." She nodded toward Seth. "These guys inhale food. Is study table over already?"

I nodded and frowned my disappointment.

"You soon learn to stock up on snacks and hide them in your room," Kayla said. "Under lock and key. If it gets out you're hiding food, you'll never see it again. This time of night, your best bet is the grocery store or Lates, which is run by dining hall services. But it's across campus."

I sighed. "That's a long walk when you're weak with hunger."

Kayla laughed. "If you're really on the edge of death, I'll drive you."

"Hang on." Seth pulled a key from his pocket and held his finger to his lips. "Don't tell anyone." He unlocked a cupboard and tossed me a granola bar.

I peeled back the wrapper and took a bite. "I am forever in your debt."

"Don't tell him that!" Kayla gave Seth a playful shove. "He'll find a way to call that debt in."

The way Seth looked at Kayla, I thought for a minute he had a thing for her. But it was clear from her end she just considered him a friend.

"How are you adjusting to living in the house?" Kayla asked.

She had just given me the opening I needed. "It's only been a day. Generally, I love it! Except for the sleeping porch." I made a heavenward glance.

She laughed. "Doesn't everybody. You'll get used to it."

"Lucky houseboys," I said. "You guys have your own rooms."

Seth got a wolfish look in his eyes as he wiggled his eyebrows and grabbed Kayla around the shoulders. "Damn, I would rather be sleeping in the sleeping porch with you girls."

"Shut up!" Kayla laughed and pushed him away. "I bet you would. Seth is the reason we have the no-dating-the-houseboys policy."

"But fraternizing with the frat boys is perfectly okay. Encouraged, even." Seth was ostensibly still teasing, but there was an edge to his voice.

"If you're talking about Eric, then shut up again," Kayla said. "What I do in private—"

"Seriously, Seth," I said. "What do your parents think of their son living in a sorority?"

He shrugged good-naturedly. "As long as it helps pay the bills, they're all for it. Why do you ask?"

"Just curious." I tried not to let my true motives show.

"Are you polling all the houseboys? Is this for, like, Psych 101? The effects on the male psyche of living with one hundred women in tight quarters, or the guarding-the-harem-effect on non-eunuch males." He laughed again.

When he saw my expression, he paused. "Oh, I get it. I saw you walk back to the house with Zach this afternoon. You're trying to figure us out so you can figure him out. Good luck with that!"

"No—" I tried to act casual.

Seth slipped his keys back into his pocket. "The girl protests too much!"

"Seth, leave the pledge alone." Kayla's eyes twinkled. "All of us have had a crush on one of the house guys at one time or another."

"Have you, babe?" Seth studied her too intently, like he wished she were crushing on him.

Kayla laughed. She was an easy flirt. "Oh, yeah. I'm not saying on which one, though. Or when."

Seth shook his head. "If it was Dillon, I'll have to throttle you."

She shrugged. "I'll never tell."

He leaned close to Kayla like he was conspiring to overtake the house. "Should I give the little pledge the scoop on my roommate and dispel her romantic notions of him?"

"If you're hoping for transference, let her down gently, Seth." Her laugh was perfectly flirtatious.

Easy to see why guys fell for it. If I could flirt as beautifully as Kayla did...

"I'll do my best." Seth focused his attention back on me. "You're wondering why a guy like Zach, with everything going for him—high school big shot, jock, practically perfect GPA, hot, according to the girls I overhear, anyway—chose to be a houseboy? Aren't we all?

"Did he tell you his dad is some kind of big shot at a Seattle advertising firm? And his mom and stepdad own a furniture store and rake in the money?

"They're crap parents. They cut him off after high school. Don't give him a dime for college. I should know. I've seen him struggle to get by and scrape up gas money to go home for break. He even donates plasma for cash when he has to and volunteers for those odd psych experiments that pay you a few bucks for your participation. Working here beats being a professional plasma donor, I guess."

"*Why* did they cut him off?" The words came out before I thought. They were too breathless and eager. I couldn't understand it. Zach seemed like the perfect son. What had he done to tick them off?

Seth turned to Kayla. "We have an inquisitive one on our hands." His gaze returned to me. "I dunno. Because they're psycho?"

I frowned and tried to match their teasing tone. "I hope it's not hereditary!"

Seth crossed his arms and leaned against the counter next to Kayla. "Yeah, you and me both. I share a room with the guy." He laughed. "Relax, Zach's fine. Normal. His parents divorced when he was little, like four or five. He feels responsible for it. Like he broke up the family. That's all I know."

Kayla chimed in. "Little kids get lots of funny ideas and blame themselves when their parents divorce. Like if they'd just been perfect enough, good enough, it wouldn't have happened. I've seen it happen to friends. Maybe that explains Zach, the overachiever."

"It hasn't seemed to impress his parents," Seth said. "They just let him keep believing he's the source of all evil. My educated guess, as a guy who got an A in Psych 105, is that it takes the pressure and responsibility off them."

I frowned, my heart breaking a little for Zach.

"Don't feel too sorry for him—he claims living in the house has been good for him. That he's learning how to relate to girls as people, not just sex objections." Seth laughed again like that was the funniest thing he'd ever heard.

Kayla shook her head. "Ignore Seth. Zach's a good guy. I totally believe him. He's like a brother to all of us here." She shot Seth a pointed look. "As he should be."

"You would believe him," Seth said, like she was incredibly trusting. He turned to me. "Don't get any ideas about bagging Zach. He's a tough nut to crack." Seth grinned like guys do whenever someone mentions nuts. "And believe me, others here have tried."

"If you mean Morgan," Kayla said, "she hasn't given up."

"It's been two years. You'd think she'd get the message," Seth said.

"Apparently not." Kayla hopped down from the counter. "If you want to stay on Morgan's good side, stay away from Zach. She double-dibbed him her freshman year." She took my arm. "Finish your granola bar so we can get out of here. While you were at study table, your new big sisters left a clue to who they are on your desks. At the end of the week, the bigs will reveal themselves. Let's go see what you got."

As I took the last bite of my granola bar, she looked back over her shoulder, blew a kiss, and waved with her fingers. "Bye, Seth."

Even though she lived out, I hoped Kayla would be my big. When we got to my room, Em was already there and I had a shiny red apple on my desk.

"An apple? Nice," Kayla said, giving nothing away. "Especially if you're still hungry." She winked. "Gotta run. See you later." She walked off.

I went to my desk and picked it up. "This is real clear. So it means my big is from in state? That's ninety percent of the house."

Em was sitting on our bed. "Or from apple country."

"Or interned at Apple." I plopped down next to her. "Do we know anyone who has interned at Apple?"

"No. What kind is it?" she asked.

"Red delicious. Do you think that's a clue? Maybe she likes red?" I grinned and took a big, juicy bite. Then I handed it to her for a turn.

"Eating the clues. Nice."

"What did you get?" I asked.

"A bag full of pink jelly beans." She took a bite of apple and wiped her mouth with the back of her hand as she handed it back to me. "That's good."

"Who likes jelly beans?" I said.

"Or pink?"

"Are they pink lemonade jelly beans? Cotton candy?" I asked.

"Cotton candy, I think."

"Maybe the hint is that they like fairs or carnivals or cotton candy," I said.

"It's hopeless."

"Not hopeless. We just need more clues." I was thinking of Zach. I just needed more clues to what made him tick. I wanted to know everything about him.

Tuesday was my lab class day. There was no one as interesting as Zach in any of my classes. As for Zach, he was missing in action at the house. I ran into Paul, Dillon, and Seth, who teased mercilessly, but I seemed to just miss Zach. We still had that paper to write for The History of Rock and Roll. I texted him, asking him to schedule a time to meet. He texted back, asking for my email, saying he would email me what he thought of the music so I could write my half of the paper and I should do the same for him.

He was clearly avoiding me. I wasn't going to let him off the hook that easily. The basement where the guys lived was technically off limits to us. I didn't care. I waited until I saw Seth leave the house and the stairway to the basement was unguarded, then I darted down with my heart pounding.

The main floor of the house was gorgeously decorated and built for show. Our rooms and the sleeping porch were more plain and modest than the main floor, but still decent. The basement was another matter altogether—bare wood beams overhead, pipes interspersed with them that clanked and banged as water rushed through them. Concrete walls. The scary furnace.

It was hotter down there than in the house, which didn't make sense until I realized it wasn't air conditioned. I worked my way past a utility sink, a workroom filled with tools and odd items like snow shovels and spare bits of wood and pipe. I found a hallway that led to two large bedrooms, one on each side of the hall. I had a fifty-fifty chance of choosing Zach's room. Luckily, the door to one room was open, spilling light into the hall. I peeked in and saw Zach sitting on his bed with his laptop in his lap.

The room was cheerier and brighter than the hall. Posters hung on the walls and it was fairly well picked up. Not too many socks on the floor.

"Hey, stranger!"

He had his headphones in and didn't hear me. I touched his foot and he jumped.

"Crap! Alexis?" He pulled his headphones out. "What are you doing here? You're not supposed to be in the basement."

"I'm looking for my study partner. We have an assignment to finish. I won't leave until I find him. Seen him?"

"Oh, shit. Shut the door before someone sees you." He set his laptop beside him on the bed.

I shut the door and sat next to him on his twin bed, cradling my laptop.

"I told you to send me your answers," he said. "I already emailed you my thoughts.

"I had some questions. It's easier to discuss things in person."

"You could have called."

"Would you have answered?"

"I thought we already talked at the College Grind."

I stared at him. "We listened to the playlist. What are you afraid of?"

"Losing my job."

I touched his arm. "For doing homework with your partner?"

"Damn it, Alexis." He left what he really felt unsaid. "I'm almost done with my paper. Let's get this over with."

I withdrew my hand and rested it on my laptop. "Wait! How are you almost done?" I frowned. "I haven't given you my answers."

He stared into my eyes. "I watched you while you listened to the playlist with your eyes closed. Everything you felt was written on your face."

"No!" I said.

"Is that too stalkerish?" He held my gaze.

I liked it. "I just don't like thinking I'm so easy to read. Let me see what you've written."

He picked up his laptop and handed it to me as I set mine aside on the floor. As I read, my mouth fell open. What he had written was beautiful, the way my face changed as I listened to each song. He'd captured what I was feeling almost exactly. He couldn't have known that part of my enjoyment was being there with him. "You could see the beat of the music coursing through me?"

He smiled. "You like to move."

I tried not to blush and kept reading. "'Though Alexis felt the lyrics and tone of fifties music are cheesy, at times, they still resonated with her as authentic and timeless. The themes of love moved her. She found it impossible to sit still when listening to the pulsing rhythms that gave birth to the modern rock era.'" I looked up at him. "The rest is impressive, and scarily accurate. This conclusion is a little generic."

"Is it?" He didn't blink.

"You pulled back like there was suddenly an editor on your shoulder. What themes, specifically, are timeless?" I asked.

"How about people being all wrong for each other?"

"I don't know what you mean?" I was being deliberately obtuse.

"Elvis Presley's 'That's All Right'? The first rock and roll song to hit the charts? Parents warning their son that girl he's fooling with isn't any good for him?"

"Would your parents warn you off me?"

"They don't have to." His voice was hard. "I'm smart enough to figure it out myself. Alexis, you know we can't start something. There's too much at stake for both of us."

I swallowed hard, thinking we already had. "We aren't." But I was lying.

"The girls in the house are like my sisters. That's all any of them can be. That's the way the system works." He held my gaze until I looked away guiltily.

He was right. But that didn't change the way I felt.

The second part of our assignment was to write about how music affects you personally. I returned my attention to his paper and kept reading. "Music saved your life?" I watched him, waiting for his reaction.

"It hasn't yours?"

I frowned. "No, I don't think so. It's gotten me through some rough times, like heartbreak."

"No? Someone broke your heart?" He acted like that was news.

I couldn't tell whether he was teasing me or not. I laughed. "You think I'm too hard-hearted for that to happen?"

"No, just wondering what kind of douchebag would let you go."

My heart raced. If he was flirting with me again, he was killing me. "Getting your heart broken is part of growing up. I should thank the douches who broke mine before for making me more discerning about who I trust." My heart screamed at me to trust Zach, and wished he would trust me. "How did music save your life?"

He hesitated, staring at me like he was debating with himself. Finally, he shrugged. "I don't usually tell this story."

"It's for class. You have to. You want us to get an A, right?" I nodded, encouraging him.

He made a point of sighing so heavily he made me laugh.

"You started it," I said.

"Okay, but only because you coerced me." He took a deep breath. "Starting the story is always the hardest part. You have to picture the scene. My mom has a big, wooded lot, nearly an acre. The house is set far to the front of it, toward the street, which leaves a big expanse of private backyard.

"After a particularly nasty fight with her, where she kicked me out, again, I took my iPod and walked into the woods to think. What was I going to do now? She was already on the phone to my dad to take me. I heard her as I walked out. I only heard her side, but I could tell he was pushing back on the idea. He didn't want me either. Living with Dad was just as bad as living with Mom, just a different kind of hell.

"They bounced me between them, each hoping I would stick with the other until I went to college. They wanted me out of their hair and lives. They were done dealing with me.

"I stood out there in the cool of a June evening, listening to my music and thinking as the sun set. School was out for summer. I felt lost and trapped.

"How in the hell was I going to make it through summer until football season started again? How was I going to deal with life? I wanted out. Just wanted to lie down and die."

He licked his lips and got a faraway look in his eyes. "One particular song always made me feel like I could fly. I sat down and listened to it over and over until I felt my spirits soar. Until I felt just enough hope to keep me going. That if I could hang on long enough, I could find my place in the world.

"A wild rabbit hopped out from beneath a tree and stared at me, wiggling its nose. I'll never forget that. I told it to go away. Pointed at it. It just looked at me, wiggling its nose like it wasn't afraid of me.

"It was like a sign. If that rabbit could be face me down when I was so much bigger than it, I could be brave, too. I knew everything was going to be okay. I got up and went back in the house to deal with my shitty parents."

I put my hand on his arm again. "I'm sorry, Zach."

"About what?"

"Your crappy parents." I rested my hand on his shoulder.

"Don't be. I survived." His grin was melancholy. "I survived it all. The summer after my freshman year, I went home and lived with my mom again. I berated myself the whole time for not finding a way to live anywhere else and still have money for school. I was suffocating, had nearly the same desperate feeling. It was so powerful, it scared me.

"That night, I had a dream that I was flying over campus. So free and light and happy. That song was playing. I was flying to that song.

"When I woke up, I looked at the lyrics in a different way, and realized it had been talking about flying all the time. I knew I'd made the right choice. I haven't looked back. I haven't felt that desperate since."

"That's beautiful, really awesome." I choked up. "What song were you listening to?"

He shook his head. "That's private. Between me and the song. I'll never tell anyone."

"But why?" I turned eyes wide with wonder on him.

"Songs are powerful at bringing up memories. Like party songs make you crave a beer. And songs you heard in elementary school bring back memories from that time. That song has the power to bring me to my knees with the memories it calls up, both good and bad. I listen to it when I need reminding. Or really need to fly. I won't give anyone the power to use it against me ever again."

"I wouldn't—"

He took his laptop from me and set it aside. Then he gently cupped my chin and tipped my face up until our eyes met. "I believe you think you wouldn't. But in life, you never know." He stared into my eyes.

Our lips were inches apart. I closed my eyes, trying to hear a song that made me feel like I was flying. His lips came down on mine, soft and warm. The first gentle strains began to play.

As his kiss grew more insistent, the music grew louder in my head. I slid into his lap, wrapped my arms around his neck, and opened my mouth and my heart to him.

No one else had ever made me hear music or soar like I was flying. He slid his hands around my waist and up beneath my blouse.

I couldn't get enough of him. When his mouth left mine to sear kisses down my neck, I gasped. His hand brushed my breast and I was on fire, wanting his touch everywhere.

Necking is like a dance. One passionate move and then the next until I ended up on my back with Zach braced over me, kissing me in the chasm between my breasts. I pressed his head to me, wishing his lips would never leave my skin. "Zach."

It was the wrong thing to say.

He pulled back, bracing himself above me and staring down at me with dark, tortured, determined eyes. "I can't do this. You have to go."

He rolled next to me and ran his hands through his hair, still breathing hard. "We're playing with fire, Alexis. My head knows the right thing to do, but my heart is talking faster. If I'm not careful, I'll start listening to it. I don't do emotional commitment. And I'm not risking everything for a quick screw."

His words stung. "That's a crappy thing to say," I said. "I should go."

He grabbed my wrist. "I'm sorry. That came out wrong. I didn't mean to imply..." He ran his hand through his hair again and begged me with his eyes. "If things were different..."

"But they aren't." I straightened my blouse and ran my fingers through my hair like a comb as he sat up next to me. I scooped up my laptop.

"All the girls get a crush on one of the house guys at least once. That's what Kayla says. It's a rite of passage." I tried to hide my disappointment and hurt behind a light tone. "Nice to get mine out of the way right off." I grabbed my laptop and headed for the door.

"Wait!"

I didn't listen to him. I threw the door open just as Morgan came down the hall.

Zach swore beneath his breath. "*Perfect* timing."

Morgan's eyes narrowed when she saw me. "She's not supposed to be down here." Her voice was like ice and judgment.

"Chill, Morgan," Zach said as he shrugged off the intimacy between us. Though if Morgan had half an ounce of emotional intelligence, she would feel the tension crackling between us. "That's what I told her. She didn't know the rule. It's my fault. We have a class assignment together. I wasn't answering her texts, so she came to find me. We should have taken it to the study room."

Zach was a good enough actor to fool her. Morgan smiled. "Not another overeager academic achiever! She'll ruin our reputation." She laughed like that was an insult.

"Someone has to keep the house GPA high enough to keep you off suspension," Zach said.

"Too bad houseboys' grades don't count." Morgan's gaze lingered on him. "Don't let it happen again," she said as I brushed past her.

"It won't." I shot a hurt look at Zach. "I promise."

Her laughter echoed down the hall as I left.

CHAPTER EIGHT

Zach

I almost lost my head and spilled everything to Alexis. There was something about her that made me want to trust her. But girls like her didn't fall for guys like me. Not guys with a past and family like mine.

It was bullshit, really. On the surface, I wasn't someone any normal parents would object to. Not even Double Deltsie parents. Not if I wasn't a houseboy. I got good grades. Didn't get into any more trouble than was usual for a guy my age. My parents were firmly upper middle class. Some of the girls would be surprised at how well off they were, given how cash strapped I always was. From the outside, it looked almost like I rebelliously insisted on living the servant life.

It was all the crap you couldn't see. All the stuff we'd spent my lifetime hiding and all the resentment it caused. Those were the deal breakers.

Alexis was normal, completely normal with a happy childhood and parents who doted on her. Maybe too much, but who was I to judge? Too much was better than not at all. She didn't need my shit messing it up.

I was still stunned that I had come so close to confiding in her. I blamed the music and the sexual tension that charged the air whenever Alexis came around. I cursed fate for throwing her in my path. But then, that was nothing new. I cursed fate a lot for what it had thrown at me. I'd learned early that life wasn't fair. You had to find a way to deal with it and even the odds.

Alexis frightened me for the way she made me feel. Or could if I let her. She was the first girl I'd known that made me even consider doing something different, finding another job and way to get by. The problem was, I wasn't ready to give up living in the house for a girl I'd just met and barely knew. And the simple act of getting to know her better would put everything in jeopardy.

For all that, some of the girls in the house were total drama queens. And some were too stuck up to talk to me or treat me as anything but subservient. And the house as a whole had a rep for being snooty and snotty. Most of them treated me like a brother. They'd become like family to me. All the family I had for now. Too much to risk. I had to harden my heart against Alexis. It was the only way.

# # #

Alexis

On Wednesday when I arrived in class, Zach was already seated. All the desks around him were completely filled with girls. Geeds. Indie-music-loving girls who laughed as he flirted easily with them. His message was clear—stay away. He could get a girl who didn't come with complications.

The problem was that whenever I saw him, my heart beat faster and I felt a smile blooming.

Lingering after class, waiting to walk back with him, would have seemed desperate. I would have swallowed my pride and done it anyway, except I had to get back to the house to prepare for our open house that evening. I caught up with Emily in our room after our pledge class had finished decorating the house and dinner was over. We stood in our bras and panties, trying to decide what to wear, tossing dresses and discarded choices on our bed.

Our door was open. A pledge named Sarah and her roommate Katie knocked on the doorframe. "What are you girls wearing to the meat market tonight? Let's all coordinate."

"The meat market?" Laurel, the other live-in pledge, was walking by. She joined them in the doorway.

"That's what Kayla calls it." Katie flashed a lopsided grin and stepped inside. Sarah followed her and took one of our desk chairs.

Laurel came in and flopped on the bed in the middle of the heap of dresses. We were all in a similar state of undress—hair and makeup done. Wardrobe choice to be determined.

And there we were—the five chosen ones. All of us blond, except for Em, who was already considering bleaching her hair. I wondered what I had in common with the other three and how I had beaten them out for top choice. They were all pretty and polished, confident of their appeal in the way popular girls are. Inside, I was as insecure as anyone. Only my mom's training gave me any polish of confidence.

"The frats really come through and size us up and we're supposed to just grin and bear it?" If you couldn't hear Sarah's tone, you would have thought she was complaining. But the thought clearly excited her.

"You'll think that's great until you see some of the frat guys!" Em surveyed another dress, frowning. "Peter Smith, like, the jerkiest, nerdiest guy from my high school, pledged." She shuddered. "Creepo. No idea how he made it into *any* frat, even the Lambda Rhos."

"Yeah, but the good houses like the Tau Psis will be coming through, too," Sarah said. "You take the good with the bad. I went to high school with the Tau Psi president, Dakota Bradley." She sighed heavily. "Smoking hot. Any girl who gets his attention is lucky. His social media says he's not in a relationship."

I fought to keep a straight face. Was Dakota really interested in me, or just flirting? No idea. But my ears perked up. If Sarah had gone to high school with Dakota, she had also been in school with Zach. Given the circumstances, the odds were high that they ran in the same social circles.

"House guy on the floor! Handyman coming through!" Zach's voice suddenly rang out.

Our door was just four down from the stairs. Katie, who was leaning against the wall and the closest person to the door, made no move to close it. Instead, she smiled devilishly. "It's just the houseboy. No one closes their door for the houseboy. They're like family."

She was right—I didn't hear a single door along the hall close.

I was standing by my open closet door, wearing pink thong panties and a lacy bra in full view of the hall. I might have ducked behind the closet door, but I didn't think or move fast enough. In the next instant, Zach walked by, glancing into our room as he passed. His gaze slid appraisingly over me until I tingled all over. Our eyes met and held for an instant that felt like time stood still. His sparkled with desire.

He frowned like he was angry with himself, and me, looked away, and walked by. He'd seen everything. Including the way my breasts budded with desire when he looked at them. As much as he was fighting it, our chemistry was undeniable.

Katie laughed and slammed the door shut too late on purpose. She broke out into a gale of giggles. "Whoa, Alexis! Good job."

Sarah was fanning herself. "There goes *the* most popular, hottest guy from the class two years ahead of me. If Zach had pledged a frat, I would be *all* over him. What was he thinking taking a job as a houseboy?" Her laughter was bubbly and contagious. At least, the other three joined in. "I still might be," Sarah said. "If Alexis drops her guard."

I blushed. "It's nothing. There's nothing between us."

"Tell it to the judge. You're guilty as charged." Sarah twirled a lock of hair around her finger, smiling angelically while her eyes danced with devilment.

Em rushed to my defense. "Give Alexis a break! If she says there's nothing there, she means it. Besides, I've heard Morgan already spit on him her freshman year. Everyone knows better than to cross her."

"Nasty Morgan." Sarah frowned. "It's weird the way things turned out. Dakota was always Zach's second. And now he's *the* one to catch."

My mouth went into motion before I could stop it. "What happened between them?"

"Oooh, good girl! You've been doing your research. Information is power!" Sarah's estimation of me had just risen several notches. I could see it in the way she looked genuinely impressed.

"I was at the party where it happened. But I didn't see it directly. I've only heard the rumors. They had been friends since kindergarten. Or maybe it was first grade. Early on, anyway. Practically inseparable. They intentionally decided to go to the same university. Everyone expected them to be roommates. Some people wondered if it would really work out or if they'd kill each other if they actually lived together. They were ultra-competitive about everything. It seemed to fuel their friendship, though no one understood how. Some people just thrive on competition.

"But Dakota always ran second to Zach. Everyone thought if Dakota was better at just one thing than Zach, maybe they had a chance. Unfortunately, the only thing Dakota really had over Zach was a ton of money from his parents.

"Zach was like valedictorian of his class and got a ton of scholarships. He was captain of the football team, baseball captain, and chosen as senior boy of the year. He took second place as athlete of the year to the only guy from the football team to get a Pac 12 scholarship.

"Something happened between them at a party just after graduation. It was like Dakota finally snapped. Both of them were hammered. They got into some kind of a shoving match. Everyone thought they'd let off some steam, duke it out, and go back to normal. Like they had in the past." Sarah paused, frowning.

"But this time was different. Dakota accused Zach of liking the spotlight so much that he would kill his own sister to get attention. Zach went crazy and beat the crap of him, like he really wanted to kill him. By the time they finally separated them, they had beat the crap out of each other. But, as usual, Dakota took a worse beating. Both of them would have been charged with assault, but their dads stepped in and smoothed things out.

"When he sobered up, Dakota reportedly apologized. But Zach hasn't forgiven him." She paused. "No one can figure it out. Guys toss crap like that at each other all the time. It's just trash talk. And this was pretty mild. Zach doesn't even *have* a sister. Bizarre."

Sarah shook her head like she was still trying to make sense of it.

The expressions on the faces of the other girls were just as startled and riveted as mine had to be. Something as provocative and salacious as this couldn't be ignored.

"Not forgiving his best friend over a stupid comment? That doesn't sound like Zach," I said. It made no sense.

Sarah shrugged. "I know. Anyone who knows Zach thinks he's being ridiculously touchy. You know Zach, things usually just roll off him."

Sarah shook her head like she didn't understand it either. "It has to be something deeper. They'd been competing for the same girl. It had to be about her. That's all anyone can think. But neither of them have ever said."

That evening Kelly opened the doors to the house promptly at seven and welcomed the first wave of guests into our open house. As pledges, we stood in two lines on either side of the entry in a receiving-line kind of thing as our guests, an endless line of frat guys, streamed in. Within minutes of the doors opening, the house smelled like Axe cologne in all its variations.

The members flitted about, served refreshments, and kept an eye on us to make sure no one quite literally stepped out of line. Calling the open house a meat market was a grave understatement. It was *the* meat market, the feel-you-up, rate-the-girls, and pick-your-mark event of the academic year.

I was leered at, propositioned, asked for my number, and generally undressed with too many guys' eyes to count. The entire time, I was distracted by thoughts of Dakota and Zach's fight. It was about a girl. Who? And if they'd fight like that because of one, what was I getting myself into if I came between them?

The lesser frats arrived first, staking their claim before open house hours were over. The event was an open invitation to anyone. Even Geeds. Not like many Geeds came through, though.

It was open house night all over Greek Row. All of the sororities were holding open houses at the same time. The Tau Psis took their time about coming. Like they were flexing their muscles, holding us, the only sorority that could claim to be their equal, in anticipation. Or maybe they thought they were saving the best for last.

Just when my feet were killing me from nearly two hours of standing on stiletto heels, and I was ready to be done, a ripple of excitement ran through the girls. I was the last girl in line, at the inner end next to the staircase, the last girl the guys came to before dispersing for refreshments. I heard whispers. Then I saw Dakota stroll in first. Being frat president had its perks.

He looked especially hot in a T-shirt that showed off his muscles as Kelly greeted him like he was an old friend. Unbidden, an image of those muscles bunching as he threw insults and a punch at Zach raced through my imagination. Maybe it wasn't surprising I couldn't work up even a hint of chemistry for him. Zach stood between us in too many ways. Looking at Dakota was like appreciating a fine piece of art that simply wasn't to my taste. Intellectually, I could know it was good and I was supposed to like it, but still not want it cluttering up my room. Or my life.

Kelly and Dakota chatted casually while his frat brothers waited on the sidewalk outside. It was a pure show of power by Dakota. When he began working his way leisurely down the line, he was all easy smiles and flattery. But beneath the charm, just like every frat guy who had come through, he was rating all of us like prime beef—six, nine, ten. I didn't really care what mental score he assigned me. I would be just as happy if he decided I was beneath his notice after all.

The girls were as impressed with him as he was with himself, and eager to please him. And why not? Tall, broad-shouldered, naturally charismatic guys with power and status were the goal of every girl in the house.

When Dakota reached me, his eyes lit up.

I didn't give him a chance to speak. "Dakota Bradley, welcome to Delta Delta Psi." I extended my hand.

When he took it in his, his dwarfed mine. "The girl does have a voice. A beautiful, melodic voice. I can't wait to hear you sing."

I had no idea what he meant by that. "Then you'll be disappointed. I don't sing. I even mouth the words to 'The Star-Spangled Banner.'" I flirted back with him.

"You'll sing for me." He didn't let go of my hand, holding it like he thought he could own me. His smug arrogance turned me off.

"Will I?" I flashed him a smile I thought Kayla would use. There was no way I could insult, discourage, or put him in his place with the eyes of the members on me.

He laughed. "Alexis Turner, I still don't have your number."

Before he could whip out his phone, I leaned in and whispered my number in his ear. "Think you can remember it?"

He let go of my hand, pulled his phone out of his pocket, typed a number in, and flipped the phone around for me to see. "I never forget a gorgeous girl's number."

Even with so short a pause, the line of his frat brothers was backing up behind him. I glanced down the row of men. The house guys were coming through now, welcoming us. My heart raced as I spotted Zach.

Dakota glanced over his shoulder toward the door and the houseboys. He frowned and his eyes narrowed. When he turned back to me, he was all seductive smiles. "I'll be calling you." He walked away, into the living room to talk with the members.

Next to me, Sarah reluctantly passed her Tau Psi onto me. If felt like an eternity before Zach reached me. "What are you tonight?" I asked him. "Houseboy or classmate?"

"Honored guest."

The air between us fairly crackled with mutual attraction. It was all I could do to contain it. He gave me a brief hug, the kind he'd given each new pledge in line. Nothing special about it as far as I could tell.

"You were Mr. Popular in class today," I whispered in his ear, trying to sound as teasing and flirty as I could. And keep the hurt out at the same time. I had my pride.

"I'm a good guy to get to know in that class. Music is one of my many areas of expertise."

"Along with humility?" I flipped back at him. "What are the rest?"

"Wouldn't you like to know?" His tone was rich and full of suggestion.

I flushed at the implications.

He laughed, and heads turned to look at us. "You'll learn soon enough, pledge, to make friends with the smartest person in each of your classes. For studying purposes. Hang with the top students who can help you with your homework."

"Sharing your secret to making the dean's list with me? I'm flattered."

"It's no secret. Just common sense." He studied me, his face a mask. "Looks like you've survived the meat market without too many bruises."

I grinned at his use of the term. "Barely. Being a piece of meat isn't all that fun, I've decided."

"Don't sweat it. All this effort will pay off soon. How many numbers have you collected?" His tone was teasing, like that of a big brother.

I hated the way he switched to that mode, like I was just another one of the girls. Like he couldn't feel the heat between us like I did. I wanted to break through that façade so badly. But I couldn't tell him here to just drop it and be real with me. "None."

"Really? Semantics. You gave out more than a few, though." He leaned in and whispered. "At least, you did if you were smart. The Double Deltsies expect it. Why do you think you're at the end of the line, you tempting little piece of tenderloin?"

His question, and the searching look he gave me, flustered me. I hadn't really thought about it. All I could think was, *Crap! Did he see me give Dakota my number?*

I glanced down the line toward the door, where Em was the first girl in line, and realized he was right—we were in order of preference. How could I have missed it? If Zach knew it, I was sure others had caught on. It was probably common knowledge among the frats. The target on my back had just gotten larger. I didn't reply.

"Maybe I should call you prime rib from now on." His gaze held mine.

"Don't you dare." Being so close to him, I could barely think.

"Watch out for Dakota," he whispered. "The house will give you big points for catching his eye. Don't let his charm fool you. He has a temper. When his anger is up, he'll stab you in the back."

Zach gave me a little, patronizing pat on the shoulder and walked off. I tried hard not to let my gaze follow him. If he thought he could dismiss me and the attraction between us like that, he was certifiable.

When I got back to my room after the open house, two surprises waited for me. I had another clue from my big on my desk—a miniature football with the university logo. It was cute, and not much of a clue, but for some reason it sent a chill down my spine. My big liked football? No big deal. Who didn't? Or my big liked football players, particularly former high school quarterbacks?

If Morgan was my big, I was in deep trouble. I pushed the thought away. I was just being paranoid.

Surprise number two—a text from Dakota. *Can't get you out of my mind.*

I wondered—was he really that into me? Or was I just top prize this season? And a way to get back at, and one-up, Zach.

CHAPTER NINE

Alexis

On Thursday, I received another clue from my big—a mug from the college of business. So, okay, a business major. And a lethal-looking letter opener in the shape of a medieval sword. History minor? The package was accompanied by a printed note that said, *I'll always have your back.*

Em read it over my shoulder. "That's sweet!"

I gave her an arch look, like she was so naïve. There was more than one kind of back. One of them was a quarterback. I crossed my fingers, hoping I was wrong.

On Friday in class, Zach was in the middle of his fan club again. I had to hurry back to the house for our mandatory event. The members had a Friday night surprise planned for the pledges before they revealed our bigs.

After dinner we gathered in the living room, dressed in our pledge T-shirts and jeans. Kelly called the meeting to order. "Pledges, I hope you brought your singing voices! It's serenade night!" She gestured to a couple of members.

They handed out lyric sheets.

"The frats are waiting to hear your golden voices. We've written you some special songs for the occasion. If you sing well enough, the guys might even reward you with something to drink." She winked at us.

So that's what Dakota was talking about. I glanced down at the lyric sheet I had been handed and suppressed a groan.

Beside me, Sarah giggled and Em rolled her eyes. "We're going to need a *lot* to drink if we're going to sing these."

Katie grinned at her. "I think that's the point. This is part of our initiation."

After a brief set of instructions, we headed out and strolled down Greek Row past the carefully manicured sororities, with their classic and modern architecture, to the frat district. In contrast to the sororities, the frat houses were mainly open timber frame Tudor-style architecture. Music, lots of screamo, poured out of them. Beer flowed so freely, the air smelled of it.

I hadn't lied to Dakota. I didn't sing. I played piano. I danced. But I didn't sing.

Kelly gathered us in front of the Zeta Nu house. "The first song is sung to the tune of 'Mary Had a Little Lamb.'"

And the concert began, with me lip-syncing. Sarah elbowed me. I just looked at her, like, what? If our choir was a little thin on voices, the guys didn't notice. They gathered on the lawn with a keg and applauded like fan boys. As soon as we finished, they came around with plastic cups filled to overflowing. "Drink, drink, drink, drink!" they chanted as we chugged.

"Thank you, guys!" Kelly tossed her cup in a garbage bag on their lawn and shepherded us to the next house.

It was late by the time we reached the Tau Psi house. I was buzzed and my reserves were down. I laughed at everything. Breaking into peals when Laurel tripped on the edge of the sidewalk. I caught her by the elbow and we both nearly went down in a wave of laughter.

"Last house, girls!" Kelly yelled. "Put your all into this one. It's to the tune of..." She named a popular sixties beach song.

The Tau Psis gathered on the lawn. Dakota made his way to the front of the crowd just as Kelly began the count. "Wait!"

Kelly hesitated.

"We request a solo." Dakota smiled at me.

Kelly played along. "Do you have a particular songbird in mind?"

My mouth went dry as his gaze rested on me.

"Alexis Turner."

Sarah, Em, and Laurel pushed me to the front of the group, laughing, as Kelly held her arm out in the way people do when they're introducing a new act. "I give you Alexis."

I froze beneath the streetlight that showcased me like a spotlight. Dakota stood in front of me with his arms crossed, smug and grinning, like he always got his way.

I was drunk, but I still wouldn't be cowed. Not by him. I took a deep breath and belted out the favorite song of the night. "I've been all around this great big campus and I've seen all kinds of tricks. But I can't wait to get back to Greek Row where the guys have the biggest *dicks.*"

I looked Dakota in the eye as I emphasized the last word, thinking I would have liked to say, *Where the guys* are *the biggest dicks.*

I kept singing. "I wish they all could be Double Deltsie's guys.*"

The rest of my pledge class joined in. "I wish they all could be Double Deltsie's guys."

Dakota started clapping, keeping his eyes on me. The rest of the guys broke into a round of drunken applause. We bowed tipsily. Em fell to the lawn, laughing.

Dakota stepped forward and grabbed my arm. "There! I've cured you of your fear of singing in public. You have a beautiful voice. You should sing more often."

I wanted to tell him to go to hell, but it was too impolitic until I had more clout, like member status at least. You don't diss the president of the Tau Psis in public before all his frat brothers. "And you must be tone deaf."

He laughed and took my hand, squeezing it tightly. "Come. Have a beer with me."

He pulled me to a keg and poured me a fresh red plastic cup of beer. I almost sloshed it on him as I took it.

He didn't seem to care. "Let me show you the house." He pulled me across the lawn, up the stairs and into the house that pulsed with music. In the living room, people were dancing.

"Music! I love dancing," I yelled over the din.

"Wouldn't you rather see my puppy? I'll give you a house tour," he yelled back.

Before I could answer, he pulled me past the crowd, down a hallway, and into a large bedroom. He closed the door with his foot as a Pomsky puppy bounded toward us. "I was supposed to take him back last Monday, but the guys decided to keep him and make him the house mascot."

I set my beer down on Dakota's desk and bent to scoop up the puppy. "I think he's grown already. Aren't you cute, baby." I nuzzled the puppy to my cheek and stood. Even though he was weaned, he still had puppy breath as he yawned like a sleepy baby.

Dakota butted up behind me, hands on my hips. He pressed the hard bulge in his pants into me as he squeezed my hips. "Like it?"

My heart raced like I'd walked into a trap. I got the feeling he wasn't talking about the puppy.

"He's adorable." I stroked the little guy behind the ears as Dakota wrapped his arms around me from behind and petted the puppy.

Then he lifted the hair from my neck and pressed a hot kiss on my skin, sucking until I was sure he'd given me a hickey. "I could use a little of that attention, too." He squeezed one of my breasts and breathed hotly in my ear.

My head was foggy, but quickly sobering as it became clear what he wanted. "I should go."

The door burst open.

"Damn it, Dak!" Kayla stood in the doorway with her hands on her hips, wearing that amused, flirtatious look she was famous for. "The old puppy trick? Again? Really? Stop teasing the pledges and go pick on a girl with enough experience with frat parties to handle you guys." She walked over, took the puppy from me, and handed it to Dakota.

"Impeccable timing, Kay. You're going to make a mean mom someday." He was obviously trying to tease, but his voice had a hard, frustrated edge.

"I'll take that in the spirit it wasn't intended—as a compliment." She laughed. "You know this is our big reveal night. We're on a tight schedule. We don't have any time for...dallying." She was expert at soothing his ego at the same time she was rescuing me. She grabbed my hand and pulled me to the door. "If you want to spend time with Alexis, you'll have to ask her on a real date and give her a sporting chance to appreciate your charms."

She blew him a kiss from the door and pulled me into the hall and outside through the crush of frat guys. I realized then that she was totally sober. When I thought back through the fog clouding my mind, I couldn't remember seeing her drinking.

"Never let a frat guy get you alone in his room when you're drunk. If you're going to go there with him, make sure you want it."

I tried to protest. "I didn't. He just took me—"

"I know. Been there as a pledge, done it. Been rescued myself by an older sister. Dakota's slick; the smoothest operator in the Greek system. FYI, he has a reputation as a love-them-and-leave-them guy.

"The guys love new pledge classes—easy targets. Like shooting fish in barrel, as my grandpa likes to say. You'll learn quickly enough." She sighed. "I expected more from Dak. He's favored you with his attention. Good for you. A lot of prestige comes with being the girl he's after. Just don't get a head about it." It was what she was expected to say, but her tone wasn't completely complimentary.

"A word of unsolicited advice about Dak—he loves the chase and lives for the conquest. Once he's gotten what he's after, he notches his bedpost and stops calling. If it's status you want, string him along as long as you can. After it's over, remember it's not you. It's him. Don't spend too long crying over him." She herded me into the group of pledges waiting on the sidewalk.

I thought about what Kayla had said about Dakota as we walked back to the house. I wasn't going to be anyone's conquest.

We settled on the floor of the living room at the house. Kelly started a speech about how our big sisters would guide us as we became members and become our best friends and mentors. A whoop and the sound of chanting male voices from outside stopped her mid-sentence.

The front door to the house burst open. A group of naked guys streamed in wearing nothing but neckties and mounds of strategically placed shaving cream.

One paused in front of me. "The Tau Psis thank Alexis and the Delta Delta Psis for their song, and return the compliment!"

A clump of shaving cream fell with a plop on the carpet, just missing my crossed legs. My eyes went wide. I blushed, mortified by being singled out.

Sarah nudged me. "You've caught somebody's eye. Only a house pres could order this."

All around me girls were squealing as the guys dashed by, dripping shaving cream from those dicks we'd sung about.

Kelly rolled her eyes. Someone started singing again. "I wish they all could be Double Deltsie's guys."

By the time the guys streaked around the room, most of the shaving cream was on the floor, not the dicks. The girls were laughing and squealing so hard we could barely breathe.

As the last of the guys waved goodbye and ran out the door, Kelly shook her head and grinned like this had all been part of the plan. "The Tau Psi pledges showing off their dicks."

She shook her finger at us. "You girls should know better than to sing to them. It only encourages them!" Then she laughed and called the members up to the front. "That concludes the entertainment portion of our program. The big moment has come. Bigs, introduce yourself to your littles!"

I crossed my fingers as Kayla came toward me and walked past. Even though she lived out, Kayla would be the perfect big.

Em nudged me. Morgan was making her way toward me. My stomach felt sour. *No!* When she sat down beside me and flashed me her drunken smile, I felt positively sick.

"Welcome, little sis!" She pulled me into a hug.

I played along and smiled back at her, acting like I was totally thrilled. Like this was a big honor. "I guessed it might be you!"

"You did?" she said in a sly tone. "What gave me away?"

"Your love of football," I said. "Your room is plastered with posters."

"A lot of girls like football." Although she sounded sweet, Morgan was baiting me.

"Yes, but only one of them has my back." I stared her down, knowing it wasn't true. Zach would never go for her.

She smiled coyly, like she was glad I understood her message. "And always will." She gave me a one-armed hug around my shoulder. "As long as we understand each other, we'll get along great."

Then I felt really, seriously sick. I jumped up and vomited into the nearest wastebasket.

Zach

It was a perfect Saturday afternoon for a football game—clear and warm with a hint of a breeze. Seth, Dillon, Paul, and I sat in the student section away from the Double Deltsie group intentionally. As much as I loved the girls, they didn't appreciate football as anything more than a social event, a chance to see and be seen. And the frat guys were always hovering too closely to them.

I was pleasantly buzzed from pre-gaming with the houseboys before we came to the stadium. Plus we had a stash with us. If you were careful, it wasn't hard to sneak booze into the stadium. Dillon and Seth were on their way to getting totally hammered, becoming more lively and boisterous with each play.

I drank slowly enough just to keep a buzz on and numb the frustration of being in the stands, not on the field. Damn, on a day like this I itched to play. I could almost feel the ball in my hands, the weight of the helmet on my head, the thrill of calling the plays. The camaraderie with the guys. Days like these were torture. I even missed Dakota. My days on the field were over. Watching the game was only second best.

Speaking of Dakota, he was seated in the middle of the girls next to Alexis. It shouldn't have bothered me. I should have been glad he distracted her. I didn't need the complication of her in my life. Of all the guys on campus, did it have to be Dakota?

Even from here I could feel his smugness in the glances he cast in my direction. I had warned Alexis off him. What more could I do? I had hoped she'd had more substance than to go for him. But he was the prize catch. Being his girl was a status position.

I hoped she didn't trust him with any secrets. Dakota would eventually stab her in the back, like he had me.

He seemed to be ignoring the new pledge Sarah. Didn't he remember her? She made me nervous. For two years I'd been lucky. No one who knew me from high school had pledged the house. Until Sarah. She'd been a punk sophomore when we were seniors, but she'd been on the fringes of our crowd. Not that either Dak or I noticed her much at the time. We had other girls in our sights.

I couldn't remember exactly, but I had a vague memory she'd been at the party where Dak and I had our falling out. Maybe it was only my fear that put her there.

If she was, she heard everything. If she wasn't, she'd heard the rumors. Total shit for me either way.

I told myself the rumors couldn't do any damage now, that no one would believe Dak's ridiculous drunken accusation. That years of hiding the truth had almost erased it. He hadn't even dared to bring it up again. I couldn't mention it to Sarah without calling unwanted attention to it. I had to play it smart.

So I was friendly when I ran into Sarah. Like people are when they share the bond of going to school together. And treading carefully at the same time. She'd made it clear she could easily still crush on me if I wanted her to. I wasn't like Dak. I didn't use girls. Not even to get what I wanted. And in this case, I didn't mean sex.

I glanced up into the crowd. Dak was sitting next to Alexis, trying to work his charm on her. He loved football as much as I did. It must have been hell to sit in the middle of that vapid crowd and still enjoy the game. No one deserved it more than he did.

But there was something about Alexis' face as she watched the plays. Like she was really, intently watching the game. Every once in a while she leaned over to say something to Dak. And when she did, his face lit up. He gestured toward the field and looked like he was making some kind of point. Showing off his knowledge. His chest even puffed out.

Seeing them together reminded me of how much I'd lost. I looked away and focused on the game just as we made a fifty-yard gain. Seth handed me our flask.

"I'll drink to that!" I took a long, cool pull of cheap whiskey.

At halftime some of the girls from the house stopped by to say hi. Seth flirted with them as usual. It was pointless, but there was no use reminding Seth. He knew what our status was.

The third quarter got interesting. Seth and Dillon "left for the snack bar." Which meant they were trolling for girls. I was so absorbed in the game I didn't look up when someone scooted right next to me on the crowded bleacher bench. The student section was always packed and in motion.

"Yes!" I sprang to my feet and pounded my fist in the air as our quarterback broke through a pack of defenders and sprinted to the ten-yard line before being tackled.

The person next to me put their fingers in their mouth and let loose with an earsplitting whistle. And then she squealed and hooted. My heart pounded into overdrive as I recognized that voice and caught a whiff of a familiar perfume. When I turned to look at the newcomer, Alexis smiled back at me.

"Hey, stranger!" she said. "Do you guys always segregate yourself from the girls? Is it by choice? Or another one of those dumb unwritten rules?"

I stared her down. "I'm off duty and trying to watch the game, pledge."

"So am I." She grinned at me. "And apparently I'm the only one. Have you ever tried to watch some serious football with that crowd?" She rolled her eyes.

I couldn't help grinning at her. Why did she have to be so perfect? "A time or two. Why do you think we're down here?"

"Then you know what I mean." She grinned back at me. "They don't know a shotgun formation from a homerun."

I laughed. "That's two different games, pledge."

"That's my point." Her eyes sparkled. Her lips were moist.

I couldn't stop thinking about kissing them. Damn dangerous thoughts. "What happened to *QB2*?" I couldn't help reminding her he'd been number two.

"He's no fun to talk football with when he's drunk. I ditched him."

"Playing hard to get? Nice move. Not many Double Deltsies have the guts to make the president of Tau Psi chase them."

"I don't want him to chase me," she said. "I want him to leave me alone." She glanced at the field as they got ready to snap the ball. "Now either talk football and watch the game or shut up."

"Yes, ma'am."

Alexis surprised me with her insight and knowledge of the game. I found myself discussing plays and strategy with her. "Where did you learn so much about football?" I asked her.

"I like sports. And athletes." She grinned at me. "I watched a lot of football with my dad. And I played summer league girls' rugby."

I turned and stared at her. She was, like, maybe 110 pounds soaking wet. "No."

Her grin deepened. "Yes. Wing. I'm fast and I have game sense."

"At least you weren't in the scrum." I couldn't believe her. "If you tell me you like to tackle—"

"I do! I love it." Her eyes lit up.

I couldn't tell if she was teasing me or not. "I don't. I'd rather carry the ball and run."

"That's because you're a showoff." She bumped me with her shoulder.

She was driving me wild with the way my body reacted to her. Worse was the way my head couldn't resist her. If I had been able to conjure up the perfect girl, Alexis Turner would have been it. I liked her way too much. If we hadn't been in public, I would have kissed her. Instead I balled my fists and made myself watch the game, trying to block out her nearness.

Halfway through the quarter, I saw Dak looking for her. When he spotted her with me, he scowled and turned away. But I knew Dak. The prize was suddenly even more valuable now that he thought I wanted it. I cursed silently. For two years I'd avoided him. I didn't want to get in a pissing fight with him now.

"You just made Dak mad," I said to Alexis.

She shrugged. "So?"

"You're not using me to make him jealous?" I asked.

She turned her gaze on me. Her eyes snapped fiercely. "Never."

Then something happened on the field and the crowd erupted. "Crap! Worrying about Dakota made us miss the play." She stuck her tongue out comically.

That's my girl, I thought, wishing she could be, as the two Tau Psi pledges who'd tried to dunk her in the river walked by in the aisle and gave me the evil eye.

We won the game with a nail-biter last-minute field goal kicked from the outer edge of our kicker's range. The crowd was on its feet. Beside me, Alexis jumped up and down. Everyone was hugging everyone else. Somehow Alexis ended up in my arms. She fit just right beneath my chin. I picked her up and swung her around as she picked her feet off the ground and hollered for the team. I had to make myself put her down.

We walked back to the house together. "Come out with us tonight and celebrate!" she said when we reached the door.

I shook my head. That was such a bad idea. "Sorry, pledge. Only the chapter president has the power to invite the houseboys along."

"Crap! This isn't a house event. Just some of us hanging out. It's not like you're a servant." She was cute when she was indignant.

"Yeah, technically, I am." I winked at her. "Besides, I have dinner duty."

She wrinkled her nose. "You mean you have to set the table?"

"Are you trivializing my work?"

She blushed.

I shook my head. "On Saturdays, dinner is a buffet. I put the casseroles Betty left in the oven and set out the bread and salads. But it's way more important duty than that. The main thing is to make sure the girls eat something before they go out drinking."

I arched an eyebrow. "The girls like to skip dinner to save on calories. Drinking on an empty stomach is asking for trouble. I'm damned tired of being woken up at four in the morning by drunk girls who've been locked out."

"Shouldn't our house mom do that?"

She was so naïve.

"Yeah. But why would they wake her and get in trouble when they can tap on our windows and avoid the whole mess?"

"So you're all softies?" Her voice was full of tease.

I liked the way she smiled and teased way too much. "Don't let it get around. The last thing we need is the pledges catching on."

She grinned. "So you what—force-feed the girls?"

"Ply them with bread." I sounded so damn responsible. "Eat a roll before you go."

She laughed. "Dinner doesn't last forever. After you're done scrubbing the pots and pans—"

"I'm on call."

"On call? You really are an indentured servant." She was hot even when she frowned, and especially when she pouted on my behalf. "Like, what kind of emergencies are there likely to be around here tonight?"

"The usual kind of dire situation that requires clear thinking and immediate action," I teased. "Too many blow dryers, curling irons, and flatirons plugged into one circuit at once, blowing the breaker."

"That is dire."

"Yeah, the hair must be perfect before the girls go out. You can see it's hopeless. I'm absolutely essential personnel around here tonight. Without me, what would the girls do?"

"You know how to fix these circuit breakers?" she said.

"A flip of the switch."

She arched one eyebrow. "So it requires skilled labor?"

"Absolutely. See you around, pledge." I walked off toward the basement. It was safer down there.

# # #

Paul was on shift with me. We took turns with Saturday and Sunday dinner. He was off after the dishes were done. He took off to party with friends. The house cleared out about ten. Yeah, it was shitty having to work Saturdays. But sometimes I enjoyed the time to myself when the house was nearly deserted. I microwaved a plate of dinner and sat in the living room to watch the big-screen TV as I ate.

I had just started to eat when Morgan staggered down from upstairs. "Zach? Are you on duty tonight?"

"Yeah. I drew the short straw." I set my plate on the coffee table in front of me. "Shit, Morgan. Have you been drinking alone again?"

She walked over and slid into my lap, straddling and facing me. Her breath stank of gin as she pressed her forehead against mine. "My bad."

"Why, Morgan? You're funny. You're hot. Get out there with the girls. Go pick up a guy." I reached past her and picked up a roll from my plate.

"I don't want just any guy, Zach." She cupped my face. "You know who I want. Why don't you want me?"

When Morgan was drunk, all her social regulators failed. Fortunately, she usually didn't remember what she said.

"Morgan, baby." I broke off a piece of roll and held it out for her to bite. "Eat something to absorb all that alcohol you chugged."

She pushed my hand away and inched her lips toward mine. "You're the only guy I've wanted since I came to school." She rubbed her crotch against mine. "I could make you feel so good, baby. So, so good."

"Morgan, you know it's no good. I can't have a relationship with the girls in the house." I'd been using this excuse since we met. For all her Double Deltsie looks, Morgan and her neediness had never tempted me.

I pulled her hands away from my face as she kept doing a bump-and-grind in my lap. I would have had to be a eunuch for my body not to react to what she was doing.

She felt the bulge growing uncomfortable in my jeans. "You like it, baby. Let me take you all the way. No one has to know. Everyone's gone," she whispered. "No one will see us." She leaned down and kissed me as she tried to unzip my jeans. The next thing I knew, her tongue was down my throat.

CHAPTER TEN

Alexis

I ignored three texts from Dakota before I finally responded and begged off, claiming a migraine. Then I shut off my phone. He could think I was flirting or playing hard to get. Or he could realize the truth—I wasn't into him. I only wanted to spend time with Zach.

I used the same migraine excuse to bail on going out with the girls, claiming the sun and the booze had brought one on. When the house finally quieted down, I started down the stairs to find Zach. I was halfway down them when I spotted Zach in the living room, sitting on a sofa with Morgan on his lap. I didn't think it was possible to literally see red, but I did.

The little bitch!

She was clearly bombed as she did a bump-and-grind on Zach's lap. And oblivious to how not into her he was.

Zach's voice carried over the volume of the TV up the stairs to me. "Morgan, you know it's no good. I can't have a relationship with the girls in the house."

I swallowed that down, knowing he was right. And I was wrong for pushing one. But there was an attraction between Zach and me that couldn't be ignored.

Zach was way too understanding and kind with Morgan. But she kept pushing. I glared at her. She wouldn't get away with this. I was going to stop her.

I turned and silently went back to my room. I looked around, wildly searching for an idea. My blow dryer caught my eye. I grabbed it and Em's. And both our curling irons. My flatiron. I ran next door and borrowed Sarah's, too. I took them all back to my room, plugged them in, and turned them all on at once.

When the breaker tripped and the blow dryers went silent, I turned my phone on and called Zach.

"Yeah?" He sounded breathless when he picked up. I heard him mumble something to Morgan.

"I have an emergency," I said. "I can't do a thing with my hair, and my blow dryer just died."

"Died?" He sounded relieved.

"Yeah, I think I tripped a breaker."

"Hang on. I'll be right there."

I was sitting on my bed, waiting for him when he arrived. When he knocked on the door, I yelled at him to come in.

"Where's the emergency?"

I pointed to the sockets stuffed with every hair-taming device I could find.

"Are those *all* on?" He turned to me, looking like he appreciated the situation and was trying not to laugh.

"They were until the power went out."

"You were using all of those? At once? Curling and straightening?" He shook his head and gave me a comically skeptical look.

"I told you I was having a bad hair day." I laughed. "Close the door and get in here." I jumped up and shut it for him.

"You look great to me." His voice was husky.

"Great! Then it worked." I turned serious. "I was saving your ass from Morgan."

His face became a mask. "You saw that?"

I couldn't tell what he was thinking. "Kind of hard to miss a lap dance like that right in the middle of the living room."

"Fuck."

"I'll say." I kept smiling at him. "What if someone less tolerant and understanding than me, like Kelly or one of the other girls, had seen you?" I ran one pointer finger over the other, making that *naughty, naughty* motion.

"It's not what it looked like. Morgan gets horny when she's drunk, but she doesn't mean it."

I laughed and moved in until I was standing toe to toe with him. "Nice try. Sure she does. She wants you." I singsonged the words, teasing him, wanting him.

"And you thought I needed saving?" His gaze held mine.

"You didn't?" We were so close, but we weren't touching.

"Shit, pledge, don't tease me." His voice was ragged.

I went up on my toes, trying to look him in the eye.

He took my face in his hands and pressed his mouth to mine. His kiss was gentle at first, a nibble. A brush of the lips, like he was trying to hold back. I leaned into him and opened my mouth to him, hungry for his kiss. I ran my tongue around the inside of his lips until he shuddered, but it was me who was going weak in the knees.

No guy I had ever kissed had tasted as good, smelled as good. Felt as good as he dropped my face and wrapped his arms around me, cupping my butt and pulling me into the hard bulge in his jeans.

I wrapped my arms around him and pressed into him. That kiss was both desperate and gentle. Passionate and mind-blowing. I forgot we were in the sorority house. That at any minute Morgan could come storming up to see what was taking Zach so long to flip a switch. I just fell into him and kissed him. And kissed him and kissed him until he pulled his lips from mine and trailed kisses along my neck.

I arched my head back, exposing my neck, begging him to feel my pulse beating for him, moaning softly as he made circles with his tongue on my tingling skin. He lifted the hair from my neck to suck my ear. He froze and I knew he'd seen that stupid hickey.

"It's nothing," I whispered. "It doesn't matter."

"Shit!" he said, tracing it with his finger. "Dak?"

I didn't answer. I clutched the back of his head, holding it to me, begging another caress. But his lips remained still.

He covered my hands with his and lifted his face to mine. "You could be *the* girl, pledge." He took a deep breath and pulled my hands away from his head. He took a step back and folded my hands in front of me, still covering them with his. "That's why I can't do this to you. It's not fair."

"No! Zach, wait. I know it's not fair. But they're just stupid house rules." In my rush to make my point, I slurred my words together, afraid he'd leave before I could finish. "Your job's on the line, I get that. But we could work around it. We can be careful. No one will know."

His eyes were dark and soulful. "Like now? This is careful? Morgan's probably prowling the halls, looking for me right now."

"I know. I was dumb. But we could be better. We could meet outside the house—"

He shut me up with a hard, desperate kiss. "If it was just the house crap, we could deal. But I come with too many issues. I'm not going to saddle you with my shit." He turned away and started pulling blow dryers and curling irons out of sockets.

"I have my own crap." I couldn't keep the desperation out of my voice. "Everyone does."

He unplugged another blow dryer with so much force the cord snapped back and prongs slapped him on his bare arm. He didn't even wince as it began to welt. "Not like mine." He sounded angry.

I watched him finish unplugging the rest with a lump in my throat. I'd met him just over a week ago and yet I felt my happiness slipping away. A door closing on what could have been something wonderful and once in a lifetime.

He walked to the door. "Hang on. I'll have the power back on in a few." He stepped into the hall and disappeared as I listened to his footsteps retreat.

I stood like I was lost in a trance. Until the light over my dresser came back on. And the whoosh of a blow dryer broke the silence and I jumped, startled. He'd missed one. Yeah, my love life might blow. But I wasn't giving up.

Two weeks passed and August slid into September. The days were hot, but the nights were cool. The leaves were changing colors. Greek Row was alive with red, yellows, and oranges. I loved walking to class with the rustle of leaves overhead, the crisp crunch of fallen leaves beneath my feet, and blue sky above.

I was no closer to getting close to Zach, though. He sat with his adoring group of girls in class and avoided me at the house. Once I managed to convince him to sit in the study room and discuss the sixties music we were listening to in class. I felt like we were opening up to each other, then he backed off.

Dakota had mysteriously backed off apparently, too. Maybe he'd gotten the message.

I thought maybe a little jealousy would get Zach to reconsider what he was missing. I accepted an invitation to a date dash with a cute guy from one of the middling frats. I met him in English 101. He was funny. And desperate to get a date or face punishment.

A date dash was a crazy animal. The members of the house announced a house event that would take place in less than twenty-four hours and required a date. Pledges were absolutely required to attend with a date, or face being ostracized and punished. It made for a lot of desperate guys begging any girl they could find to take them on. I took pity on Kirk.

He pledged his eternal gratitude and we had a good time. But we'd gone as friends and that was the way it stayed, at least on my part.

Homecoming was only a month away. At our weekly house meeting, Kelly called on Shelby, our homecoming event coordinator, to present the annual philanthropy fundraiser.

Shelby cleared her throat. "This year we'll be competing in a powder puff football tournament."

A chorus of boos broke out.

Shelby looked around the group for the culprits. "Can it! I didn't pick the event. We were outvoted last spring by the frats." She rolled her eyes and made a disgusted face, like, *Men!*

"Flag or tackle?" someone asked.

"Flag." Shelby stared at us, daring us to boo the news again.

Too bad. Tackle sounded good to me.

"What is the guys' part in all this?" someone else asked.

"I'm getting to that!" Shelby sounded put out. Clearly, she wasn't in favor of this idea. "Let me ex-

plain for those of you who are new. This is a fundraising event as well as a competition. We'll partner with a
frat. The guys and the girls each have a competition.
This year, the guys will take part in a Mr. University
pageant. We get points for each guy who signs up. And
the finalist and winners get more points for their team.

"The winner of pageant gets one thousand dollars to
donate to his team's charity. The winner of the football
tourney gets five thousand. The team that raises the
most money wins a trophy and the prestige that comes
with victory.

"Almost every frat on the row has issued us an invitation to partner with them. As you know, there are
more of them than us. Which means we can be choosy
and some of them will be left out of the fun."

Sarah raised her hand. "Which house has the most
football players?"

"Good thought," Shelby said. "But the college players are restricted by league rules from playing charity
events during the season."

"Former high school players, then," someone else
volunteered.

"That would be the Zeta Nus," someone else called
out.

"Don't forget the Mr. University pageant," Kelly
said. "The Tau Psis are some hot boys and they have a
fair share of jocks. They've both invited us."

We took a vote, but it ended in a tie between the two
frats three times in a row. The house was equally split
on what was more important—winning the pageant or
winning the tournament.

Shelby gave up. "We have to respond to the frats by Friday at five. Think about it and we'll take a vote by secret ballot on Friday morning. In case of a tie, our leaders will make the final decision."

On Thursday, I went to study table time with my pledge class. I was working on a paper for English when five guys wearing masks and Zeta Nu sweatshirts burst into the study room. I looked up from my laptop, mildly curious as they scanned the room like they were looking for something.

"There she is!" One of them pointed to me. "Grab her!"

Before I could move, the biggest one, one who could have been a former high school linebacker, pulled me from my chair and tossed me over his shoulder.

"Put me down!" I pummeled him with my fists.

He was impervious to my attack on him. Which was when I realized he was wearing football pads.

Two other guys circled us like they would defend us from any attackers. Two others kept the entrance clear.

Em stood up to protest. "Where are you going with her? Put her down now!"

They ignored her, too. And the other girls who joined in.

As the big guy raced to the exit with me on his shoulder, one of the other guys issued an ultimatum to the girls chasing him. "We have one of your pledges. If you want her back, you'll have to negotiate her ransom. Call us. You know where we are."

Out on the street, the big guy tossed me in the back of a waiting car. We peeled out as the girls spilled out on the lawn, yelling at them to stop.

CHAPTER ELEVEN

Zach

Kelly burst into our room without knocking as Seth and I were studying. She was breathless and her eyes were wild. "The Zeta Nus have stolen one of our pledges!"

Seth looked up from his laptop and laughed. "So call the campus cops."

Kelly put her hands on her hips. "We're not calling the campus police. This is just a dumb prank. The Zeta Nus are demanding a ransom, and I refuse to pay. You have to go get our pledge back."

Seth turned to me. "I don't remember anything in our employment contract about rescuing kidnapped pledges, do you, Zach?"

"I don't remember an employment contract," I said.

"Shut up!" Kelly's voice pitched high when she was excited.

"What are they demanding?" I asked. "If it doesn't involve nonconsensual sex, give it to them."

"They're demanding we accept their invitation to be their partner for the powder puff football tournament. And I'll be damned if I'll accept it now! That will just encourage them to try these kinds of stunts in the future. We don't negotiate with terrorists." Her eyes flashed with anger.

"Terrorists? That's a little extreme." Seth didn't look like he was moved to act.

Paul and Dillon wandered in after hearing the commotion. "What's this about Zeta Nu terrorists?" Dillon asked.

"Great! You're here, too." Kelly grabbed Paul's arm. "Did you hear what I told Seth and Zach?"

Dillon shrugged. "Who did they take?"

I hadn't even thought to ask. It was inevitable that we were going to have to make a rescue attempt, no matter whom they'd kidnapped.

"Does it matter? Will it make a difference?" Kelly was trying to tug Paul toward the door.

He shook her off. "It might."

"They took Alexis, okay? Grabbed her right out of study table. Tossed her over their shoulder and hauled her out kicking and screaming." She looked around the room at us desperately. "Now will you guys *please* go get her? The Zeta Nus are animals. She's probably scared to death by now."

I swore beneath my breath and stood up. "If the Zeta Nus beat the shit out of us, you're footing the medical bill."

"Like they could take us on," Paul said with false bravado.

"Are you crazy? This is suicide," Dillon said. "There are four of us and over a hundred of them. And they're big and mean."

"We can try to reason with them." I grabbed a sweatshirt.

"Yeah, right. That's a good plan." Seth stood and grabbed Kelly. "Why don't we take her along as a shield?" He laughed as Kelly shook free.

"Always the gentleman," she said. "You don't have to coerce me. I'm coming with you."

"No you're not." Seth picked her up and set her aside. "I was only joking. We'll get Alexis and be right back. You stay put."

It took less than ten minutes to walk to the Zeta Nu house. On the way there, we joked and discussed a strategy. In the end, we strolled in the front door. Several dozen guys lounged around the living room like nothing out of the ordinary was happening. And they were all big.

"You have one of our pledges," I said. "We would like her back."

One of the biggest guys got in my face. "Who's 'we,' houseboy?"

I'd faced badass guys like him on the football field. But there I had the advantage of speed. I couldn't tear out of the frat house without Alexis. I had to use my wits.

"Come on," I said as Seth, Paul, and Dillon backed me up. "Let's be reasonable. Give us back the girl."

"Are they willing to pay the ransom? Have they accepted our invitation?" The big guy was obviously a senior member.

Seth spoke up. "You'll have to talk to Kelly."

"And by that, he means sweet talk her," I said. "She's furious right now. And in no mood to meet demands."

"Fuck." The big guy made no move to get Alexis.

"Look," I said. "I have some experience on the field. I quarterbacked for the state 4A champs my senior year. I'm telling you this in confidence: the Double Deltsies are hot to look at, but as far as football talent, they've got squat. They're the kind of girls who are worried a helmet will mess up their hair and catching the ball will ruin their manicures.

"I understand wanting to be around hot girls." I nodded toward my fellow houseboys. "Why do you think we put up with the shit in this job?"

The Zeta Nu grinned like we understood each other.

"But we don't even *watch* football with them, let alone attempt to play it—do we, guys?" I looked to Seth, Paul, and Dillon for backup.

"No way." Seth shook his head. "We refuse to sit with them at games. We could if we wanted to, but their inane drivel about everything but football is enough to make you want to slit your wrists."

"Absolutely." Paul nodded.

"Positively," Dillon said. "Check out where we sit at the next game if you don't believe us."

I sighed and nodded. "Too high a price to pay, even to be around hot girls. The only girl with even an ounce of potential is the pledge you stole. The rest don't know an I-formation from a hole in the wall. One girl isn't going to make a team. Especially a slight girl like her."

The big guy stared me down. "Yeah, but they're hot."

"For serious athletes like the Zeta Nus? Not worth it, man. Find some other way to get close to them."

The guy frowned like he was thinking about what I'd said. "What about Mr. University? They have a ton of beauty queens who know all about pageant crap."

I waved a hand, brushing the thought away. "Look at you guys." I pointed at him and a few others who were lounging around, listening with interest in case they got the opportunity to fight. "You're jocks. You're built. Why do you need them?" I sighed and shook my head. "The Mr. University contest is only worth a fifth of the football tourney, anyway. Focus on football. What do you guys want to be known as? Beauty queens? Shit, that's going to hurt your image."

He looked at me with some respect. "So what would you do, QB?"

"Scope out the girls' rugby team. They're a club sport. They aren't governed by the same rules as the varsity sports. Those girls know how to play. They also know how to take direction. They're coachable."

I leaned in and whispered the name of a sorority to him as I held up four fingers. "Four girls on the rugby team, including the team captain. Look it up yourself if you don't believe me.

"They're just a midlevel house. But they have decent fundraising potential in the lesser homecoming events, too. They would be flattered by your invitation. Play their hearts out for you. Probably take you to the championship game, at least."

He stared me down. "Why are you telling me this?"

I grinned. "I've been tasked with getting our pledge back. No one gave me any restrictions on how I was supposed to do it. I'm trying to get the job done without getting the shit beat out of me and my friends."

The big guy roared with laughter and slapped me on the back. "I like you, QB. You got guts." He motioned to one of the other guys. "Get them their pledge."

We crossed our arms and waited. A few minutes later, Alexis came down the stairs. Her face was set in anger. You could practically see steam coming from her ears. Until she saw me and her face softened and lit up. She ran into my arms. "Zach!"

I scooped her up and carried her out of the house while the others covered my back. Damn, she felt good in my arms. "Are you okay?"

"Fabulous. And spitting mad. They locked me in a filthy room that smelled like stale beer and ripe socks." She wrinkled her nose and wrapped her arms around my neck. "Then they quizzed me about football and wanted me to give them the rundown on the other girls in the house."

She was so damned adorable when she was excited. Her eyes flashed with indignation and her lips were moist and full. It took all my will not to kiss her in front of the guys. Or laugh at her fury. "What did you tell them?"

"Zach!" She gave my shoulder a gentle shove. "It's not funny!"

"What? I asked a simple question!" I faked being affronted.

"I told them if they wanted a homecoming queen, we were their girls. Two of our members are up for it. If they wanted girl jocks, like girls who could actually play football, they should look someplace else."

I held her tighter. "Is that *all* they did?"

"Yeah. What did you think? That they tried to take advantage of me. *Please!*"

I started laughing.

"Hey!" She pushed my shoulder again. "What's so funny? It was incredibly boring in there. And disgusting. I didn't even have my phone."

"Sounds terrible. Maybe you should write your story—my fifteen minutes as a hostage of the Zeta Nus."

"Shut up." Her voice was softer.

Seth, Dillon, and Paul were congratulating themselves on a rescue well done.

"Frat rats," Seth said. "They didn't even put up a fight. Shit."

"Like you wanted a fight!" Dillon said. "What were we going to do to them? Pee on their carpet?" He laughed. "QB here outsmarted them. Good thinking, Zach." Dillon gave me a playful shove.

Alexis looked up at me. "What did you tell them?"

"About what you did—the Double Deltsies aren't the best lady jocks on campus." I grinned at her. "Then I might have given them a strategy for winning the tournament. But that's all hearsay."

Seth backed me up. "Didn't hear a thing about that. Did you guys?"

"Not a thing," Paul said. "As far as we're concerned—we asked for you back and our menacing presence convinced them to turn you over."

Alexis laughed and looked up at me like I was her hero. I didn't need her encouraging me like that, or the way she felt so good in my arms.

I'd gone half a block, hardly realizing I was still carrying Alexis.

"I can walk, you know," she said.

"Really?" I set her down so suddenly she squealed, startled. "You could have told me way back there."

"Like you thought my legs were broken." She grabbed my arm and leaned her head against it. "My hero! All of you!" She broke free and hugged Dillon, Paul, and Seth as we walked. When she took my arm again, she asked about Kelly. "I hope she didn't cave to their demands. I am *not* playing powder puff ball for them."

"Hell no!" Paul said. "Kelly has balls."

"She has someone's," I said, and laughed. "Looks like you'll be playing for Dakota," I whispered to Alexis, trying to hide how unhappy I felt about that. "I hear he's the Tau Psis' head coach."

Alexis

Half the house was mad at me for tanking our chances of partnering with Zeta Nu. Like it was my fault they kidnapped me while I was minding my business and writing my English paper. I wasn't too happy about it myself. In all likelihood, I'd just been thrown back in Dakota's path. He'd been ignoring me these past weeks. I couldn't decide if he'd lost interest or if I was on his bad side. You didn't turn down the president of the Tau Psis without repercussions, faked migraine or not.

Kelly called an emergency meeting after Zach and the guys returned me to the house and issued a statement. "Delta Delta Psi doesn't deal with kidnappers and extortionists. In light of the Zeta Nus' behavior, the house leadership has decided to accept Tau Psi's invitation to be their partner."

Kayla was at the house with a nerdily cute guy she introduced to me as her cousin, Dex. He was some kind of genius who'd stopped by to help her with her homework. It was hard to see the family resemblance—like, there was none. But there was clearly family loyalty and affection.

When he heard about the prank and my adventures, he just shook his head. "Dumbass Zetu Nus. They let their dicks guide their decisions instead of their brains. Hot girls before football skills." He rolled his eyes.

Kayla gave him a playful scowl. "Hey! Was that a slam? We're great fundraisers and fun to hang with, too."

"Uh-huh. I'm sure that was their thinking exactly. Those fundraising skills sold them." He made a point of sighing heavily. "They wouldn't be the first person to fall for a pretty face, would they, Lala?" He shook his head. "Looks fade, Kayla. Brains endure."

Kayla glared at him. "Shut up, Dex. When are you going to let that drop? Justin is a nice guy, but he's not my type."

"Justin?" I said.

She sighed. "Justin Green, a guy in one of my classes who's a friend of Dex's."

"He's going to be rich someday, Lala. Then you'll be sorry." He took a deep breath. "You and the Zeta Nus have a lot in common." Dex shook his head again. "Those amateurs! They should have seen the holes in their plan from the beginning. If they'd been smart, they would have made the Tau Psis look bad and swooped to the rescue."

"They're not as dumb as you think." Kayla lowered her voice to a confidential whisper. "They paired with the girl jock sorority house before we even had a chance to formally refuse them."

Immediately I saw Zach's hand in their decision. But I kept my mouth shut. The houseboys were absolute heroes in the house. I wasn't going to ruin their moment.

"That should have been their obvious first choice." Dex shot Kayla a conspiratorial look. "It's amazing that they suddenly saw the light right after they released your pledge." He turned his gaze on me.

I held up my hands in protest. "Don't look at me! Why would I help them?"

He grinned and whispered to me. "Then you have a couple of smart houseboys. You might suggest they train as hostage negotiators." He winked.

According to Kayla, Dex and his parents were legendary in the family for their pranks.

Dakota wasted no time getting our team ready for competition. He called a Saturday afternoon practice on the intramural field. Sarah, Katie, Laurel, Em, and I walked with the other girls from the house. Most of the living-out girls met us there. We were already becoming cliquish. The five of us live-ins were tight.

The Tau Psis were already on the field when we arrived, tossing the ball around and showing off. A collective sigh rippled through my fellow pledges.

Em's eyes went wide as she watched one particular Tau Psi. "I spit on that one. His name's Carter. He's in my Gen Ed class. I Facebook stalked him. He's single." She shook her hand like she'd been scorched. "Whoa! He's hot."

I stared at her. "Why didn't I know about this?"

"I'm private about my crushes." She was still staring at him. "And waiting for a function with the Tau Psis so I can get to know him better before I declare myself. Now's my chance."

Sarah was unimpressed. She dated a different guy every week, sometimes two or three. I had no idea how she did it, but there were weekends when she had a date on Friday night, a Saturday lunch date with a different guy, and a third date on Saturday night. She was still shooting for a record four dates per weekend. She just hadn't found a way to fit a Sunday date in.

Laurel had an on-again, off-again boyfriend back home and was currently in the "on" state and having a hard time remaining faithful. And Katie was just Katie and having too much fun flirting with whoever was handy.

Dakota waved us over. "Welcome, ladies! I'll be your head coach this season." He gave us some general instructions and passed out a sheet of rules. "If you lose it, look the rules up online." He gave us a web address.

"Today we're going to partner up, one guy with one girl, and practice the basics so I can see where we stand. Everyone line up—guys facing girls."

Em maneuvered herself opposite Carter. I tried to look for a guy who knew his way around a football.

Dakota pulled me out of line. "Not you. Alexis, you're the girls' team captain. You're my partner."

"A frosh! Are you kidding?" Morgan's eyes flashed daggers. "She hasn't even tried out."

So much for my big cheering me on and supporting me.

"She doesn't need to. She knows her game," Dakota said. "Now drop and give me five pushups."

Morgan's eyes went saucer wide. "What? You have to be joking."

Dakota stared her down. "Never give your coach lip. Drop and give me five before I make it ten." I thought his lips were twitching, like he was trying to hold back a laugh.

Morgan shut up and did five girl pushups. I would have done the regular guy kind just to show him. But that was me.

"Everyone else pair up. The guys know the drills. Get on it!"

Dakota took my arm and led me to a prime spot on the field. "If you get lost, follow our lead." He whispered to me. "How good is your arm?"

"Let's find out."

He tossed me the ball he was carrying.

"Go long," I said.

He ran across the field more like a running back than a quarterback. I let the ball fly.

He had to run for it. "Nice spiral, captain!" He laughed and threw it back, hitting me right in the hands with enough force that it smarted. I didn't flinch or worry about breaking a nail like he might have expected.

"Wiseass!" I threw it back. It wasn't lost on me that I was one of the few girls in the house who could throw the ball so that it spiraled. The rest were all elbows and terrible form.

We tossed the ball back and forth, playing catch until Dakota called to the girls to watch my form and then explained how to correctly throw a ball.

When we moved on to practicing plays, I noticed two guys sitting on the hill overlooking the field, watching us—Zach and Seth.

Dakota must have seen them, too. "Alexis, you've played rugby, I hear?"

I nodded.

"You know how to tackle?" he said.

"Yeah. Why?" I frowned, not getting where he was going. "We're playing flag."

He ignored my question. "And fall so you don't get hurt?" He didn't wait for me to answer. "Let's show them how it's done."

He called the girls over. "We're playing flag football, right?"

The girls nodded.

"That's all fine and good. Until we come up against a team we need to intimidate. If we 'accidently' tackle them once or twice..." He shrugged as a devilish smile spread across his face. "We'll take a penalty. But we'll also scare the shit out of them and get them to back off. The game will be ours to lose." He gave some brief instructions. And demonstrated some moves on me in slow motion. "On my count, Alexis, take off at breakneck speed. I'll demonstrate how to tackle you." He took a deep breath. "One, two, *three*!"

I sprinted out. Dakota took off after me. He was fast on his feet. He took me down hard, tackling me from behind, landing on top of me. He was breathing hard in my ear and pressing up against me with a bulge in his pants. He lingered longer than necessary. "You made me work for that. Good job, Alexis."

He smacked me on the butt as he got up. When he gave me a hand up, he pulled me too hard, directly into his chest.

When I looked toward the hill, Zach and Seth were gone.

By the time practice was over, I was bruised, grass-stained, and needed a shower. As Dakota dismissed us, he grabbed my arm. "Not you, captain. We need to talk strategy. Come to the SUB with me. I'll buy you something to drink."

CHAPTER TWELVE

Alexis

"I'm a mess," I said to Dakota.

"So am I." He slung his athletic bag over his shoulder and winked at me. "It's okay. I like messes." Then he ran his gaze over me with a look on his face that said he wasn't lying.

We made small talk as we walked to the SUB. In the food court, he ordered a large fries and a couple of pops. We found a table that overlooked the practice field where another frat/sorority team was practicing.

"Never hurts to keep an eye on the competition." He shoved the fries to the center of the table to share.

He was dead serious about the game and winning the tournament and the homecoming trophy. We discussed the team and practice.

"You were impressive out there today," he said. "I mean it."

"Thanks." I rubbed my shoulder. "You could have gone a little easier on me."

He shrugged. "Why? The other girls won't. I thought you knew how to take a hit?"

I sighed. "Not from a wall of solid muscle."

He grinned like I was flirting with him.

"And don't keep drawing a bull's-eye on me. You name me captain without seeing me in action in a single practice? What's that about? You made my big furious."

"Morgan? Don't worry about her." He laughed. "You know football and love the game. As far as taking a hit, I meant the other teams. The Zeta Nus' girls will eat you for lunch. They're going to use the accidental tackle play, too. Bet on it."

"None of them will be as big as you are." I took a fry and dipped it in ketchup.

"Don't count on it." He winked. "Zach came out to watch the practice. What's the deal with you and him?"

I stared at him and tried to hide what I felt behind nonchalance. "Nothing. He's one of the houseboys. They don't date the girls. And we don't mess with them."

"Sounds good in theory." He took a drink, looking like he didn't believe me. "Hearts and hormones don't always follow the rules."

I ignored his statement, more interested in what he could tell me about Zach. "I could ask you the same thing—what's the deal between you two? Archenemies? Nemeses? I hear you two used to be inseparable."

"Where did you hear that? Sarah?" He held my gaze.

I shrugged. "It's common knowledge."

"Nice dodge. You're not a journalist. You don't have to protect your sources."

I laughed. Dakota was as smooth as a politician. He wasn't going to tell me anything else unless I startled it out of him. "I heard something else—I heard you said he'd kill to get attention. Has he?"

As he stared at me, I watched him struggling for an answer. "That was shitty of me. I was hammered. I lost my temper. I never should have said what I did."

I leaned forward. "Is it true? He's an attention whore?"

He paused. "He always has to be number one. When the spotlight trails off him for even a second, he'll do something outrageous to get it back. That's just the way he is."

I led him on, playing sympathetic because I wanted to know more. "As his friend, that must have been hard to deal with."

He looked at me like he'd found an ally. "You're right. I put up with that shit for years. That night he was out for all the glory again and I'd had enough. I called him out."

It might have been my imagination, but Dakota seemed uncomfortable talking about it. I couldn't help feeling he was holding out on me. That there was more to the story, something that he either didn't want to tell or refused to admit.

"I said some shitty things. Aired our crap in public. I'm sorry about that. If I could take it back, I would." He shook his head and took a deep breath. "I apologized. Repeatedly."

Dakota paused, looking lost in thought. "If he wouldn't have made such a big fucking deal out of it, no one would even remember. He could have laughed it off, but he didn't. He didn't like the reflection he saw when I shined the mirror on him."

Dakota paused again and reached across the table to grab my hands in his. "I don't know what Zach has told you about me. I'm not such a bad guy, Alexis. He and I are a lot alike, which is why we were buds for so long."

He squeezed my hands and stared at them. "I like you, captain. There's something between us. I know you feel it, too." He sounded sincere as he lifted his gaze to mine.

I stared back at him, unable to answer. No, I didn't feel it. I felt like I was watching a romantic movie where the two main characters are trying to pretend they have chemistry and the audience doesn't buy it. Maybe Dakota was just trying too hard to impress me.

He gave me a half-smile. "This is going to sound like self-serving bullshit. But it's my duty to warn you— Zach doesn't let girls get close. Don't expect him to let you in, either. Just when you think he's all yours and the two of you are soul mates, he'll cut you loose and break your heart. I've seen him do it too many times before."

I hadn't noticed it before, but away from the frat, Dakota was much more real. I liked this Dakota better.

He reminded me of Zach. Dating him would be so much less complicated. But my heart wanted Zach.

Dakota looked me straight in the eye. "Do I have a chance with you?"

"Impress me," I said, trying to buy time while I sorted my feelings out. "Then maybe."

Zach

I had Saturday night duty again. I volunteered to take Seth's shift. The house was quiet. I was finishing the last of the dishes when Alexis walked in and lingered in the doorway, watching me work. I saw her from the corner of my eye. She didn't say a thing. Just watched like she was trying to figure me out.

I broke the silence first, refusing to look directly at her for fear of giving my feelings away. Of letting her see how stupidly happy she made me just by showing up. "Don't you ever go out on Saturday night?"

"I might if the right guy asked me." There was enough flirtation in her voice that I would have had to be dead to miss it.

I glanced at her. Shit. She wasn't wearing any makeup. Her face was freshly scrubbed. Her hair was pulled back in a French braid down her back and she was wearing sweats and a crop top. The fresh reality beauty of her made my pulse pound.

"That's no excuse," I said. "You can't find a party on Greek Row? Step out the front door and you'll run into one."

She gave a simple shrug of her shoulders. "Maybe I don't feel like partying. Maybe I'm tired. It was a rough practice today." She rolled her shoulders and winced, making her point.

I believed she was sore, but not the part about being too tired to party. The only time the girls were too tired to party was if they were down-and-out sick or in the middle of menstrual cramps. She was too perky for either.

"It's not surprising," I said. "Dakota banged the hell out of you out there." The words slipped out and had a dual meaning that I hadn't intended and came straight from my subconscious. I cursed my stupidity for letting my jealousy and fear slip through.

Her eyes lit up and I thought, *Crap, she sees right through me.* It was part of what thrilled me about her. And part of what scared me shitless.

"He hits hard and likes to do a full-body slam," she said.

And linger way too long, I thought. "Why the hell was he teaching the girls to tackle?"

"To scare the other team into thinking we're badass rule breakers who will crush their bones." She cocked her head. "You watched part of our practice."

It was like she was calling me out and looking for some kind of reaction from me.

"What do you think of our team's chances in the tournament?" she asked.

"QB2 has his work cut out for him." I turned back to the sink, rinsed the pan I'd been holding in my hand almost forgotten, and set it in the dish drainer.

She came up behind me and went on her toes to whisper in my ear. "Any tips for me?"

I felt her heat behind me and the brush of her breasts against my back, tempting me to do things I shouldn't. "Do you want to avoid Dakota?"

I was testing her, speaking in code because there was no way in hell I was coming directly out with my feelings.

"Naturally." Her words brushed my ears like a breath of a breeze.

They shouldn't have made me so damned happy. But the way she sounded, she knew what we were really talking about. "Dakota always hits with his right side to the player's left. Stay to the left of him and he won't be able to take you down."

She put her hands on my shoulders. "Anything else?"

"Dak is a player." And I meant that in every sense. "Not a coach." I stared into the window over the sink, watching her reflection as she peeked over my shoulder. "Coaches don't get down and dirty and tackle players."

When I looked over my shoulder at her, she grinned and gave me a seductive look that made my pulse beat even faster. "Not ever?"

"Why are you here?" I grabbed a dishtowel to dry my hands, turned to face her, and leaned back against the counter.

She looked up at me, completely guileless. "I'm parched."

I bet she was. I was, too.

"I need water." She reached around me and grabbed a glass from the cupboard next to the sink, brushing against me as she did. "*And* I was hoping to run into you. I could use your help getting ready for the tournament."

"You already have QB2's special attention. Why do you need me?"

"You just said he isn't a coach. I need real coaching."

I stared at her.

"*Please*, Zach. I'm team captain. I can't let the others down. You're one of us. You *have* to help me."

I dried my hands. I should have told her no flat out. But I couldn't. "You're cute when you beg."

"So you'll help?"

"Yeah. Sure. Anything for the house." And her. When it came to Alexis, I was a stupid fool.

"Thanks! You won't regret it. I'll work hard." She grabbed my damp hands, went up on her toes, and kissed my cheek. Her perfume filled my nose, and the heat of her nearness made me force myself to hold myself in check. Before I did something stupid, like kiss her back for real, the way I dreamed of doing.

She laughed and ran her hand down the inside of my forearm. "You missed some suds!" She wiped a blob of suds off my arm and trailed her fingers down it in a feather-light touch that made me shiver in the heat of her nearness. Then she blew the suds at me, sending tiny bubbles into the air as she laughed like a combination between a siren and a delighted child.

She caught my arm again as I blew the bubbles in the air back at her. She traced my tattoo with her thumb. "July fourteenth—"

I pulled my arm away. "It's just a date."

She frowned, looking almost hurt by my curtness. "And an angel?" She looked up at me with sympathy. "A cutesy, girlie angel, like for a little girl. That doesn't go with your image." She paused and whispered. "It's more than just a date. Who died?"

I never talked about it. But something about Alexis made me want to share it with her. "My baby sister."

"Oh." Her eyes went wide. She grabbed my hand and squeezed it reassuringly. "I'm sorry."

I nodded. "Me too. Her death blew our family apart. My parents couldn't handle it." I took a deep breath, trying not to sound as ragged as I felt. "I don't know why I'm telling you this."

"Because I asked. And sometimes it helps to talk."

The look of sympathy on her face was beautiful and genuine. "Yeah, I guess you're right." I grinned. "You did." I paused. "They divorced less than a year after she died." I had to swallow my grief. All these years later, survivor's guilt still gutted me.

"Oh," she said again.

This was where people always faltered. They never knew what to say. What else could she say? What could anyone say? Nothing took the pain away or changed what happened.

"I don't remember her," I said, surprising myself. I never admitted that to anyone, either. "Except from pictures. My only sister and I can't remember the sound of her voice or picture her face."

Alexis pulled me into a hug and pressed her head against my chest, not saying anything. I wrapped my arms around her and rested my chin on her head. Her hair was still damp in the braid and smelled fresh, like shampoo.

"What you're feeling is too complex for words," she said. "You need music. And its healing power." She paused. "Want to listen to some together? If you want to, only if you want to, you could share a song that makes you feel better. Or we could do our homework together?"

Right then, I knew I loved her. Crazy as that sounded. She was the first girl I'd met that really got it and me. She didn't try to get me to talk about it. She knew exactly what I needed.

"Sounds great to me." I took her hand. "My room? Seth's out until dawn or later. We won't be disturbed."

We held hands as we sneaked into the basement. I felt lighter just being with her. In my room, I pulled two beers out of our mini-fridge and tossed one to her.

She grinned as she caught it. "I thought this was an alcohol-free house."

I arched an eyebrow. "You're kidding, right? What kind of a stash do you have?"

She laughed.

"Seventies rock cries out for beer." I screwed the top off my bottle, brought up the playlist for class on my laptop, and ran it through my speakers.

Neither of us spoke as we sat on my bed, leaning against the wall, drinking and listening to seventies rock. I had two more beers to her one. Led Zeppelin's "Fool in the Rain" came up.

"We heard that the first day in class," she said.

We sat on my twin bed, hip to hip, thigh to thigh. Somehow moving closer with each song.

Her eyes sparkled. "My dad says this is late-seventies party music." She rested her chin on my shoulder.

"Too bad it's not make-out music," I said, teasing her, watching for some kind of green light from her as the buzz of alcohol tore down my defenses.

"Isn't that what they did at parties? The whole goal?" she whispered, smiling.

I set my beer on the nightstand, tipped her face up, and kissed her the way I'd been dreaming of since I'd met her—with the full force of my passion.

She slid into my lap. I lowered her onto the bed, kissing her neck and sliding my hands beneath her crop top. "You are so beautiful," I whispered as I kissed her neck and she ran her hands through my hair.

She didn't stop me when I caressed her breast. Or when I pulled her top off. Or unfastened her front-hook bra and it fell away, revealing perfect breasts, hard and excited for me.

I was in awe as I bent and sucked one. In awe that she let me touch her, that she wanted it. That a girl this perfect wanted me the way I wanted her. She gasped and pressed my head against her breast like she was afraid I would back off. I didn't have that much willpower.

No, I was the only fool around here, risking every-thing because I couldn't stay away from this girl.

I ran my hands down the flat planes of her stomach and the gentle curve of her hips. I slid them beneath the waistband of her sweatpants, beneath the thin, soft material of her panties into the heat between her legs.

I kissed her, ferociously, with the intensity of everything I felt as I rubbed the nub between her legs in a way that made her moan into my kiss.

I lost myself in her as she stroked my chest and unzipped my jeans. I was asking for trouble. Somewhere that voice in my head was warning me this could all be my undoing. But I didn't listen. I was too buzzed. Too horny. Too desperate for Alexis.

I was too selfish. I wanted once, at least once. When she grabbed my dick, I was afraid I wouldn't be able to hold on long enough.

She slid my jeans down. They got stuck at my feet. We laughed as I helped her slide them off. While I tossed them aside, she slid her sweatpants and panties off. "Let's do this, Zach. I want this."

We were both buzzed and high on music. It was such a bad idea.

She must have sensed my momentary hesitation. "It's okay. I'm on the pill."

I pulled a condom from my nightstand drawer, slid it on my dick, and perched over her as she leaned up and looked me in the eye.

"Stop teasing. I'm ready." She positioned me near her opening and wrapped her legs around me, ready to drive me in.

I saved her the trouble and drove into her, deeper and deeper with each soft moan that escaped her lips. Again and again as the pleasure built. Trying to hold on as long as I could. Waiting for her to join me at the moment of climax. It was important that I satisfied her.

It also was inevitable I would meet a girl like her— one whose mind and body defeated my defenses and tore down the wall I'd built to keep people away from who I really was. It wasn't fair to her to go this far without telling her the truth about me. How messed up and unlovable I was. But I didn't have enough willpower to stop.

She gasped and cried out. And I let go, let the waves of pleasure crash, and crushed her to me as I came and came and came with an intensity that took my breath away.

When it was over, I was breathing hard and she was smiling up at me with her eyes shining.

"I love you," I said, unable to stop myself. Like she would believe me after what we'd just done. Like she wouldn't think I was just saying it because it was the thing to do.

Yeah, this was the storm and it was lighting up not just the love I felt, but the danger that it would blow apart my whole life. I was the fool in the corner, the guy who would stand in the rain and let the warmth of her smile scorch me.

"I love you, too." Her eyes were alive with it.

My heart soared, beating for her. I pulled out, slid the condom off, and tossed it away before pulling my jeans up. I handed her her sweatpants and panties. "There's something I want you to hear."

My hands shook as I found the music I was looking for. "This is what saved my life." I grabbed my shirt and pulled it over my head, catching the wide-eyed look on her face.

She hooked her bra, pulled her top on, and sat up, listening with a rapt look on her face. I sat next to her. She took my hand in hers, lacing our fingers together.

My heart beat so loudly that I could barely hear the music over it. When the song ended, she turned to me with a look of shock and sympathy so fierce I knew she understood.

"That day in the woods?" Her voice was soft as she squeezed my hand. "You didn't tell me you had a gun."

I squeezed her hand in return. "I had the pistol to my head, a .357, ready to pull the trigger. But the song wasn't playing just then."

This was the part that was hard to explain and made me sound crazy. "I was just about to pull the trigger when I heard a voice. It wasn't spoken. It just was. It said, 'Hang in there. Two more years and you're free.'

"As I lowered the gun, the rabbit jumped out of the woods. I pointed my pistol at the bunny, but it wasn't afraid. It stared back at me."

She looked up at me. "Then how did the song save you? It sounds like the voice and the rabbit did."

"Yeah, they all did. I sat on the rock, still wavering. And then I listened to the song and heard, really heard, the lyrics. They spoke to me as clearly as the voice. I knew that if I killed myself, my mom would be getting exactly what she wanted—attention and sympathy. And I would be throwing everything away." I swallowed hard. "I went back in the house and put the gun away. And here I am." I looked at her, expecting to see horror.

Instead, she smiled at me with scorching heat. She made me so damned happy it was scary.

"I'm glad you did." She kissed me lightly. "I'm glad you listened to that voice deep inside you that knew best."

She thought the voice was my conscience. I didn't correct her, but I would swear it wasn't.

As I leaned down to kiss her, a loud tap on the window startled us. We broke apart like we were about to be caught by our parents.

"Zach!" Morgan's drunken voice was muffled through the window. "Zach, turn your damn phone on! I know yurinthere. I can't find my key. Get up here and let me in."

Shit. Perfect timing.

CHAPTER THIRTEEN

Zach

I knew this could happen, that we could get caught. "We have to sneak you out of here. I have to let her in. She won't go away. She'll stay there and puke in the window well."

"Stupid Morgan." Alexis's eyes were narrow, but her voice held a tinge of fear.

I took her hand and led her to the stairs to the kitchen. "Go! I have to let her in our entrance." I brushed Alexis' lips with a kiss and watched her disappear up the stairs.

"Zach!" Morgan was pounding on the door. Any minute now she'd wake Carol.

"Coming!" When I opened the door, she fell into my arms, smelling of weed and beer. "You've been smoking."

"I'm so hungry, Zach. So hungry." She clutched my shirt. "You're such a good guy to let me in. Such a great guy. Take me to the kitchen."

"Didn't you eat before you left?" I grabbed her arm and helped her up the stairs that led directly to the kitchen, hoping Alexia had disappeared. "I warned you, Morgs—you have to eat or you get drunk way too fast. And smoking always makes you hungry. You know better. I don't like cleaning up your shit."

Morgan laughed. "You're hot, even when you lecture. Zach"—her breath stank as she stuck her face right up in mine—"do me before we go upstairs."

If she hadn't been so wasted, she would have smelled Alexis' perfume and the scent of sex on me and gone ape-shit crazy. I lucked out that way.

I pushed her away, gently. "You're high, Morgan. That makes you horny and hungry. Between the two, food is the obvious choice. You won't regret it in the morning."

"I would never regret you, Zach."

We both knew that wasn't true. But that didn't matter. I wasn't interested. I took her arm and led her to the kitchen.

Everything was locked up. I hadn't grabbed my key and there was no way I was going back downstairs to get it. As I looked around, Morgan went to the one unlocked cupboard in the place. All it had in it were things the girls wouldn't grab to eat—shortening, jam, condiments. Morgan grabbed an industrial-size tub of raspberry jam. She hauled it to the counter, pulled a bowl from another cupboard, reached into the jam with her bare hand, and scooped a blob into the bowl.

"Crap, Morgan. Use a spoon," I said.

She ignored me, jumped up to sit on the counter, and attacked the jam with her bare hands, getting as much on her face as in her mouth.

"Damn it, Morgan!" I raced across the room and grabbed her wrist. "You're going to make yourself sick."

"Leave me alone, Zach. If you were really concerned about me, you would have made love to me. This is yummy." She held a scoop out to me to lick off her bare fingers. "Want some?"

"You're crazy." I backed off and watched as she scooped handful after handful into her mouth, until the bowl was empty and her face, hands, shirt, and arms were sticky with jam.

"More!" She hopped off the counter, leaving raspberry handprints for me to clean up.

I grabbed her by her sticky wrist. "That's enough for tonight."

"You're cutting me off?" She fell into me and left a sugary red jam print on my T-shirt.

"Friends don't let friends eat gallons of jam drunk." I led her to the sink and positioned her in front of it. "Let's get you cleaned up and put you to bed." I turned on the water and stood behind her, reaching around her to test the water as I waited for it to warm up.

Morgan rubbed the back of her head against my chest like a cat looking for attention. "You smell good, Zach." She giggled.

I smelled like sex with Alexis. I stuck her hands beneath the running water and lathered them up, washing them like I would a little kid's.

"Your hands are big and strong." She giggled like that was funny and backed her butt up against my crotch.

I imagined she was thinking about hand size being indicative of dick size and was trying to find out for herself if it was true. "Wash your face."

"Wash it for me." Her voice was petulant and flirty at the same time as she gyrated against my crotch.

I made a teepee around her, pulling my crotch out of rubbing range, and cupped a handful of water, playfully rubbing it on her face. She licked my fingers as I tried to rinse the jam off her. She caught me off guard and managed to suck my pinkie into her mouth.

"Need some help?"

My heart dove for my stomach at the sound of Alexis' voice. Alexis and Emily stood in the doorway to the kitchen. I wish I could have warned Alexis off. Coming in just now and seeing Morgan wasted and making a pass at me was asking for trouble. Morgan would have her head in the morning. The house rule was to ignore Morgan when she was in this state and let the house guys, particularly me, deal with her.

"We heard voices. Is everything okay in here?" Em took a step toward us.

I extracted my finger from Morgan's mouth.

Morgan glared at them. "Go away! This is none of your damned business."

Her fierceness stopped Emily short. Alexis' eyes snapped. She was undeterred. She came forward, pushed me out of the way, grabbed a dishtowel, and handed it to Morgan. "Dry your hands. We'll take you upstairs and help you to bed."

Morgan made an angry growling noise.

Alexis didn't back off.

"As your little, this stays between us. It's my responsibility to help you when you need it. Just like you'd look out for me." She took Morgan's arm and looked at me. "Thanks, Zach. We'll take it from here."

The girl had guts. That was just one of the things I loved about her. And gave me more reason to worry.

Alexis

I woke up late Sunday morning with a smile on my face to my phone ringing. I grabbed it, hoping it was Zach. Nope. Mom. Bleh.

I answered groggily. "Hey, Mom," I whispered, trying not to wake the sleeping girls around me.

"Morning, Alexis! I guess it's still morning. For a few more minutes, anyway. Did I wake you?" Her voice sounded too perky and seemed to echo through the quiet sleeping porch. Half the girls were still in bed.

Almost noon? Was it really that late? "No, I had to get up to answer the phone." I slid out of bed and went into the hall to take her call and have a little privacy.

Mom laughed. "Sorry!" She didn't sound sorry at all. "I couldn't wait to share. Good news, kiddo. I'm coming to campus on Tuesday!"

"What?" I leaned against the wall and rubbed my sleepy eyes. "Why?"

"Recruitment trip for the company," she said.

"But you don't usually do college recruiting." I was hoping I could talk her out of it. Mom was head of human resources. She usually sent less senior people on college recruitment trips. Only execs the company was interested in got her direct attention.

"I usually don't. But I'll make an exception when I can get a free trip to see my kid."

"That's great, Mom." It was horrible.

"I'm coming on Tuesday. Flying into that cow pasture the university calls an airport at the ungodly hour of eight in the morning and out at six in the evening. Exhausting. My flight leaves here at seven. I have to be at the airport before six and it takes at least forty-five minutes to get there from home. I won't get home until after eight that evening.

"I have a busy, full day of interviews and meetings, but I kept lunch open for you."

"Excellent." I let out a sigh of relief. How much trouble could she cause me in a lunch hour? "Where do you want to meet for lunch?"

"At the house, of course!"

"What? Why? The food is really not that great here." I said a silent apology to our cook Betty. Lunches weren't actually that bad. But I didn't want to chance Mom running into Zach.

"I don't care about the food. It's the company that's important to me. And I want to see your room and the house and meet your sorority sisters. We won't have much time, but we'll just have to make the most of the little we do have. Tell the cook to set an extra plate for me!"

She meant Zach, Seth, Dillon, and Paul. The house-boys set the table.

"Sure, Mom."

"Fabulous! Now, tell me, are there any cute guys? What about that frat president who seemed interested?"

"No, Mom. There are absolutely no cute guys on this campus," I said.

"Tightlipped about your love life?" She laughed. "I'll extract all the details out of you on Tuesday. Right now I have to run. See you soon, sweetie. Love you."

She wouldn't be extracting any details. Not if I could help it. I texted Zach, reminding him he owed me some coaching. I wanted to warn him in person to stay away from the house during lunch on Tuesday. But mostly I just wanted to see him.

I got a big, dumb smile every time I remembered the way he'd said he loved me. And how he proved it by being so vulnerable and sharing his private song and secrets with me.

I had to put a lock on that smile when I was around him in the house. Or maybe just period at the house. I didn't need any questions.

I went to my room, grabbed my towel and bath tote, and headed to the showers.

Morgan entered the bathroom at the same time as I did, her eyes red and puffy, hung over. She glared at me. "Your phone call with your mommy woke me up."

"Sorry. I don't have any control over her."

Morgan's eyes narrowed. "Then turn your phone off or keep it in your room." She grabbed my arm. "And a word to the wise, my drinking is my business. No one interrupts when I'm around Zach. Word of that raspberry jam gets out, I'll make your life hell. Tell your roomie, too. I don't need your help. Either of your help." She squeezed tightly.

I refused to wince.

Which irritated her more. "Got it?"

I stared her in the eye and nodded.

"Good." She dropped my arm. "Consider this your first—and last—warning. I'm only giving you slack because you're my misguided little. I haven't been doing my job about educating you on how to be a valuable part of our community. Consider this your first lesson, too." She walked into a stall and slammed the stall door behind her.

When I got in the shower, a finger-shaped bruise was already forming on my arm. I didn't need a hot shower. I was already steaming. Morgan had been coolly aloof and conspicuously missing as far as being a big went. Em, Sarah, and Laurel all got along with their bigs with varying degrees of compatibility. But their bigs were all reliable mentors and genuinely tried to help. Even if Em's was usually so busy she had little time for her.

It was like Morgan had chosen me so she could make sure I was isolated and ignorant and stepped in as many messes as I could without the guidance of a big. She didn't scare me. Not now that I had Zach.

When I got out of the shower, I had a text from Zach. He wanted to meet at an intramural field across campus far away from Greek Row. This one bridged the edge of a big dorm complex and the outer edges of university-owned apartments. It wasn't a place any of the girls were likely to go.

Don't wear any sorority gear.

Like he had to warn me.

I caught the edge of brunch and grabbed a bowl of cereal just before Seth and Dillon cleared it away. There was no way I was going to have any toast with jam. Not after seeing the way Morgan had dug into it.

I headed out of the house toward campus. Zach was waiting for me by the main library on the mall at the heart of campus. I grinned when I saw him with an athletic bag slung over his shoulder. I ran into his arms and kissed him like I didn't care who saw. It was careless, but it felt right. Besides, the mall was deserted this time of day.

He caught me and held me tight as the athletic bag banged against my thigh, returning my kiss with the bruising passion I felt.

"Wow. That's some greeting. You can say hello like that to me any day." His eyes sparkled. He looked as happy as I felt.

"Even at the house?"

"Maybe not there." He let me go. "Until we figure things out."

My heart flew at the thought of him wanting to figure things out. The simple statement spoke to me of commitment. "Until then, our status is 'in a secret relationship'?"

"Yeah, I guess that's it. Can you live with that?"

"If it's the only way to be with you. It has a thrilling, dangerous excitement to it."

"Good thing I like danger." He smiled, took my hand, and squeezed it. For a second, I thought he was going to let go. Then he laced his fingers through mine, like fate be damned, as we walked to the play fields.

I think we both felt nervous. I know I did. I felt the tension melt away when we were well out of Greek territory and into the heart of Geed land, where no one knew us and there were no expectations and stupid, artificial class differences between us.

It was a sunny afternoon, and warm for late September. When we reached the field, Zach set his bag down and pulled out a football. The play fields were on a hill and had views of the surrounding rolling hills. It was a gorgeous time to be out with the guy I loved. I looked around, so happy that I tried to commit this moment to my memory as something I would never forget. I just hoped it never turned into a melancholy memory.

He pulled his sweatshirt off and tossed it on his bag, revealing a tight black athletic shirt, sculpted biceps, and the tender inner skin of his arm that held the tribute to his little sister. The beauty of him, all of him, inside and out, made me emotional and fierce. I *knew* we were right together.

The walk up the hill had made me warm, too. I stripped off my sweatshirt and dropped it next to his. "Are you ready to play some fierce football?" I was laughing and flirty. In love with being with him.

He frowned and caught my arm. "What the hell is this?" He ran his thumb lightly over the bruise Morgan had given me.

I sighed. "Morgan grabbed me this morning on my way to the shower and warned me to keep my mouth shut and leave you to her."

He swore beneath his breath.

"She doesn't scare me," I said.

"She should," he said. "Leave her to me next time. I can handle her." He paused. "What you saw last night—"

"Was nothing. I know." I took his hand. "I trust you."

He cupped my face and kissed me. In his embrace, everything in my world was warm and sunny. I never wanted to leave that place, but the kiss ended too soon when two Geeds walked by and yelled at us to get a room.

Zach grinned at me. "Jealous douchebags." He bent and pulled a football out of his bag. "Time to play ball, QB."

"QB?" I said.

"Come on. No false modesty. You're the only girl in the house with any game sense at all. The only girl who gives the ball a spiral. Dak has already singled you out as captain. That means you'll be QB1. We need to work on your arm and your throwing form." He tossed the ball to me and started running. "Hit me, QB."

Watching him run, I wondered why no one had recruited him for college ball. His form was perfect. And I mean every aspect of his form. He was pure eye candy and smooth motion as his muscles rippled and he pulled away from me.

He waved at me to throw the ball. I shook my head, giving him more distance on me. Waiting until he was at the edge of my range. Then I let the ball fly. And threw short. He had to dive for the ball, but he caught it. So much for me showing off. However, he could not show off enough for my tastes. He got up. "Too much elbow, pledge. Keep it in. Like this." He threw the ball back and hit me in the chest.

"Nice aim," I yelled back. "But I'm not a moving target."

"Shut up and throw!"

I tossed it back.

"Too much arm," he said. "Put your body into it."

"Too much arm? If I had half the bicep bulk you do, you would never have been able to catch up to that ball."

He grinned. "Then do what I say and put that hot body into it."

We practiced throwing. He ran me through some simple plays. Time flew by too quickly.

We took a break. He pulled his phone out and checked the time. "I have to get back to set the table for dinner soon." He rolled his eyes. "Shit, that sounds like I'm a little kid. Come on in, Zachy, and set the table for dinner." He laughed.

"Crap! That stupid sorority." I pushed him playfully in the shoulder. "One more throw?" I tried to take the ball from him.

He held it out of my reach. I grabbed his arm, trying to pull it down and grab the ball. His bicep was like a rock. I could have hung on to it all day long.

I reached up, stroked his cheek, and kissed him. While he was distracted by my tongue tracing his lips, I grabbed the ball. Laughing, I broke away and made a run for it.

He took off after me. I was fast. He was faster. I wove and dodged. He anticipated my moves, dodging and weaving in sync with me. We both put on our competitor/game face. I ran toward the woods at edge of the field and a clump of trees and bushes like it was the end zone. Zach understood intuitively what I had in mind.

Just as I reached the trees, Zach tackled me from behind, plowing me into a thick bed of fallen leaves. He was gentle as he took me down and he held his weight off me. We lay there, laughing, as I cradled the ball beneath me. He reached around me, like he was trying to bat the ball away. Then he kissed the back of my neck and sucked hard, like he wanted so much more than the ball.

I rolled over suddenly, looked him in the eye, and held the ball out to the side. "Is this what you want? Come get it."

He lowered his lips to mine and knocked the ball away. "No. This is what I want."

I wrapped my arms around his neck and kissed him back, letting him suck my lip. He ran his tongue on the outer edges of my lips until I shivered with pleasure, inhaling the scent of moist soil, dry leaves, and him. When we kissed, I lost track of time.

He was the stronger willed of the two of us. He pulled away first and leaned on his elbows, staring down at me. "You deserve so much more than I can give you right now, Alexis." His voice was low and soft, but hard with conviction at the same time. "I wish I could take you out on expensive dates. To concerts and events and dinner and all that crap. But right now, I'm flat broke."

It took a lot of guts, and swallowing his pride, for him to admit that.

"I don't care." I meant it. "It doesn't matter. We can't be public right now, anyway."

"It might matter. In the future." His expression was serious. "I won't always be broke. When I get out of school, I'm going to make good money. And shower you with all kinds of fabulous shit."

I laughed and kissed him lightly. "And we won't have to be secretive anymore."

He rolled off me and sat up. "Yeah, about that. I've been trying to think of a way around our situation. And coming up stumped. I checked the job boards. There's nothing. For now, I'm stuck. I need my sorority job."

I sat up, too. "I know. I wouldn't want you to give it up now, anyway." I wanted to reassure him and let him know I wasn't greedy or unreasonable. "We'll be careful."

"Maybe at semester something else will open up," he said. "Right now, no one is even looking for roommates. All the housing and the campus jobs are filled."

"I don't want you to give up the house." I wanted him to understand I knew he needed it. "We'll think of something."

"One day at a time?" He pulled a leaf from my hair and took my hand.

I squeezed his hand to reassure him. "One day at a time."

He stood, pulled me to my feet, and grabbed the football.

Something about being at the edge of the woods made me think of what he'd told me last night. "Zach?"

He looked at me curiously.

"You haven't ever thought of killing yourself again, have you?" I swallowed hard. "Because if you ever need someone to talk to, you can always talk to me."

His face became a mask. My heart pounded like I had really messed up.

"I don't have clinical depression." He spoke calmly. "I never have. I had a trauma when I was little that scarred me and made me feel like I didn't deserve to live. I realized that day in the woods that I've been given my life for a reason. And there's no way I'm going to squander it."

"Oh." I let out a sigh of relief and felt a smile blooming, knowing better than to press for more details, no matter how horrible and wild what I imagined might be.

"To answer your question, I felt unworthy for so long, it became a habit. Sometimes those feelings come back. But I have ways to cope now." He grinned at me. "And even more reasons to go on." He put the football in the bag and handed me my sweatshirt.

I pulled mine on at the same time he pulled his on.

He slid the bag over his shoulder and we began walking back. He gave me a lopsided grin. "Any dark secrets you want to share with me?"

I made a face. "My mom is coming to campus on Tuesday for a recruiting trip. She's eating lunch with me at the house. Does that count?"

He laughed. "You were holding out on me. If that's the darkest secret you have, I have it easy." He looked at me, suddenly serious. "Do you want me to make myself scarce?"

"No!" I decided without thinking. My original plan had been flat-out wrong, I realized. Why should I hide him? "I think you should meet her. Casually. If she meets you, she'll see how awesome you are and be happy when we eventually tell her how we feel about each other."

He shot me a skeptical look. "Do you really think she's going to be happy you fell for the houseboy? From what I've gathered, that doesn't sound like your ultra-Double Deltsie mom to me."

"You aren't going to be a houseboy forever," I said, evading his question.

He put his arm around my shoulder. "And another thing—let's keep this football practice secret, too. Enjoying tackling and really loving sports isn't Double Deltsie behavior. It will ruin their rep."

I shook my head and laughed.

He grinned. "The perils of being the favorite pledge."

"Someday someone is going to have to explain to me why I am."

"That's easy," he said. "You're totally lovable."

CHAPTER FOURTEEN

Alexis

Zach saved me a seat in class on Monday. The girls he had been sitting with shot me dagger looks, but I didn't care. Even though we had to keep things quiet, I was too deliriously happy to worry about the opinions of others outside of the house. Except for Mom's. Mostly because she held the purse strings and the power of parental disapproval over me.

I was that desperately wanted child, the one my parents had tried for years to conceive. The one they went through round after round of fertility treatments and expense to get. I was the product of one weak egg that somehow made it through in vitro. And implanted. And lived. And thrived when the doctors said it was almost impossible for Mom to get pregnant and carry a child to term.

Dad told me that was why I was so strong-willed and vital. That I had wanted to live so badly I defied every odd. I didn't know about that. I didn't feel so strong-willed now.

I was the child of my parents' early middle age, born when they were in their early forties. I carried the weight of their posterity on my shoulders. As much as they loved me, they had also invested everything in me. Including their dreams.

I had always done what they had asked. Carried their dreams forward, even going through recruitment and becoming a Double Deltsie because that's what they wanted. I even tried to be a good Double Deltsie. But more and more my dreams were diverging from theirs. Mostly because of Zach.

Yet I knew if Mom and Dad met him, they would like him. If they could just get past him being a house-boy, they would see he was everything they wanted in a guy for me.

I was nervous on Tuesday as I waited for Mom to arrive at the house. I had put on my makeup and done my hair. Dressed in the right clothes. I looked full-on Double Deltsie. I hoped it was enough.

I was sitting on the sofa in the living room when Mom walked in the door. I hadn't realized how much I'd missed her until she called my name and held her arms wide open for a hug.

"Mom!" I ran to her.

She hugged me and then held me at arm's length to look at me. "Gorgeous! Sorority life agrees with you. You are the perfect Double Deltsie."

Only because I was trying to fool her, and everyone else, into thinking it. Only because I was trying to please her. Inside I was miserable and a fake.

She looked around the house, beaming. Glowing with memories. Even though she was nearly sixty and gray-haired and it was almost impossible to picture her as a young, hot Double Deltsie, her rapturous expression gave a hint of it.

"The place has changed." She inhaled deeply. "But it still smells the same."

"Smells the same?" I frowned, skeptical. "Like what?"

She laughed. "Like laundry soap, cleaning supplies, youthful perfume, and bodies. Like dust and old house and fresh paint. And salads and sandwiches and soup. Like being young." She shrugged. "It's a scent all its own. Unique and unmistakable."

She took my arm. "Show me around! Show me the house! I have to see your room and what you did with it. We'll have to be quick, though. I only have an hour."

I took her to my room and introduced her to Em, who had gradually been highlighting her hair until she was almost blond now. Mom looked around the room like she approved of it and Em.

"I almost forgot," Mom said. "I brought you something." She pulled a velvet jewelry box out of her purse and watched me with rapt attention while I took it. "Open it!"

I popped the lid, revealing a Delta Delta Psi neck-lace with a diamond glittering in the center. And yeah, it was a diamond, not cut glass or a crystal. And the chain was 14K gold. "It's...gorgeous. You shouldn't have." My heart fell at the sight of it. She was way too into this.

"Nonsense! I ordered it the minute you accepted your bid. I was going to save it for Christmas, but I couldn't wait." She took the box from me. "Let me help you put it on."

Em was sitting at her desk. She came over to admire it. "Wow! Awesome."

I wished it were hers, not mine. I would give up it and the house for Zach.

Mom beamed. Em joined us as I showed Mom the rest of the house. Mom told stories about just about every room in the place, sharing secrets I had never known about her. Throughout the tour I gave Mom, the other girls admired my necklace. And Mom beamed with pride.

I ended the tour in the dining room. As we'd planned, Zach was working the lunch shift. Even though he was dressed casually, he was wearing a but-ton-front shirt and had freshly shaved like he had fixed up for the occasion. My pulse raced. He was so smoking hot. And friendly and charming as the girls talked and joked with him.

Mom had to see he was more than an ordinary houseboy.

He was restocking the salad buffet when we came in. I grabbed a plate and led Mom through the buffet to where Zach was putting out a fresh bowl of grated cheese. I don't know how, but Mom seemed oblivious to him. Almost pointedly so. Even after Em started talking with him.

Until I cleared my throat. "Mom, this is Zach. One of our four awesome house guys. No house tour is complete without meeting them. Zach, Mom."

Mom's eyes narrowed, like she was taking stock of Zach. "Do you boys still live in the basement?"

"Yes, ma'am." He smiled at her.

She didn't extend her hand, just nodded curtly. "Another Double Deltsie tradition maintained. Nice to meet you, Zach." And then she moved on, like he was a server at a restaurant buffet and of absolutely no consequence unless she needed another helping of something.

I was stinging at her snobbery. How could she not notice how extraordinary he was? I had to resist shooting Zach a look apologizing for her. It was so odd to be in this position. Mom was usually the queen of social graces, an absolutely smooth and charming hostess or guest. I felt the social slap she'd given Zach as if it had been a physical slap across my face.

I was quiet as we took our salads to one of the tables and Em and I sat on either side of my mom. Mom didn't seem to notice as she ingratiated herself with my sorority sisters. Acting like she was one of them. And at the same time, reveling in her superior alum position. Talking about being on the national board and all the accomplished Double Deltsie alums she knew.

We were going places. We were going to be big somethings. We shouldn't let anything, or anyone, particularly a boy, hold us back. I might have been super sensitive, but I thought she was making a particular point for my benefit.

She held up the success of Amber Ranklin, a young alum, in Mom's opinion, anyway, who was the youngest university regent. Maybe they were just being polite, but Em and the other girls made a point of paying close attention, sucking up to Mom. Impressed by her accomplishments.

And I thought, *Crap, that's why I'm the top pledge. No one wants to tick Mom off.*

And so Mom's legacy continued.

Zach walked past the table, carrying a fresh pot of soup to the buffet line. I couldn't help noticing the way his biceps bulged and how he was trying to ignore us. But I knew he had to be curious and wished he could sit and join us so I could really show him off. And Mom could get to know him.

"Do the houseboys still cook Sunday breakfast?" Mom spoke loudly, like she wanted Zach to overhear. Like she was putting him in his place.

Em responded. "Oh, yeah! Zach makes mean scrambled eggs with cheese. I look forward to Sundays just for them."

"How nice," Mom said, still too loudly. "A boy who can cook." She made it sound like it was his only skill.

Laurel and Sarah joined us, saving me from thoughts of telling Mom off. I introduced them to her.

She sucked them into her circle, promising to use her connections in HR to help girls get key internships.

I had set my phone on the table. When it buzzed, I glanced at it. A text from Dakota. *Come to the date dash with me tomorrow?*

I ignored it.

"Aren't you going to answer that?" Mom asked, taking a breath from talking with the other girls nonstop.

"It's just a text." I shrugged like it was no big deal. The phone buzzed again. A second text. *The pres has to set an example. You get a free T-shirt. It glows under black lights. Am I enticing you?*

"From whom?" she asked.

Laurel leaned over my shoulder. "Dakota Bradley! President of Tau Psi," she said for Mom's benefit.

I wanted to elbow her.

Mom beamed, like this turn of events just kept making her happier and happier. She gave me a knowing look. "*And?* What does he want?"

"Probably just wants to schedule a practice for our football team," I lied. I hadn't told her much about that, either. She wouldn't approve of me playing tackle football, even if it was for the sorority's charity.

"Liar!" Sarah was sitting on the other side of me. She glanced at my phone. "He's practically begging to take you to the Tau Psi date dash tomorrow night. Hardhearted wench!"

"The Tau Psis are having a date dash tomorrow?" Em perked up, looking excited, hopeful, and despondent at the same time.

I knew that cocktail of emotions, waiting for a guy to call. Hoping he will. I hoped her Tau Psi crush would invite her.

"Don't keep the boy waiting," Mom said. "Tell him you'll go."

I shook my head. "Maybe later."

"Don't be shy! You can text him in front of us. You are so *lucky*!" Laurel explained to Mom about how prestigious the house was and how gorgeous Dakota was. Like Mom didn't already know. "You can't say no."

Kelly walked by just then. "No to who?"

"Dakota asked her to the date dash tomorrow."

I glared at Sarah for giving me up.

"She's right. You can't say no," Kelly said. "It's an unwritten rule. Dakota asking one of our pledges is, like, a huge honor. The frat president doesn't usually ask *anyone* to date dashes. Only the pledges are required to attend." She gave me an encouraging smile, beaming like she was incredibly pleased.

I looked at them helplessly. Zach was clearing things behind us. I was sure he'd heard every word.

"There's no good reason for you to refuse him." Kelly paused. "Unless you have a secret boyfriend we don't know about?"

My heart felt like it fell into my stomach and landed with a crash. For a second, I thought Zach and I had already been found out. When I realized I was about to give us away if I didn't act, I smiled, shakily, and typed a response. *A free T-shirt? How can I resist?*

Kelly and my mom broke into eerily similar proud smiles. *Crap!*

After lunch, I walked Mom out, going all the way to the sidewalk with her. I thanked her for the necklace as I hugged her goodbye. "Hope your afternoon meetings go well. Have a safe trip home and kiss Dad for me."

"Will do." She looked me in the eye. "Stay away from that houseboy. Zach," she said, catching me by surprise.

I thought I had been pretty stealthy about my feelings for him.

"I don't know what you mean." I put on the innocent act I had perfected during high school.

"I think you do." She looked me in the eye. "That's why you introduced us." She took a deep breath. "He's a handsome boy, I'll give you that. Charming in his way. I can see how he'd catch your eye." She sighed. "Totally stupid of your house mom to allow such good-looking boys to live in. Trouble."

She took me by the arms. "You're destiny lies with the house and a great life after college. Don't let a crush on a *houseboy* your freshman year mess that up. Give that frat president a fair shake, Alexis."

I watched Mom walk off, feeling desperate and hopeless. Then I realized—there was a solution. I just had to be brave enough to grab it.

CHAPTER FIFTEEN

Zach

I waited for Alexis in front of the SUB. When she saw me, she flew into my arms and kissed me like she'd missed me as much as I had her.

"Hey, whoa!" I said, pulling away when I finally got the willpower to. "Someone like an avenging Double Deltsie might see us." I tried to sound light and teasing. But I was seething inside, railing at everything.

"I don't care!" Her eyes flashed. "Zach, I am *so* sorry about my mom." She rolled her eyes. "I didn't think she was such a snob. You heard?"

I nodded. Her mom could diss me all she wanted. I'd learned to let crap like that roll off my back.

"Yeah?" She sighed. "Don't tell me you told me so. You were so right. I was just stupid." She paused. "You heard the part about Dakota and the date dash, too?"

"Afraid so." It was hard to sound casual when I was burning with jealousy. I took her backpack from her and flung it over my shoulder as we started walking toward the door.

"I'm not going. I refuse." Her face was set and stubborn. She looked fucking gorgeous to me.

I grinned at her. "That's the spirit. How are you going to get out of it now?"

"Easy."

"Easy?" I repeated, and raised an eyebrow.

"Yeah, now that I've made up my mind."

She was damned cute when she was fired up.

"I know how to solve our problem." Her tone put me on guard.

"Yeah? How's that?" I held the door for her as we walked into the SUB. We were supposedly "studying" together.

She passed through in front of me and dropped the bomb. "I'm going to quit the sorority."

I caught her arm. "Whoa!" I studied her to see if she was serious. "We need to talk this out."

She smiled at me. "A guy who wants to talk. That's cute."

"I'm serious, Alexis. This is serious shit."

She shrugged. "There's nothing to talk about."

"Really?" I said. "That's bullshit."

The cafeteria was packed with students studying. I bought us each a pop and found a table in the corner out of earshot.

We didn't say another word until we were seated opposite each other across the table. I brought it up. "You can't quit the Double Deltsies. Once a Double Deltsie, always a Double Deltsi. They don't let you out. Quitters ruin their rep."

"I can. I'm not a member yet. Not for another week." She leaned forward as she grabbed her cup of soda. "Think about it. If I quit, I don't have to go out with Dakota. You won't lose your job if we get caught. And we can date and not care who knows."

I nodded. "Good plan. Screw everyone." I paused and tried to sound completely reasonable. "What happens when your parents go ballistic on you?"

She shrugged like "no big deal." But she squirmed, giving herself away. She had no idea the trouble she was about to step in. I loved her too much. Even though it ran counter to everything I wanted, I couldn't let her throw away her relationship with them.

"You can handle their disappointment?" I studied her. "Are you sure? That necklace your mom gave you. Her hopes are pretty high."

She shrugged again.

I wrapped my hands around hers, which were wrapped around her paper cup so tightly she was about to crush it. "Damn, you don't know how much it means to me that you're willing to make that sacrifice for us." I paused to emphasize my point and stroked her hands with my thumbs. "But I can't let you do it. We'll find another way."

She looked me square in the eye. "I don't need your permission."

"I get that. But we're a team, right? If this is for us, we have to agree and prepare." I smiled at her, trying to make her understand. "Have you ever defied your parents on something this important before?"

She hesitated and grinned like she was trying to win me over and divert my attention. "You mean like over a guy?"

"Over anything that would piss them off so badly they cut you off," I said. "The truth."

"No. But maybe the time has come."

Her answer didn't surprise me. I saw the pleaser in her, like in my little brothers. Being the most-loved child had its own set of pressures.

"You're an only. You don't have any siblings who have tested the waters. You have no idea how badly they'll react."

"I have an idea—"

"Yeah. We both have an idea. But we don't know *how* hacked off they'll be. Or how long they'll hold a grudge." I held her gaze, trying to make her see what she was risking. "They'll cut your money off. Best case, they'll only threaten to. Money gives them power. Money and the guilt trip they'll throw at you."

"Why are you fighting me? I thought you would be happy!" Her eyes pleaded with me, but were rapidly filling with hurt. "We can be together openly. Screw everyone else and all these stupid rules!"

I clasped her hands tighter. "No argument here. The rules are crap," I said. "If you drop out of the house, you'll never get back in. Not to the Double Deltsies. Not to *any* house. Your mom will be supremely pissed about that. *Forever.*" I tried to keep the emotion out of my voice. "It's not easy to fall from grace. Take it from me."

"Zach..." Alexis' eyes filled with pity.

Shit. I hated being pitied.

"Don't give your parents another grudge against me. I don't want it to be me, the guy you threw your life away for, against them." I tipped her chin up. "It's like you said. I won't be a houseboy forever. Chill for now. Agreed?" I gave her my best pleading look. "For me?"

She sighed. "For *now*. But what about my date dash with Dakota?"

I fought not to blow all the progress I'd made. "Shit. That sucks. I'm wild with jealousy. Not that I would ever take you to a crappy frat party. You deserve better."

She grinned. "Where would you take me?"

I just grinned and raised an eyebrow.

She laughed. "If only! What do I do about Dakota?"

"Text me throughout the night. Definitely don't drink. Refuse all house tours. And bail early." I grinned. "It wouldn't hurt to wear his ex's favorite perfume. Just saying."

Her eyes sparkled. "You're awful! What else?"

"Cinnamon breath mints. He hates those."

She laughed. "That's it? He isn't, like, deathly aller-gic to something I could wear?"

"Vicious! You want to kill a guy just because he wants to get it on with you?"

"Not kill. Just disable."

Shit, I loved it when her face lit up like that and she threw my crap back at me.

"A date dash is just an excuse to get a girl to have sex with you. Dak was known as 'hands' for more than the way he handled a football. If he lays one finger on you, call me and I'll come and beat the shit out of QB2."

"My hero!" She faked a swoon.

I leaned across the table and brushed her lips with a kiss that made me wish weren't separated by a table and so much more. I lowered my voice. "I've heard of a few things you can dump in a guy's beer that take him out of the mood as soon as he starts vomiting his guts out."

She made a disgusted face. "What! That's awful."

"Yeah," I said. "The things you learn living in a so-rority house." I smiled and shook my head. "I love you, pledge. I can't believe I'm encouraging you to go on a date with my ex-best friend. Sometimes reality bites."

"Doesn't it?" Her smile made me weak in the knees. "I love you, too." Her words were even better.

Alexis

Sometimes love was a crazy, wild thing that made you do stupid stuff. Like going on a date with someone else when I only wanted to be with Zach. Yeah, going out with Dakota was good for hiding my relationship with Zach, but I still hated it. And part of me wanted insane jealousy from Zach. Not reasonableness. Not logic. But that was only the fantasy part of me that thought passionate jealousy was romantic in the abstract. Like kissing the steps where I'd walked. Or tossing rose petals in my path.

Em was glowing when I got back to the house. "I'm going to Wasted Wednesday!" She bounced off the bed in our shared room and took my hands so I could bounce with her.

I didn't feel bouncy. "What?"

"Wasted Wednesday. You know, the Tau Psi date dash? Carter asked me!"

"That's fab!" I got it now and bounced with her. "We can get ready together."

Dakota texted me to wear jeans and be prepared to lose my shirt—for the one he was giving me. Very funny.

Em spent hours on her hair and makeup getting ready. I made a valiant attempt at pretending to be excited. Carter and Dakota asked us to meet them at the frat house.

Em was full of details. "Until eleven, it's a closed party. Then anyone can show up." She made a face to show her disgust at the shortness of the exclusivity.

I was planning to ditch way before eleven.

When I returned from the bathroom to grab my stuff and head out, there was a water bottle filled with juice on my desk.

Zach texted me. *Carry this water bottle around. Pretend it's spiked. The guys will think you're drinking and leave you alone.*

I smiled to myself. He really was my hero.

I grabbed the bottle. When Em came back to the room, we headed downstairs together.

Kayla caught us as we were about to head out for the date dash. She eyed my water bottle. "Bringing your own booze. Smart plan. That's what I always do." She winked.

I had renewed respect for her and Zach.

Em was filled with nervous excitement and gushing about Carter as we walked to the Tau Psi house through the crisp autumn evening and the parties pounding from frat houses. Half a block from Tau Psi, I texted Dakota that I would be there in minutes and popped a cinnamon breath mint in my mouth.

When we showed up, he was waiting on the front porch of the house, holding a beer and leaning against a pillar beneath a light. Impervious to the cold, he was dressed in jeans and an official dark blue date dash T-shirt that showed off his toned arms and trim, athletic form. The light lit a halo around his hair. His face was set in the easy smile of a popular guy who was used to making girls' hearts pound. The power and prestige of his status and position on campus alone should have been enough to light me up. I thought, like I had a zillion times before, *He should make my heart dance. But he doesn't.*

Compared to Zach, Dakota was a distant number two.

Carter stood next to him. When Carter spotted us, he ran to Em like an eager pledge puppy. Dakota, too cool to be bothered, waited for me to come up the steps and get a full-frontal view of his T-shirt with its glowing white letters and stenciled pair of praying hands.

"Pull Out and Pray Date Dash," I read, and looked him in the eye. "I thought this was Wasted Wednesday."

He nodded toward the water bottle filled with juice in my hand. "You couldn't wait to get started?"

I grinned. "I was getting a jump on what I thought was the theme."

"'Jump' fits the theme." He winked, took my hand, and pulled me toward the frat house that pulsed with music and smelled like beer and hot bodies.

Carter and Emily fell in behind us, oblivious to us now.

A pledge at the door ran his gaze up and down me. "Small?" He held up a folded pink T-shirt.

"Good eye," I said as I took it from him. I shook it out as we walked in. On the back was a silhouette of a cowgirl riding bareback on a bucking horse. And the slogan, "It's better bareback."

I turned to Dakota. "The eternal optimists."

He laughed and pointed. "The bathroom's over there if you want to change." He was issuing a challenge, daring me to be a chicken and change in the bathroom.

I called his bluff, slid out of my jacket, pulled the shirt I was wearing off, and slipped the new T-shirt on with a shimmy. Then I flashed him a look that said,

"Who needs a bathroom?" I hoped he got the message that I was in control.

He took my jacket and shirt and tossed them on a pile on a sofa near the door. "Dance? Beer pong? Ladies' choice."

"What a gentleman! Dance, definitely." I set my water bottle down and let him lead me into the middle of the dance floor.

The room was lit with black lights that made the lettering on our T-shirts glow. Dakota was an easy dancer, too cool to go crazy with nerdy moves. He knew how to hold a girl just right, too. What he wasn't was the octopus most frat guys were, hands everywhere. And when you lopped one off, two more grew back.

Sure, he felt me up. Held me close as often as he could. Made a show of being all over me for his buddies. Call it intuition, but something felt off to me. And his phone kept buzzing in his pocket. I felt it when he held me close. He ignored it.

We danced until we worked up a sweat and got thirsty. When Dakota went to get us a beer, I texted Zach an update, typing as fast as I possibly could. Hoping not to get caught. Zach texted back so fast, it was like he'd been holding his phone, *Text me when you're ready to leave. I'll meet you and walk you back.*

I smiled and slid my phone into my pocket. I'd lost my water bottle during the dance. It wasn't where I'd set it. I went looking for it. As I passed the large picture window in the front room, I spotted Dakota on the front sidewalk by himself, with his back to me.

I frowned and headed out to check on him. It didn't look like he was out for a smoke. He definitely wasn't getting a beer. He didn't hear me approach. I stopped in my tracks as I overheard his end of a conversation.

"Baby, no! Be fair." He looked up at the sky like he was pleading with someone for understanding and let out a breath that curled upward in the cold. "It's nothing. We're just dancing. For show. No, I haven't made a move. No, she doesn't suspect. No one does. Babe, I told you this is important. It's part of my image. I have to go to these functions.

"I'll ditch soon. I'll think of some excuse. I'm being *completely* faithful." He ran his hand through his hair.

I thought, for just a second, about sneaking back inside and letting him off the hook. Then again, this could play to my advantage. "Everything okay?"

Dakota jumped—like, physically jumped. "Gotta go. We'll talk later," he said to the person on the phone. "Alexis!" He forced a smile and slid his phone into his pocket.

A forced smile is so easy to spot. It doesn't reach the eyes. His looked worried and sad.

"What are you doing out here?" he asked.

"Looking for you." I came up even with him, shivering in the cool of the evening. "So I'm a decoy date."

I don't know why, but I found that funny. And it was fun to confront him. Fun to have power for once. All this time I was using him as a decoy and thinking he had the hots for me and he was using me the same way. I fought to hold my laughter in.

"How much did you hear?" Even in the dim light, his guilty expression and tone gave him away.

"Everything I need to. More than enough to realize I've been used!" I tried to sound indignant, which wasn't easy while fighting laughter.

"Alexis!" He turned to face me and grabbed my arm. "I'm sorry. I'm—"

A giggle slipped out. Maybe it was relief. Maybe I should have pretended to be indignant longer and strung out his suffering. "So I'm your beard now?"

"Beard?"

And then the implication hit him and he dropped my arm. "No! *Shit.*" He ran his hand through his hair again. "I'm not gay."

His phone buzzed in his pocket. He pulled it out and glanced at it. "Shit," he said again. "Just a sec." He typed out a text and put his phone away again. "That was a girl. *My* girl."

I crossed my arms like I was mad. "Your secret girl?"

He took my arm again. "Are you pissed?"

He couldn't see that I was relieved? Maybe I was a better actress than I thought. "Probably."

He stopped short. "Probably?"

I shrugged. "Depends on what I can get out of this situation."

"I need to talk to you. In private." He looked around. "Like, really in private. Now. My room."

I put my arm around his waist. "Are you offering me a house tour? The girls warned me about those. Never go to a frat guy's room alone unless you mean business."

He shook his head. "Very funny."

I grinned. "Ready to put on a show? If I'm going to be your decoy girl, we might as well make it look good." I batted my lashes at him.

"Stop that." But he smiled and wrapped his arm around me, sticking his hand in my back butt pocket.

"No pinching," I said.

He laughed.

I'd been to his room, the presidential suite, as it was, once before. It had gotten messier since. It was a typical guy's room. Laundry piled on a chair. Wastebasket overflowing with beer bottles. Smelled vaguely of gym socks and unwashed bodies. As Dakota shut the door, I looked around for the puppy. "Where's the Pomsky?"

"Mom insisted I send him home to her to train. She didn't think we were taking good enough care of him. Damn, he had so much attention here, he was spoiled. She claimed you shouldn't spoil a dog. That it ruins them.

"She's probably doing the same thing right now that she accused us of. She fell in love with him and bought him all kinds of pampering crap, like this special bed that's nicer than mine. I wouldn't bet on her giving him back anytime soon. I think he's become my brother the dog. She likes him better than me now."

"Poor baby," I said to Dakota.

"Him or me?" He flashed that charmer's smile.

I plopped onto his bed so hard I made the springs groan. I was thinking that he and Zach had been quite the killer pair of hotties. I patted the spot next to me on the bed. "People are going to expect to hear some headboard pounding in here."

He raised an eyebrow. "That's going to be tricky without a headboard." He sat on the bed next to me.

I started bouncing. And moaning. "Oh, oh, oh, oh! Harder, Dak! Dak, Dak, Dak!"

"Shut up." But he grinned.

"I'm doing all the work here," I whispered to him. "Help me out. This is for your rep we're maintaining."

"Maybe I want to lie back and let the girl do all the work for once." His eyes danced.

"Sexist. Bounce!" I bounced until the bedsprings groaned.

"Damn, you're a bossy woman." He grinned and joined in.

With our combined bounce power, the bed rhythmically hit the wall.

"Turn on some music." I pointed to the speakers on his desk next to the bed. "People always think they can cover sex with music." I rolled my eyes. Since when did that ever work?

"What do you like?" He reached for the speakers.

"Whatever turns you on."

He paused the action to put on the music I'd asked for. It caught me off guard. I bounced into him so hard he had to grab me to keep me from slamming into the desk. I screamed and laughed as he laughed with me.

I broke into another round of giggles as he turned the music on and a cheesy sex song came on. The kind guys always think turns girls on.

"That's your sex music?" I asked. "I have a few things to teach you."

"Hey! Can it. This is the music the guys expect."

"Good point." I realized we'd both stopped. "We're losing our rhythm."

"Crap." He flashed me a devilish smile and bounced so hard it sent me flying and into another gale of laughter.

When I caught my breath, I asked him the important question. "Do you like screamers? Should I scream for you? Since we're faking everything else, I'd happy to fake that, too."

"Give me a few more minutes. I have epic staying power and everyone knows it. Let's give them something more to talk about."

We both cracked up. He bounced the bed so hard, I slammed against the wall and bumped my head.

"Ouch! Showoff! Give me some warning next time." I rubbed my head.

"Sorry. But I am supposed to be fucking your brains out."

I couldn't help it. I cracked up. "Not literally!"

He just grinned. "We're coming to a soft spot in the music. Get your scream on. I want everyone to hear this. Make it real."

"Make it real!" I rolled my eyes and let out a faked scream of ecstasy to end all faked orgasm screams. Just as the slats holding the mattress slid out and the mattress crashed to the floor. I tumbled on top of Dakota. We were both laughing so hard we could barely breathe.

"That should do it! Damn, I've never broken the bed before." He looked at me with admiration.

"Something to shoot for," I said into his ear when I finally caught a breath. "No one can say I'm not a good fake lay." I was lying on top of him and staring into his eyes as the music filled the room with its boom. He was a hot, gorgeous guy. And still, he just felt like a friend. I untangled myself from him and rolled off next to him to finish catching my breath.

Someone pounded on the door. "Everything okay in there, Dak?" The deep voice was amused, teasing.

"Go away, shithead!" Dakota grinned at me as we heard laughter and the sound of retreating footsteps.

I wiped tears of laughter from my eyes with the back of my hand and tried not to laugh again as I caught my breath. Dakota turned the music down now that the fake deed was done.

"I've never had so much fun having fake sex," he said. "Thank you."

"Do you always thank girls after sex?"

"After mind-blowing fake sex, yeah."

"Mind-blowing!" I grinned at him. "I'll take it!" I leaned back against the wall and caught my breath, wondering at the weirdness of having so much fun with Dakota when I'd been dreading this night. Seeing a glimpse of what he could be like and why he and Zack had been best buds.

"Now that I've given you what you want," I said with a tease, "we have to talk. This girl—why are you keeping her a secret?"

"Shit, I'm thirsty." He got up and got a beer from his mini-fridge, neatly avoiding the question. "Want one?"

"I'll take a pop or an energy drink if you have one."

He tossed me a can of pop. I tapped on the top and opened it cautiously.

"Her name's Jordan." He popped open his beer and plunked down next to me on the mattress that was still on the floor. "Faking sex with you was easy—you smell like her. Like her perfume and cinnamon. That's just another thing I like about you, Alexis. You remind me of her in all the good ways. Which is why I feel like shit using you."

Oh, crap! Jordan wasn't his ex. She was his current. And Zach, with his good advice, had made me an ever more delicious morsel. Another burst of laughter slipped out. "And yet you did."

"I can explain." He chugged his beer like he was working up courage. "Jordan and I are off-again, on-again. She goes to community college back home. Whenever I leave for school, she freaks, goes insecure on me, and breaks things off.

"When I first saw you in your Rho Gam group, we were off. There was something about you. I felt a spark."

"I'm flattered." I took a drink from my can and patted the mattress. "Should we fix this?"

"Don't worry about it. I'll fix it later." He took a drink. "You should be flattered. Jordan's the only other girl I feel that spark with. If it wasn't for her..."

I swallowed hard, touched. This evening was turning out so differently from what I'd imagined. Dakota was different than what I thought. "Thanks." I meant it. "So I take it you got back on at some point?"

"Just after the open house."

A light bulb went. I spoke without thinking. "That explains why you didn't text or call me for weeks!"

His eyes lit up. "Did you want me to?"

"If things were different. Don't make things more awkward." I bumped him playfully with my shoulder. "Tell me about Jordan."

He shrugged. "Not much to tell. Except my parents hate her for no reason. We dated in high school and went to prom against my parents' wishes. When we broke off when I left for school my freshman year, my parents did the dance of joy. Since then, we've kept our relationship from them. It's easier that way.

"Then there's my rep here at the house. The guys expect their fearless leader to date the hottest girls in the Greek system. To maintain the house rep."

"You mean me?" I primped my hair and laughed. "I really am flattered."

"Half the guys here would kill to be with you, Alexis." His voice became soft and completely serious.

I really was flattered. Embarrassed, I brushed it off. "Keep talking. My ego's hungry."

He shoulder bumped me back. "We agreed I would date and go to the functions."

"So you have to text her during the event and reassure her. Does she always freak?" I asked.

He looked me in the eye and shook his head. "She used to think it was funny...until you."

"Oh," I said as the laughter I'd felt evaporated.

"The other girls I took out weren't threatening to her. I chose them that way. But you..." He took a deep breath. "That day at practice when I took you to the SUB and asked you about Zach, that was a serious question. The way you answered it, I knew I didn't have a real shot with you. I'm fucking tired of being second to Zach."

"You would have dumped Jordan for me?" I violated my own don't-make-things-awkward policy by asking.

"I might have. I like you a lot. Life would be a lot easier."

"For both of us," I said, seeing that he understood. "If we were really into each other."

He snorted. "Yeah. My parents would love you. You're just their type."

"Judging by your tone, I'm not sure I should be flattered by that," I said.

He grinned. "They *usually* have pretty good taste." He paused. "Except about Jordan. They think she's not in my league—not connected enough, wealthy enough, pretty enough. But damn, she's funny and she makes me happy. I should tell them to screw it. I will when I graduate. Until then..."

"You should!" I said, dreaming about doing the same thing.

He stared ahead like he was looking at nothing, his face a mask. "Jordan Facebook stalked you. She doesn't like you. Says you're too hot. Too perfect and too perfectly sorority."

"That's too bad," I said. "I was going to propose being your decoy girlfriend. Guess she wouldn't go for that."

He turned and focuses on me. "Seriously?"

I shrugged. "Why not?"

His eyes narrowed. "You need a decoy boyfriend, don't you? To keep Zach a secret."

Dakota knew the consequences of Zach and me being together better than anyone. I didn't even need to throw my mom's disapproval into the mix. With the way he was able to reach Zach, he could be either our strongest ally or our worst enemy. He'd already guessed at how Zach and I felt about each other. He could blow the whistle on our whole relationship.

I pursed my lips as I weighed all that. Finally I decided to go for broke. What did I have to lose? I could deny anything. "Would that affect our fake relationship?"

His gaze remained steady. "No. I owe Zach one."

He didn't elaborate.

"So we could do this?" I said. "Hang out at the necessary functions, flirt at football practice, and fool everyone so we could have real relationships with someone else?"

He nodded. "We'll be the it couple of the season."

"You can convince Jordan?"

"She'll see the light when I tell her how you feel about me and Zach and why you're doing it. She'll be happier knowing I'm not leading you on and you're doing the same thing I am." He paused. "You think Zach is going to buy into it?"

I honestly didn't know. "Yeah. When he sees the merits of our evil plan."

I expected Dakota to grin at my humor. Instead, his expression remained serious, "Alexis, just one thing. I wasn't bullshitting when I warned you about Zach. I didn't have an agenda except to protect you. Zach is dealing with some serious shit. It's not the kind of thing that will just go away."

I hesitated, wondering if I'd missed something about Zach. Wondering how much to say. "He's told me about...things."

"Everything?" Dakota perked up.

"How would I know?" I was putting Dakota on the spot, but I had to ask. "Do Zach's parents really hate him as much as he says?"

He snorted again. "You obviously haven't met them." He took another swig of beer. "Yeah, they do. If anything, he underplays it."

My mouth fell open. It wasn't like I didn't believe Zach. But I'd been hoping he was mistaken. "Why?"

Dakota just stared at me.

"Come on!" I begged. "I need to know. I have the feeling you do."

He stared ahead without focusing. "He should be the one to tell you. I lost the best friend I ever had because I spilled his secret once. Damn, I miss him sometimes."

I swallowed hard, touched by his show of raw emotion. Sad that things had ended badly between them. "Would you like to be friends with him again?"

Dakota focused on me and smiled sadly. "Yeah. Like it's going to happen. Maybe when hell freezes over."

"We could try. I could help." I was getting in deep, maybe too deep. "But I have to know what I'm dealing with."

That sparked something in Dakota, like he was thinking about it. "Part of it's my story to tell. No one can blame me for that." He paused when he realized he was talking out loud. "*If* I tell you, you can't let him know you know." He frowned. "He'll figure out how you found out."

"I won't tell him. I promise!"

"Promises can be broken. Take it from me." His frown deepened and he looked deep in thought. "You're friends with Sarah, aren't you?"

I nodded.

"Ah, shit. If she ever remembered what she actually saw at the party that night, she could tell you." He looked like he was waging battle with his conscience.

I didn't tell him she already had. But it made no sense to me.

Finally, he sighed. "I'm only telling you this because you seem like you really care about Zach."

"I love him!" I blurted without thinking.

He studied me like he was trying to determine if I really meant it. "Then you should know before you get in deeper." He paused again while I waited, holding my breath. He took a deep breath. "He killed his little sister."

CHAPTER SIXTEEN

Alexis

I gasped like the air had been knocked out of me. Suddenly what Sarah had told me about the fight between Zach and Dakota made perfect, terrible sense.

"What? No! How?" I felt sick, wishing I could take back the question. Not believing it, but the look on Dakota's face was so earnest and all the evidence pointed to it being true.

He nodded like he didn't like thinking about it either. "Yeah. Backed over her with the car."

I started trembling. Trying to picture the date of her death on his arm. And the angel. He said he didn't remember her. But if he'd hit her with a car, he had to be old enough to drive...

Dakota set his beer down and covered my hand with his. "When he was three and she was, like, one and a half."

"What?" The horrible images in my mind skidded to a stop, replaced with something worse. "How could a three-year-old—"

Dakota squeezed my hand. "You're icy cold." His touch was warm and reassuring. "Tragic accident. He doesn't even remember causing it. Shit, he doesn't remember his sister, and that kills him. Everything he's missed not having a sister. Everything she missed. Everything that got fucked up because of it.

"If you ask me, that's why he loves the house. It's full of sisters. Then you came along. And he doesn't love you like a sister, sister."

My eyes filled with tears. I swallowed against a lump in my throat that wouldn't go away. I felt like crap for upsetting Zach's world. I was asking him to give up too much for me.

"He needs someone to love him," Dakota said. "Unconditionally."

I looked at Dakota through my tears. "Did he tell you any more?"

Dakota's eyes shone with sympathy. "He doesn't remember much. Just vague snatches of images and emotions. His mom crying and screaming at him. Being in big trouble. Incredible sadness. And sirens.

"His bitch of a mom claims she left the kids buckled in their car seats in the car in the garage while she carried groceries into the house. Somehow Zach got out of his seat. He apparently knew how. His mom said he must have let his little sister out of her seat, too. That she didn't know how to do it herself. And opened the car door for her because she was too little to do it." He sighed. "Nice of that bitch to lay a guilt trip on him. She has no clue what really happened. No one does."

He paused. "Zach's mom said he was fascinated with driving. He must have gotten into the driver's seat while his little sister was playing behind the car. Somehow he knocked the car into gear and backed over her.

"His mom found him sitting in the driver's seat, pulling the handbrake, and crying for help. His sister was crushed beneath the back tire. They lifebirded her. But she was dead before she arrived at the hospital."

"Oh my God! Oh my God! Oh my God!" I just kept saying it over and over as wave after wave of horrifying images crashed through my mind. It was easy to see why Zach couldn't live with himself. Why he thought about killing himself. Why he wouldn't forgive Dakota.

Dakota put his arm around me. "His mom never forgave him. His parents blamed each other and divorced. They each moved separately to Seattle from Yakima, remarried, and hushed the whole thing up. They never even brought her up. It's like she never existed. That's crappy, too. Another reason for Zach to feel guilty.

"The idea was to protect Zach from the stigma of the tragedy. I was the only person he ever told. And I threw it up at him in a drunken rage at a party shortly after graduation." Dakota swallowed hard. "I was jealous and tired of always playing second to him." He hung his head and pulled his hand back from mine.

"Accusing him of killing his sister to get attention was the shittiest thing I've ever done." He paused. "Now you know why he won't forgive me. Still think you can help? Still want to be my decoy girlfriend?"

I grabbed his hand, feeling both their pain and hating Zach's parents. "*Yes*. More than ever." I had to ask the question. "Is the guilt over his sister's death why he almost killed himself?"

Zach

I waited for Alexis in the shadows on the corner, watching as Dak walked her to the end of the sidewalk and she waved goodbye. Hating that I had to be that guy, the one in the shadows.

Something had changed between them, relaxed, like they were suddenly friends. I saw it in the way Alexis waved exuberantly and her casual, happy posture. Deep in my gut, jealousy burned. Not the kind you would expect. Not like I imagined Alexis had shifted her love to Dak. I felt excluded. And frustrated that the only two people I'd ever trusted had suddenly become tight. I was on the outside. Estranged from one. Desperate not to lose the other.

I balled my hands, wanting to slam them into something, preferably Dak's face. Why had I talked Alexis into going to the date dash with him? I was a victim of my own logic. In trying to solve one problem, I'd created another. My damn mistake. In the years we'd been in college, I'd made Dak a cardboard villain and forgotten how charming he could be.

Alexis ran down the sidewalk to me where I waited next to a clump of bushes. When she saw me, she broke into a smile and ran all out, like she couldn't wait to throw herself into my arms. Ran like an athlete—with perfect form, grace in motion, arms pumping, strides long, hair blowing, breasts bouncing. Damn. Breasts bouncing. I got hot just watching those two scoops of perfection.

She ran to *me*. She was mine. Not Dak's. *Mine*. My love for her burned hot and bright. Damned if I could control it. Damned if I wanted to. I opened my arms for her. She slammed into me with so much enthusiasm she nearly toppled me, and her with me, into the thorny barberry bushes behind me.

I caught her, and myself, just in time. "Whoa there, QB!"

"Hey to you, too!" She wrapped her arms around me and lifted her face for a kiss.

My breath caught. Even in shadow, she was so damn beautiful. Love sparkled in her eyes. As corny as it sounded, I was the luckiest guy alive. I wrapped my arms around her waist and lifted her off the ground so her feet dangled.

She laughed and bent her knees so her feet hit that awesome ass of hers. "Am I glad to see you!"

Before I could reply, she dropped her legs and climbed me like a stripper pole, pausing to rub against the bulge in my jeans that had grown hard and pulsing. "Someone's happy to see me, too!" She wrapped her legs around my waist and cupped my face in her hands, stroking my cheeks in a way that sent shivers down my spine.

I grabbed her butt, desperate for her. Wanting every part of her, body and soul. "Likewise."

I didn't hide the hoarse desire in my voice as I pressed my lips to hers, knowing we could be caught any minute. Half the Double Deltsies were at the Tau Psi party she'd come from and could walk by without warning. The danger of getting caught fueled the thrill.

She tasted like cinnamon breath mints and smelled like tainted perfume. If those scents hadn't been such a turnoff, I would have lost control right there. I cursed myself for suggesting she imitate Jordan. Too many unpleasant memories.

She kissed me back, openmouthed and eager. I was consumed with thoughts of making love to her. Horny for her. "Another kiss like that and I'm going to take you right here in the bushes."

"Promises, promises." Her laughter turned to a frown and a pout. "I wish one of us had our own place. Somewhere safe and private we could go..." She ran her hand through my hair.

I kissed the hollow of her neck, running my tongue in a circle around it until she gasped. "Seriously, pledge, only that awful perfume you're wearing is stopping me."

"You mean Jordan's?"

My heart stopped. I pulled back and stared at her. "Shit! How do you know her name?" I paused and swallowed hard.

"Dakota told me. The perfume reminded him of her."

"He told you about her?" My heart pounded. Things were worse than I imagined. "Just how good a time did you have in there?"

"I had a fantastic time!"

It wasn't what I wanted to hear.

She dropped her legs from around my waist until they dangled again and she reached for the ground. "But not the way people think I did. Don't believe the rumors." She laughed like she was flirting. "Frat guys exaggerate."

"What the fuck? What rumors?" I set her down with my heart beating out of control.

She took my hand and laced her fingers through mine. "The mind-blowing sex I had with Dakota." She squeezed my suddenly limp fingers in hers. "It was all faked. Just sound effects."

She laughed again. She was clearly trying to lighten the mood, but her voice shook like she was nervous. "We got carried away and broke his bed. That's what happens when you bounce too hard. Just like Mom used to warn."

"You were alone in his room?" I scowled and turned took a step toward the frat house, ready to beat the shit out of Dak like I had promised.

She held me back with our locked hands. "We faked it for a reason."

I froze. "Are you screwing with me? You faked sex with Dakota?"

"Yes." She stroked the hand she was holding as she looked me in the eye. "Don't be angry. Just listen, okay? I have so much to tell you!"

I stared at her, trying not to blow up and blow things. Remembering how I'd lost my best friend by losing my head. The excitement in her voice fueled the jealous burn in my gut, threatening my control.

She leaned in to me. "Can you keep a secret?"

"Is that a rhetorical question?" Shit, I kept a secret better than anyone I knew. But how would she know that?

She laughed, still trying too hard. "Brace yourself for some scandalous gossip—Dakota only invited me to this stupid date dash as a cover! He's in love with some-one else."

"What?" I frowned, confused. "Why?"

"Because he's expected to date the hottest sorority girls." She stroked my arm and laughed. "And I'm evi-dently one of them. And she's not up to standards."

She mocked herself, but she was wrong. She wasn't one of the hottest girls. She was the hottest.

"He doesn't want to date the hottest girls? What the fuck is wrong with him?" I didn't trust Dak.

"He's in love with someone his parents, and frat brothers, don't approve of. Sound familiar?" She rested her head against my shoulder. "Delicious irony, huh?"

I had to ask, though I had a sick feeling I knew whom. "Who?"

She smiled like she was happy I asked and eager to share. "Jordan."

The bottom fell out of my stomach. I masked my expression so I didn't give anything away.

"They're keeping it secret. Like we are. While I was using him, he was using me. He went to get a beer and I caught him outside talking to her on the phone. Checking in with her! And she was pissed he was with me."

"I can't believe Dak had the balls to get back together with her." Things had just gotten more complicated.

"His guts are our good luck." She kissed me again, just a quick brush of lips.

I was startled by the sweetness of it. It was enough to get me hard again. A burst of laughter stopped me short. A group of drunken girls was stumbling toward us.

I untangled our fingers. "We'd better get back to the house before we got caught. If anyone asks, you texted me to come walk you home."

"I hate this," she said as we started toward the Double Deltsie house, walking side by side while I ached to touch her.

"How long have they been back together?" Morbid curiosity was hell.

"On and off since he graduated."

I bit back a curse, remembering how Dak and I used to know everything about each other. I was still pissed at him. But I guess you could be pissed and still miss someone.

"There's something you should know," she said as
we turned the corner. "Dakota knows about us. He figured it out."

I stopped short and stared at her. "If he figured it
out—"

"Don't worry. He knows you better than anybody.
No one else will know, especially now. Dak and I have
agreed to help each other. We're going to be in a decoy
relationship. Go to enough functions together, flirt just
enough, to throw everyone off and leave us free for the
relationships we're really in. No one will have any reason to suspect a thing."

How could I feel so cold when my heart was beating
so fast? She sounded so confident and assured of her
plan's success.

"Zach?" She looked at me with concern.

"Dak was my best friend. Now I'm supposed to
watch you act like his girlfriend?" I shook my head.
"No! I can't do it. I don't trust him."

"Why?" She grabbed my arm. "He has as much to
lose as we do. If he betrays us, I'll out him to his frat
brothers and parents for the fake he is."

I couldn't speak. I didn't want to tell her why.

"He's sorry for what he did to you." She sounded
sincere, like she really believed him. "He told me all
about it. He misses you. He wants to be friends again.
That should count for something."

The pleading in her voice felt like a slap. Dak had
sucked her in. If she was going to be on his side now...

My mouth went so dry with fear the words stuck in
my throat. I searched her face for some clue she knew

the dark truth about me. "What, *exactly*, did he tell you?"

"Exactly what you told me before." She stared at me like she was waiting for me to flinch.

Shit, I had the feeling she knew something.

"He said he got drunk at a party and spilled a secret you'd asked him to keep. He wishes he could take it back," she said. "I believe him. It's hard to fake regret and guilt like that." She paused. "He's trying to make up for it now by helping us. Let him help. All of us win this way."

I shook my head. She knew more than she was telling me. I grabbed her by both arms. "Tell me the truth. *All* of it. No lies of omission. What did he tell you? What do you know?"

CHAPTER SEVENTEEN

Alexis

Zach held my arms too tightly. The planes of his face fell into hard, worried lines. His muscles were taut and tense, like he could snap at any minute. Maybe I should have been afraid. Instead, I ached for him.

I made a split-second decision. Right here. Right now. This was going to end. Either Zach was going to trust me and let me love him. Or he was going to break my heart. But I would be damned if I would betray Dakota. I stared into Zach's eyes and ramped up my courage, raising my chin like I wasn't afraid. "He didn't tell me anything I hadn't figured out already myself."

Even though the lighting was dim, I swore Zach paled. If I backed down now, I lost him.

I made my voice as gentle as I could and still maintain control. "I know about your sister, Zach. And the accident. It doesn't change how I feel about you."

He was stone silent, scarily so. His grip on me loosened just enough so it didn't hurt. But I felt him slipping away from me, like he was letting go emotionally, too.

I had to explain. "Sarah told me, though she doesn't know she did. She doesn't even know you have a sister. She repeated what Dakota said at that party about how you would kill your sister to get attention." I said it as gently as I could, but he flinched like I'd slapped him.

I kept talking, hoping I wasn't pushing him away with every word. "You told me about the tattoo on your arm. When Dakota said he'd betrayed you, I put it all together. I *made* him give me the details. That's it. That's all. I should have come to you. I'm sorry."

Zach dropped my arms. His Adam's apple bobbed. Once. Twice. Again.

"Do you want to talk about it?" I asked.

"Fuck! No. Drop it, Alexis." His gaze was stony.

"You were three, Zach," I said. "*Three.* You weren't responsible. You didn't even know what you were doing. You shouldn't have been left alone in a car. Your mom should have known better."

"Don't try to blame her. I ruined her life." He turned his back on me.

I was desperate. I pleaded with him. "I'm not blaming her. I know you've heard all this before. But I mean it. No one's to blame. It was an accident. A tragic set of events."

"That doesn't change things." His voice was hard and final, like death. "She's still dead." He started walking away, leaving me before I could leave him.

I couldn't let him go. But he had to come back on his own or nothing would work.

"You're alive, damn it. Live!" I took a deep breath. "Nothing can change what happened," I called after him as tears welled in my eyes.

If he walked away now, I wasn't going to get him back. I felt the urgency as my heart cracked, ready to shatter for both of us. "But you can change what happens from now on. That's what you decided in the woods. Why are you giving up now that I know the rest? I know the truth and I still love you. I'll always love you."

He froze. His misty breath rose in the dark night like he was a breathing statue.

I came up behind him with tears streaming down my face, wrapped my arms around him, and pressed my face against his back. "Forgive yourself, Zach. Forgive Dakota. Live the life your sister would want you to live."

I let the tears stream down my cheeks. I wasn't too proud not to beg. "Don't walk away from me. Don't walk away from us. I *love* you. Believe you can be loved. Let me love you."

I felt the rise and fall of his chest. I watched his breath curl out in the cool night air. And I held on to him like I would never let go and never stop loving him.

"Shit." He leaned his head back against the top of mine. "I love you, Alexis."

I came beside him and took his hand. "I love you, too."

He needed me and I needed him. I pulled him into the alley that ran between the frat houses, into the dark where a brick wall separated two houses. It smelled like chimney smoke, asphalt, stale leaves, and beer. None of that mattered. I didn't need the romance of rose petals.

"I want you. Right now." I reached for his pants and unzipped his zipper.

"Shit, Alexis. I need you so bad." He pulled up my jacket and T-shirt and lifted my breasts, kissing the mounds at the top of my bra, licking the valley between them.

When he started sucking them through the thin fabric of my bra, I gasped and shoved his pants down on his hips. I reached for his dick, stroking him until the tip was wet.

By the time he undid my pants, I was wet, too. He slid his fingers into my panties and stroked the building heat between my legs. His fingers were rough, cold, and tender at the same time as he caressed me.

I slid my jeans down and pushed his hand away. "I can't hold on much longer. Come with me." I wrapped my legs around his waist again, rubbing against him like I had earlier. This time, though, I was naked against him and barely hanging on. I slid him into me as he backed me up against the wall and thrust in deeper.

Then I hung on and held him tighter and tighter as I grasped his shoulder in my teeth to muffle the scream of pleasure building inside me. He pierced me again and again, with his hands at the small of my back to cushion it from the rough, unforgiving, unyielding bricks of the wall behind me.

I felt the tension building in him as it reached higher and higher in me. And then every muscle of his tensed and he let go. "Alexis!"

I came with him then and let the waves crash over me, trembling with the power of the climax and being with him.

When it was over, we leaned our foreheads together and panted, trying to catch our breath as its white mist gave us away in the dark.

"Wow! Just wow." I unlocked my legs from his waist and dropped my feet toward the ground.

"'Wow' doesn't even come close." He slid out of me and set me down, letting my T-shirt and jacket slide back into place.

As we zipped our jeans, I noticed the raw back of his hand. "You're bleeding!" I took it in mine. "The bricks scraped you up. Why didn't you tell me?"

"I didn't even notice." He stared at his hand, where the blood looked black in the dark. "I didn't feel a thing." He grinned. "Until you mentioned it. Now it stings. Thanks a lot, pledge." He sucked on the back of it and wiped it on his jeans. "Totally worth it. Best way to get scraped hands ever."

I took his hand in mine. "You shouldn't have done that. Blood doesn't come out."

"Maybe I don't want it to." His voice was husky. "Maybe I want permanent proof I bled for you."

When he released me, I pulled a tissue from my jacket pocket and pressed it against the scratches. "Up against the rough grain of a brick wall—think that will ever make it in a porn movie?"

"In an alley behind a frat house? Probably not." He kissed me and took my hand as we walked out of the alley.

Out on the sidewalk, where we could be seen, he let it go and shoved his hands in his sweatshirt pockets.

"Why did you stop?" I had to know. "Did I say the right thing?"

"You made all the right points. That's not why. I couldn't walk away from you." His voice broke with emotion. "I'm a fool for you, pledge. It's going to kill me watching you pretend to be Dakota's."

I hesitated, but I had to ask. "If you ever want to talk about...the accident, or your sister, I'm here. I won't judge."

He was silent a moment, like he was thinking. "Dak told you I was three? That they found me in the driver's seat pulling the handbrake?" he said.

I nodded. "Yeah. Trying to save her."

He took a deep breath. "And all I remember are sirens and being in big trouble?"

I nodded again.

"Then you know everything I do. My memories of it are like snatches of a nightmare. Disjointed and unreal. With too many gaps to fill in. If I hadn't seen my sister's grave and lived with the fallout it did to our family, I might have gotten away with thinking I'd imagined the whole thing. I might have even forgotten it altogether. How many things do you remember from when you were three?"

I frowned, thinking. "Not much."

"Neither do I." His fists bulged in his sweatshirt pockets, like he wanted to punch something. "But my parents have never forgotten. Or forgiven."

"That's really why you almost killed yourself that day in the woods, isn't it?" I blinked back tears. The whole thing was so tragic. How could his parents not love him? Why didn't they hurt for him the way I did? The story would have made me cry even if I didn't know and love Zach.

He looked at me without blinking. "I was tired of fighting with my parents and hoping they would eventually give a shit about me. I wanted to give up."

"They don't matter." I felt fierce. "You have me now." I grabbed his arm. "You promised, remember? You won't ever try that again."

He looked off into the distance. "I promised I would fight the urge. Sometimes, though, I think if I sacrificed my life for someone else's it would make everything right."

I stared at him, terrified.

He grinned. "Don't worry. Life doesn't give many people a chance to be a hero. Let's go home."

Em got back late, glowing. I was at my desk, studying for a lab exam.

"Whoa!" she said. "Aren't you the studious one! The girl who screwed the frat president in wall-pounding fury heads back early to study? Weird. You were like

Cinderella ditching the party so early." She tossed me my water bottle. "You even left this behind. What's the scoop with you?"

"I'm trying to make the dean's list." I grinned, but I was glowing, too, with the memory of Zach. The sex had been hot, but the intimacy we shared went deeper. He trusted me with his secrets now.

"Shut up!" She studied me. "Are you and Dakota an item now?"

"Maybe," I said. "You and Carter?"

She flashed me a sly grin, looking like I'd convinced her. "Definitely. I want all the details."

"You already heard all the details." I closed the notes I was studying. "Tell me about Carter."

Zach

I spent Thursday morning when I wasn't in class or working looking for a new job and place to live. Anything to get Alexis out of this decoy relationship. There was nothing. Probably would be nothing until semester. I would keep looking and hope to get lucky.

Thursday afternoon was lingerie football practice. The first day Dak and Alexis would be full out faking their relationship. There were two things I couldn't stay away from—Alexis and football. Combining them would have been like making a peanut butter cup out of chocolate and peanut butter. Great on their own. Combined, best thing ever. Except for Dak. Throw him into the mix hitting on Alexis, real or faked, and the whole sweet thing went sour. There was no way I was missing that practice.

Since last night, I'd been thinking about what Alexis had said about forgiving Dak. She was right. How did I expect to be forgiven if I refused to forgive someone else? Holding on to anger and blame had destroyed my family and the best friendship I'd ever had. The problem was me. I was going to have to forgive myself and come clean.

Alexis' love made it seem worth the effort. My life was coming into focus, becoming more and more worth living. Letting go of an old grudge was another step forward.

I walked with a group of girls from the house to the practice field, happy and tormented at the same time. I couldn't get last night in the alley out of my mind. My story about how I scratched my hand was lame. But no one had seen through it yet.

It was hell acting like Alexis was nothing special to me. Leaving her to walk in the middle of her group of friends and not come up beside her and put my arm around her like she was mine. She sparkled and laughed, totally gorgeous. I fought to keep my eyes off her.

I'd had a lifetime of practice holding my emotions in, but this was the hardest it had ever been. I nodded to her and her roommate Emily. They walked in a clump with the other live-in pledges, Laurel, Sarah, and Katie. They were dressed nearly identically in sports bras, Double Deltsie T-shirts, and short running shorts. It was a muggy afternoon. Rain threatened, but nothing could dampen my spirits. Not after last night.

Some of the girls grumbled, not wanting to get messed up. Alexis shone with the excitement of going to play.

Walking in the middle of the hottest sorority girls on campus made me the envy of every guy we passed. If only they knew. The hottest one was my girl and I couldn't admit to it.

Morgan fell in step with me. She was just as blond, thin, and put together as the others. So much so, she was what I called a sorority clone. Where was the real Morgan? She would have been as pretty as the rest of the girls if she would let go of her pettiness and insecurity. "Guess you heard about the big function at the Tau Psis last night?"

I shrugged. "Think so? Why? I don't give a damn what the frat guys do."

"But you hear the gossip." Her perfect pink, glossed lips twisted into a smug smile. She was enjoying this way too much.

I wished I could tell her how unattractive it made her. I caught a whiff of her perfume on the breeze, and an image of Alexis with her legs locked around me came out of nowhere. Crap. Morgan was wearing Alexis' brand of perfume. On purpose. Real subtle. Was she trying to kill my desire for it or entice me with it?

"Why don't you just tell me what you want me to know?" I said, knowing what it was and wishing Morgan would get over this misguided crush she'd had on me since freshman year.

"You're baiting me!" She laughed too brightly, like she was trying too hard. "Don't tell me you haven't heard the rumors about Dakota Bradley banging Alexis so hard they broke his bed. The little freshman is getting a real reputation." She shot a sideways look at Alexis's group, speaking loud enough for Alexis to overhear her condescending tone. "Someone should warn her that reaching too high could come back to bite her."

"Sounds like the job for a big," I said, trying not to clench my teeth.

Morgan ignored my comment. "No wonder Dakota made her captain. I knew right away he was playing favorites. He wanted in her pants." Though Morgan acted nonchalant, she was studying me for my reaction to this salacious news.

I knew what she was looking for and was damned if I would give it to her. I shrugged like that shit didn't matter to me. "Rough sex is his business. Does it surprise you? You saw him tackle her last practice. He likes it hard." I paused for a beat. "But making her QB was just smart game. He'd have been an idiot not to. She's the best player in the house."

I hoped that would shut Morgan up. Most of the girls in the house, including Morgan, knew about the rivalry and past friendship between Dakota and me. She was the main threat in the house to Alexis and me. I let Morgan have this victory, hoping it threw her off our scent. She'd been suspicious and jealous of us since recruitment week. Why Morgan thought putting Alexis out of reach would make me suddenly turn to her after she'd had a two-year head start and hadn't caught me yet, I had no idea.

Morgan was undaunted by my rebuff. "She changed her social media status to 'in a relationship.'" Morgan sounded so happy she might as well have sung the announcement. "She pinned a selfie of her and Dakota at the top of her page."

"Hope she's not heartbroken when she realizes it was a one-night stand and she's just another notch on his bedpost," I said. "We all know QB2 likes to play the field."

Morgan passed from happy to downright ebullient. I saw myself mirrored in her, the ugly glee I felt when bad shit happened to Dak. My gut turned over. I made myself sick. This had to end.

Sarah came up beside us. I didn't know if she'd had enough and was coming to the rescue or not. I didn't care. I was happy to have her there.

"Hey, Zach! Are you going to stay and give us pointers this practice? We could use your help. You know more about football than all the Tau Psis put together. *Including* Dakota." Sarah's smile was deceptively sunny and innocent. I had no doubt she knew what she was doing.

Ah, shit, I thought. Interfering with Dak's gig was the last thing I wanted to do.

Sarah's suggestion caught Kelly's attention. "That's right! You played high school football, didn't you?"

Sarah answered for me. "Played football? Are you kidding? He was the starting quarterback the year our high school team took 4A state! Dakota was just his backup."

I tried not to wince. Dak would hate being called "just backup."

"I had no idea you were so good, Zach." Kelly looked at me with new admiration. Sometimes the girls didn't see past the houseboy image unless pushed to remember I had another life outside the house. "You didn't get recruited and get an athletic scholarship?"

I shrugged. "Not to one of the big schools I wanted to go to. To little schools in the lower divisions." That didn't offer scholarships big enough that allowed me to even come close to paying for tuition and board.

"You gave up football to come be our houseboy! Awesome. We love you, Zach." From anyone but Kelly, that would have sounded snarky and snotty. But she was genuine.

"So?" Sarah said. "Are you going to coach? Houseboys can coach, can't they? There's no rule against it. You're one of us."

Beside her, Alexis remained quiet. But she shot me an encouraging glance on the sly.

I appreciated the girls thinking I was one of them. Not a girl. A member of the family. But this wasn't my gig.

"Please, Zach!" Sarah said.

A chorus of girls joined her. "Please, Zach! Please, please!"

"It's Dakota's team," I said, evading them. "His call."

"It's our team, too," Kelly said. "I'm house president, just like he is. I can tell him we want you as part of our team."

Crap. I could imagine how being commanded to let me coach was going to go over with Dak. "Let me handle it, okay?"

Dak was waiting for his team with a play clipboard in hand when we arrived. Now was the time to man up.

Alexis flashed me a quick, secret smile, encouraging me, begging me to stay with the team and talk to Dak. Damn, she made me happy.

Dak looked up and smiled at Alexis with a hungry look in his eyes that was hard to believe was faked. "Captain!"

She bounced on her toes and gave him a flirty wave. "Coach."

Some of the girls elbowed each other and giggled, probably remembering the rumors. It was clear to everyone Alexis and Dak had a connection. Only I knew what it really was. Even knowing, jealousy twisted my guts inside out.

I cleared my throat. Dak looked over at me as if to say, *What the hell are you doing here?* Our gazes locked. There was a moment of stony silence, like we were both getting ready for battle.

"Hey, Coach," I said, breaking it. "The girls could use a water boy and a trainer. I'm volunteering." I grinned, making a joke about being a houseboy, a servant, showing him I was willing to take a backseat to his position of power.

What Dak wanted more than anything was to be number one for once.

He stared at me as if he was trying to decide how sincere I was and whether this was an apology and an olive branch or more bullshit.

The girls held their collective breath while I held mine.

"Water boy? Shit, Zach, why would I waste good talent? I could use a good offensive coach." He held his hand out for me to shake. "Are you in?"

I took his hand and pulled him into a bro hug, slapping him on the shoulder. "Thanks, man. For everything," I whispered.

His Adam's apple bobbed. "Welcome aboard."

After the general warm-ups, Dak gave me the offensive squad to train. Morgan, Sarah, and Kelly were on offense along with Alexis. I didn't envy Dak having to pick the offensive and defensive lineups. There wasn't a girl in the house who weighed more than 140 pounds, tops. And that was our tallest girl, who was nearly five ten. Everyone else had about as much bulk as a feather.

We were in desperate need of linemen. We would have to hope we got a good schedule for the single elimination tournament. If we went up against the house known for their chunkiness, or the girl jock sorority, we were going to be in deep shit. We would have to rely on our superior coaching strategy, wits, and speed. There sure as hell wasn't much game sense on our team. That had been obvious in the first practice I'd watched.

I wasn't prepared to coach. I knew these girls. Trying anything too complicated would be an exercise in

futility. At the end of the day, they would still be sorority girls who cared more about their nails than football.

I ran them through some basic passing drills we
used to do in high school. I was used to working with
Alexis, who got it. I grew frustrated when most of the
others seemed clueless. Only Kelly and Morgan, who'd
played high school soccer, seemed to catch on at all. As
I worked on some simple plays, my team's level of inex-
perience and lack of knowledge became painfully obvious. I assigned the girls with the least skills, the ones
who couldn't run, pass, or catch, to the line, no matter
how slight they were. Crap, using that criteria, almost
all I had were linemen.

No matter what I tried or how I explained the responsibilities of each position, the girls failed. The wide
receivers were scared of the ball, afraid to jam a finger
or break a nail. The linemen were afraid to block. The
running backs never seemed to find the hole.

You would think the girls could understand the
simple running routes—fly, hook, post, five and in, and
post corner. I mean, fly, really? Pretty self-explanatory.
Run straight out. Fly, damn it! Hook, loop back.

About halfway through practice, it began to drizzle.
Some of the girls grumbled. Alexis lit up.

"Stop bitching," I said to my squad. "This is good
practice. You're going to have to play in all kinds of
weather."

Finally, I decided to demonstrate the running routes
using my three best players: Alexis, Kelly, and Morgan.

"All right! Everyone watch. I'm going to be the QB.
When I call nine, that means the receiver is going to

run the fly route, the most basic move. Alexis, you're going to receive. Morgan, you play lineman and block. Kelly, you're the wide receiver. I'll be the QB. Everyone else line up in your positions and watch." Just getting the girls to line up properly was a headache.

A girl named Kylie bounced up and down to get my attention. "I'll be the hiker!"

I rolled my eyes. "We won't use a snap or need a center for this demonstration. I'll start with the ball. Everyone ready?"

Just then, the mist turned to an all-out downpour. The girls squealed.

"Stay in position, damn it!" I screamed at them. "We're running nine. Go."

Morgan blocked me like she was supposed to. The wet ball was slippery, but I was used to that. Alexis went long, running straight up the middle for the ball. As Morgan charged me, I let the ball fly. Damn if Morgan didn't tackle me. I went down with a splash in the soggy field, landing with Morgan on top of me, grinning like she should win a prize or something.

"Nice tackle, right?" she whispered in my ear.

I rolled her off me and sat up to see if Alexis had caught the ball. She had. I grinned.

I had to scold Morgan. "You're not supposed to tackle your coach. This is just a demonstration. But yeah, great tackle. Remember, only use it if Dak orders it."

She beamed.

We ran through the plays, demonstrating and getting the other girls involved. I put Morgan back out as a receiver. The rain kept pouring down until we were all drenched and had drawn a crowd of guys, who cheered and gawked at the wet T-shirt view of the girls. Kelly, Alexis, and Morgan looked like mud wrestlers.

Alexis and I worked smoothly as a QB/receiver team. Our private practice had improved her game and given us a good sense of each other's moves.

"I can see a W, ladies! A real W," I yelled to encourage the girls.

After each play, Alexis and I conferred and joked. I didn't realize we were being too familiar with each other until I noticed Morgan watching us and frowning.

I backed off and went into coach mode. I switched places with Alexis, taking her place as wide receiver to demonstrate running the post-corner route, putting Morgan on the line to block her. I wanted to see how Alexis did under pressure.

She called the play. I took off. I was cutting back toward the corner when I saw that Alexis was in trouble. Morgan ran toward her like she wanted to hit her hard. *Shit.*

I yelled at Morgan to back off just as Alexis tossed the ball to Kelly and Morgan crudely tackled her. Alexis crumpled and didn't get up.

I sprinted back to her. "Alexis!" My heart was in my throat.

By the time I got to her, Dak was already there, helping her up and bawling Morgan out. "What the fuck do you think you were doing? You just took out the only girl here who can actually play." His eyes were as hard as his voice as he wrapped Alexis' arm around his shoulder.

Alexis was favoring her ankle, afraid to put any weight on it. I ran for the medical kit and got an instant icepack and tape, grateful to Dak for covering for us and jealous at the same time. I tossed the icepack and tape to Dak.

Dak helped Alexis to a bench and inspected her ankle, touching it so tenderly he looked like her lover.

She winced. "Sorry!"

The other girls circled Alexis, watching.

Dak dismissed them. "Good job, ladies. Practice is over! Get inside and get warm. See you all on Saturday."

The group disbanded slowly. The girls kept looking over their shoulder at Alexis. Some flashed Morgan dirty looks. I heard mumbles that this was flag football, not tackle. And Morgan had done it on purpose to show her little who was boss. A couple of others complained about how the ball smarted when it hit their hands. Another had a nail bent back. It was crap you would never hear the guys complain about.

I kneeled beside Alexis and shot her a compassionate smile. "How are you?"

Dak answered for her. "She'll be okay. She just turned it. I'll wrap and ice it and get her home. Thanks for your help today." He shot me a look, warning me not to blow our cover.

I nodded. "I'll walk the girls home."

As I gathered up the gear, I caught a glimpse of Morgan. She was wearing a triumphant look, like she saw through our charade. Or at least me. She was still testing us. I had been careless. Anyone looking for it could see how I felt for Alexis.

Dak had stepped in to play his part. Alexis played along. But we weren't fooling Morgan. She was going to be a problem. I shivered in the rain, but it wasn't from the cold.

CHAPTER EIGHTEEN

Alexis

Dakota was right. I'd just turned my ankle. I recovered quickly. Almost as quickly as the rumors of how gentle and concerned he'd been with me flew. The confirmed player Dakota Bradley was now a reformed, one-woman man. And to the public eye, I was his woman. In the weeks leading up to homecoming, I was initiated and became a member in the house, and Dakota took me to all the Tau Psi events. He stopped by the house to study with me and discuss coaching strategy with Zach. The three of us even met over coffee at the College Grind.

We posted pictures of each other on our social media pages. And gushed in the mushy, over-the-top way new couples do, laughing about it in private. In secret,

I was Zach's girl, meeting him wherever we could find for privacy. We couldn't keep our hands off each other.

In public, I walked to class with Zach. I sat with him openly. We studied together in the house, listened to music, and pored over playbooks and strategy. We watched old episodes of *Friday Night Lights* on Netflix. And no one thought anything about it. It became common to see us together, laughing and joking with each other like old friends. Because I was Dakota's girl, people missed the intimacy in the looks we gave each other.

Even better, Zach and Dakota were rebuilding their friendship and establishing trust in each other again, bit by bit. Football gave them the common bond and excuse to be friends, pushing aside the class differences of houseboy and frat pres. I didn't know what would happen after homecoming, but they way things were going, I knew we'd find a way to work it out.

Mom saw the pictures I posted and was delighted, gushing, glowing. I felt bad deceiving her. But eventually she would see that Zach was twice the guy Dakota was.

I was happy. As happy as I could be given I had to keep my relationship with Zach secret. And put all those emotions into my fake one with Dakota to make it seem real.

Under Zach and Dakota's expert coaching, our team improved. Like, really improved. To the point where the girls actually started to care and act like winners. Which made my role as captain and quarterback easier and fun. Team spirit ran high. Anytime, you could shout out, "Go Deltsies!" and someone would echo it back.

The girls who weren't great athletes kicked our fundraising into high gear. The football game was the biggest event and would win us the most points and money toward charity for our philanthropy project. But we needed every point we could earn.

We got every guy in the Tau Psi house to submit an application to be Mr. University, collecting twenty points per guy who applied. I even convinced Zach and the other house guys to apply, and sweet-talked the Greek committee into giving us twenty points apiece for them, too. They applauded our ingenuity and spirit.

The team with the most points in the Mr. University competition got a thousand dollars donated to their charity. Thanks to a lot of hustle, we were out in front. The winner of the football tourney got five thousand. There were other events to raise money, but those were the main ones. The sorority/frat team that raised the most money won a trophy. We were beginning to picture how nice it would look in our living room.

With our girls coaching the guys on how to win a pageant and Dakota and Zach coaching our girls' football team, how could we lose?

Two weeks before homecoming, Dakota was selected as a finalist for the Mr. University contest. As his fake girlfriend, I was bursting with pride, and posted pictures of him all over my social media. I even bought him a pageant sash from a party store. He donned it in good spirit. I took a picture of him and posted it online.

He never mentioned what Jordan thought of every-thing. He never mentioned her at all. Zach grumbled about our decoy relationship from time to time, and ribbed me about dating one of the most popular guys on campus while slumming with the houseboy.

The girls lobbied for Zach to make the finals, but the selection committee was run by Greeks. Geeds and houseboys didn't have a shot. I thought he'd been robbed. Despite that disappointment, life was great. I was flying high.

I had a big midterm lab report due on Thursday morning before Homecoming Week. It was freaking me out. College classes were harder than even my high school AP classes. And so much more work! I didn't go to the sleeping porch on Wednesday night. Instead, I stayed in my room, working in the circle of light be-neath my desk lamp until my eyes went bleary, intent on pulling an all-nighter if necessary to finish.

About three a.m., someone knocked on my door. When I answered, Kayla tumbled in. Her eyes were red and puffy like she'd been crying.

"Oh, crap!" she said, and sniffed. "Isn't anyone sleeping in the sleeping porch tonight? I'm looking for a bed and a place to crash. They're all full."

"Feel free." I pointed to the bed. "I have a big lab to finish. If you don't mind sleeping with the desk light on."

She came in and closed the door, looking relieved. "Great. Thanks. It's not like I'm actually going to sleep anyway." She plopped onto the bed and fell back with her arm over her head.

I swiveled in my desk chair to look at her. She lived out with a couple of roommates. But she and Eric pretty much slept over at either her place or his every night. "What happened?"

"I was spending the night at Eric's, but he was being a douchebag!" Her eyes flashed. "We had a fight. I had to get away and calm down before things really got out of hand. I couldn't go back to my place, because my roomie has her boyfriend over and I can't stand him. So I came here to crash."

I nodded, not wanting to pry. "Sorry."

"Yeah, Eric can be a real prick." She sat up, eyes flashing indignantly. "He's been flirting with this Geed who works at the College Grind. Like I wouldn't notice!" She rolled her eyes. "I caught him texting her."

"Sorry," I said again.

She talked right over me like she hadn't heard. "When I called him on it, he had the nerve to accuse me of flirting with other guys." She shook her head and laughed. "Like he's seriously jealous of Justin Green. I mentioned him, remember? My cousin's friend?"

"Sure. Now that you mention it," I said.

"He's a boy genius, like Dex." She grabbed a pillow and bunched it in her lap like she was taking her anger out on it.

I almost joked about not abusing my pillow. Then I thought better of it. She was clearly not in a joking mood.

"You've seen Eric?" Beneath her anger, she got a dreamy look on her face.

"Once or twice with you at the house," I said.

"Then you know how stupid it is for him to be jealous of anyone!" She pulled her phone out of her purse, brought up a picture, and handed the phone to me. "Justin. He's completely adorable in a little boy, puppy kind of way." She sounded fond of him.

I studied the picture. "He's in college? Serious? He looks about twelve." I wasn't exaggerating.

She nodded. "I know! He swears he's seventeen."

I gave her a skeptical look. "He doesn't look it."

"Yeah." She nodded. "And he's in this junior-level class of mine. Acing it without even trying. Some of the guys pick on him, which is crap. I put them in their place. Eric says I have to stop playing mommy. Bastard." She sighed. "Poor Jus. He's really sweet and cute in his little boy-like way. You can't see it in the picture. He's only about five feet four. And super scrawny. If he weighs 120 I would be surprised."

I tilted my head and stared at Justin's picture. "He's baby-faced."

She nodded. "Poor boy. He'd love to be a hipster, but he can't grow the beard."

I pursed my lips. "He has good bone structure. If he ever goes through puberty, grows about nine inches, gets some facial hair, and fills out, he has a shot at being hot." I handed her phone back to her.

"Yeah, he'd be irresistible." She sounded highly skeptical, like the odds of that happening at seventeen were about zero. "He has a wicked sense of humor, though. Really funny. But totally awkward around girls. He has an adorable crush on me."

Her eyes narrowed. "So you agree—Eric is being a douchebag? And totally making excuses for himself so he can flirt with the barista girl to make up for Justin having a crush on me?"

"Total douche," I said.

Her phone rang. She glanced at it. "Speak of the devil."

"Aren't you going to answer?" I asked.

"He can stew overnight. Thanks for letting me stay here. Have anything to drink?"

"If you mean alcohol, Em keeps a stash under the bed. If you mean anything else, help yourself to anything in the mini-fridge."

She got up and got herself a bottle of coconut water. "I already have a headache. I don't need to make it worse. What are you studying?"

I'd forgotten she didn't drink. "I'm writing my biology lab report. Due tomorrow and worth a third of our lab grade."

"Biology!" She made a face. "Sorry, I can't help you with that. Science is not my thing. I sucked in that class." She drank her water while I worked on my lab report and curled up to sleep.

About four thirty, I finished the stupid lab report. I was so tired, I could barely stand. No way could I make it to the sleeping porch. Two of us could fit on the twin bed. Em and I had done it before.

"Scoot over." I slid in next to Kayla. The bed groaned.

"Finished already?" she whispered.

"I thought you were asleep."

"Just dozing."

We did a dance, trying to get comfortable. The bed was old. It squeaked and creaked while we tossed and turned.

Kayla laughed. "It sounds like we're doing the deed in here." She wiggled on purpose, making the springs groan rhythmically.

"We should record this and send it to Eric to make him jealous," I said. "I'm just as attractive as Justin."

"More," she said as we turned back to back. "Taller and bigger, too."

"Thanks for that," I said with a heavy dose of sarcasm.

She laughed. "Plus you're a quarterback. Now get your shoulder out of my back."

We maneuvered around until we found a comfortable spot. Just as I closed my eyes, the door burst open, scaring me so that my heart pounded wildly.

"Caught you in the act!" Morgan stood in silhouette in the doorway. "I'll have you thrown out. Both of you—"

Kayla sat up and flipped the lamp on. "This isn't what it looks like."

Morgan's eyes went wide.

"Oh, shut up, Morgan." Kayla started laughing. "I'm not bi. Alexis is letting me crash here while she studied. I had a fight with douchebag Eric. She got tired and needed to lie down for a few hours. So I scooched over to make room. And then you charged in."

Morgan actually blushed. Or maybe her face was red with rage. Anyway, she blustered and mumbled an apology. "Sorry, Kay. I thought you were a guy."

"You need your eyes checked, Morgs," Kayla said. "What are you doing up at this hour, anyway? Stop playing morality cop and go get some sleep."

Morgan left, but my heart wouldn't stop pounding.

"That scared me spitless." I put my hand on my heart and took a deep breath.

Kayla studied me. "You don't think this is as funny as I do. Who was Morgan expecting me to be? Zach?" She sighed. "The crush that never ends."

"I'm with Dakota now," I said.

Kayla studied me. "Morgan wouldn't go stalker psycho trying to catch you with Dakota. She's only certifiable over Zach. If she's jealous, she's picking up on something between you."

I shrugged. "She's crazy. Zach and I study together for our History of Rock and Roll class. And he's helping me with the plays for our football game. If she's reading something more into that, that's her problem." But I knew it was mine.

Zach

Alexis asked me to meet her at the College Grind before football practice on Thursday. She was waiting for me at a table with two cups in front of her. When I saw her, my pulse raced in that crazy-ass-in-love way. Despite all the secrecy shit we had going on, I was the luckiest guy on campus. She was my girl. I wanted to

kiss her badly, badly enough to risk it. But when I approached, she shook her head, warning me off.

She pushed one cup toward me as I sat down. "I
suppose you've heard the rumors?"

It was cold outside. The warm cup felt good in my
hands. "What is it with you and rumors? Who am I
supposed to be jealous of now?"

"Kayla," she said with a grin. "Morgan caught me in
bed with her last night."

"What? And you didn't invite me?" I grinned.

"Shut up! This is serious."

When she explained, I lost my sense of humor about
the situation. "She burst in on you?"

"Yeah. And said she'd have us thrown out of the
house. Kayla put her in her place." She grinned. "That
part was kind of funny." She bit her lip. She looked so
cute and kissable when she did that. "We're going to
have to be more careful. No more, you know, in the
house."

We'd gotten careless, or maybe we'd started to feel
invincible. We'd been having sex in my room and hers.
"So where are we going to do it? Against the rough
brick of a wall? That was pretty hot."

"And horrible on your hands." She winked. "In the
park at midnight."

"By a study carrel at the back of the library?"

She rolled her eyes. "We could borrow a room or
rent a hotel."

"We'll think of something."

She took my hand. "I love you." She paused. "Do you
think it shows?"

"I hope so." I squeezed her hand.

"Crap. It's not supposed to. But I can't help myself." Her eyes sparkled. She frowned, wrinkled her nose, and pursed her mouth to one side in an expression that was totally, sweetly her. "We have to warn Dakota."

I held back a curse. I was tired of involving Dakota.

Seeing my look, she changed the subject. "Good news! Kayla thinks he has a real shot at winning the Mr. University pageant."

Yeah, that cheered me up. "Oh, yeah? He looks great in a bathing suit, does he?"

Her eyes sparkled. "Not nearly as hot as you. You were robbed! Stupid Greek snobs on the committee." She winked.

"Thanks, pledge," I said. "Aren't the two of you the pair? The beauty queen and the star quarterback. Only he's the queen. Nothing like role reversal."

She shook her head. "How many times can I tell you to shut up? I want to be out in the open with you. I'm your girl, through and through."

Alexis

I had the most fantastic, best practice of my life. The game was really starting to make sense to me. I'd always loved watching it. But the perspective from the field was totally different and took getting used to.

"Alexis is ready to up her game," Dakota told Zach after practice. "I'm calling a coach, assistant coach, captain meeting. Coffee in the SUB to talk strategy."

They were getting along well. Mending their relationship at each practice. I saw glimpses of the way they must have been together in high school. Insepara-ble. Easy in each other's company. And I thought, *If nothing else, I did one thing right. I got them back together. All the deception is worth it.*

"What are you saying? Are you giving me the green light to teach QB1 the *Friday Night Lights* Special?" Zach sounded totally serious as he hefted his athletic bag over his shoulder, but his eyes twinkled. "I don't know, Dak. That's a big step. Maybe we should watch some game film together first, the three of us."

"What's the *Friday Night Lights* Special?" I walked into their trap willingly as I fell into step with them.

Zach acted scandalized that I didn't know. "Come on, pledge. We've watched some episodes together. That's only the move that Coach teaches Julie that wins her and Matt's team the big powder puff game over Riggins' team. We made our own version."

"That's what I'm saying. 'Cause you can never lose with a TV show move." Dak put his arm around my shoulders.

"Got that right," Zach said.

"We can watch the game film at the house tonight," Dakota said.

"Which house?" I asked.

"Your house," he said. "Let's include everyone. They'll all need to know how to run the play. We'll call the girls together and have a movie night. Popcorn and everything." He turned to Zach. "The way we're play-ing, we have a real shot at the title." He sounded pleas-antly surprised, like a minor miracle was occurring. "The Zeta Nus are almost certain to be in the finals.

Dan Bates is coaching them and drilling them like it's the NFL." He sneered like Dan's name was anathema.

Zach explained the situation to me. "Dan was the opposing quarterback against us in the finals the year we took state. He knows a lot of our plays and how we think from studying our game films and playing us. The good news is we know his."

"He's itching for revenge. I'm half serious about that *Friday Night Lights* Special." Dakota grinned. "We might need it."

"I wouldn't mind besting Dan a second time." Zach grinned, evilly, making it clear he was the king of understatement.

All the way to the SUB, I was Dakota's girl. But when we settled into a booth, the dynamic changed. I sat next to Dakota. But beneath the table, I slid my foot between Zach's and brushed my leg against his in a way meant to turn him on. Zach gave me that quick, intimate grin of his.

Dakota ordered a large basket of fries with his coffee, and doused them with ketchup.

"Damn, Dak," Zach said to him. "You really going to eat those with the beauty pageant a week away? Think about it, man. You're risking your girlish figure for a momentary indulgence."

Dakota scowled at him. "Shut the fuck up."

Zach was undeterred. "Pledge, I hope you're keeping him off the beer, too. A beer gut hanging over swim trunks will not win us the competition. If we lose the tourney, Dak is our last hope to take the trophy."

"I have absolutely no control over him," I said.

"Only over my heart." Dakota winked at me, looking like that was so much BS.

"Speaking of hearts..." I told him about Morgan.

"Shit," Dakota said. "You were bouncing the bed with someone else? I'm damn jealous."

I rolled my eyes. "Be serious."

"I am serious," he said. "Sounds like we need to up our game. Guess I'll have to casually start shopping for promise rings."

I grimaced. "Don't buy me a ring."

"I didn't say I was going to *buy* one." He grinned. "I said I could be seen *looking* for one. You know how fast that will get the rumors going."

Zach's expression was masked. "What will Jordan think of that?"

I didn't understand it, but it seemed to me that Zach almost hesitated at her name. As if he didn't like mentioning her.

Dakota shrugged. "She understands the situation."

That was all he said. No one pushed. But his body language said she wasn't thrilled, either. The happy mood was killed. It was like a shadow had passed over it. I wondered how long we could keep this up.

It was like Dakota read my mind. "Don't worry. We're fine," he said. "We can keep this up all school year if we have to."

"And do what?" I asked. "Keep upping the lies? At that rate, you'll have to pin me at some point."

"If I have to, I will." Dakota's face was dead serious.

Zach looked away. Pinning was tantamount to getting engaged. I couldn't read what he was thinking.

CHAPTER NINETEEN

Alexis

On Wednesday of Homecoming Week, we went as a house to the all-campus bonfire with the Tau Psis. The university's football coach gave a pep talk and introduced the players. The cheerleaders led a spirit rally. We had two girls on the squad. If there had been a competition for spirit, we would have won.

I stood sandwiched between Dakota and Zach. The Tau Psis seemed to accept Zach's presence, since Dakota had named him assistant coach. I watched Zach and Dakota's expressions in the glow of the firelight, wondering if they missed the excitement of being the center of attention on the field.

The ASB officers tossed rolled bonfire T-shirts into the crowd.

"Make eyes at the guys throwing the shirts so he'll toss one this way," Zach whispered to me.

"Pimping me out, are you?"

"Haven't I been all semester? What's changed?" His tone was neutral, not teasing like it should have been.

I showed him and stuck out my chest, batted my eyes, and got the attention of one of the T-shirt throwers. Sure enough, he tossed one our direction. Zach, Dakota, and I all lunged for it. The guys had the height advantage, but I refused to let that stop me.

I jumped for it. Zach, the natural quarterback, stretched for it and caught it just out of reach of my fingertips. Dakota and I both tried to pry it out of his hands before he had a firm grip. The three of us fell, grabbing for the shirt and laughing, into a pig pile with me at the bottom. Zach right on top of me, bracing himself to keep his full weight off me.

I looked into his eyes, wanting him so badly.

I love you, he mouthed.

Caught up in the moment, I lifted my face to his instinctively for a kiss, closing my eyes so I could feel the full force of it.

Dakota hissed at him. "Cut that shit out. Give me the damn shirt so I can make a show of giving it to Alexis."

Zach swore beneath his breath and slid the shirt to Dakota before rolling off me. Dakota batted Zach away when he tried to give me a hand up, offering his own instead. I thought, *This has to stop.* I only wanted Zach.

When I was on my feet, the Tau Psis and Double Deltsies cheered when Dakota handed me the shirt and brushed my lips with a kiss that did nothing for me. It was like kissing a good friend. No zing. Almost too late, I remembered to fake it.

I shook the shirt out. "It's a small!"

"Of course it is, babe," Dakota said. "That's why he threw it to you."

The single-elimination powder puff tourney started on Thursday. Our uniforms were cute, and tiny. Sports bras and boy shorts. Cold, but effective in distracting opposing frat coaches. We handily won our first two games, surprising everyone with our blowout. As a coaching unit, Zach and Dakota were unbeatable. It was like they thought with one mind, even finishing each other's sentences. Watching them in action was pure joy for me.

Winning the first two games put us into the finals against the Zeta Nu team and their old archenemy Dan Bates. The guys had their vendetta. I had mine against those animals for kidnapping me. Our drive was strong, but they wouldn't be easy to beat.

We girls dressed for the game in full makeup and pushup cups, ready to flirt with the refs, a couple of frat guys from neutral houses, those who didn't have a team in the tourney. The other team's girls may have had us beat in athletic ability, but we were man killers.

The Zetu Nus had coached their girls well in the art of dirty play. Throwing elbows, late blocks, "accidental" tackles, all when the refs weren't looking. Add in that their girls were athletes and fearless. And their line was stocky and solid. Unlike our girls, they weren't afraid to block. We were in deep trouble.

In the first half, they plowed over our defense. Superior coaching on offense kept us on the boards and in the game. We went to the locker room at the half tied at fourteen apiece.

Dakota gave us a rousing speech. "Keep it up, girls. Keep. It. Up. Hold our heads and we can win this one. I do not want to parade around the Mr. University stage in my swim trunks. And I sure as hell don't want to win Mr. Congeniality.

"It's all riding on this half of the game. I see a W, a big W in our future! The other team isn't used to playing against girls who know what they're doing. We'll wear them down, outsmart and outrun them. If we win this, we win the homecoming trophy!"

If we won the game, we had enough points to win the overall competition even if Dakota didn't show up to the Mr. University finals. If Zeta Nu won, things got dicey. Dakota would have to place in the top three of the Mr. University contest for us to take home the trophy.

He and Zach went off to confer about strategy for the second half, whispering to each other and laughing like the old friends they were. We came into the second half fired up. But it didn't seem to matter. Dan and his girls had figured out our limited playbook and shut down my offense. Fortunately, Dakota and Zach were able to out coach him on defense to keep the game even.

The game was still tied with less than twenty seconds left to play. We had possession on their fifteen-yard line. It was third down and twelve. We'd lost yards in each of the first two downs. We couldn't break through their defense. Dakota called a timeout. He and Zach had a brief discussion about which play to run.

"You're the head coach, Dak," Zach said. "I bow to your decision. But if you want my two cents, I say we have to surprise them. Dan is guessing our offense every play and running a perfect defensive game. We have to do something that wasn't in our high school playbook."

"All or nothing?" Dakota held Zach's gaze and grinned. "Know what I'm saying?"

Zach grinned back. "It worked on TV."

Oh, crap, I thought as Dakota grinned full out and called me over.

"*Friday Night Lights* Special, QB." Dak slapped me on the back. "You can do it, girl."

I was shaking when I returned to the huddle, called the play, and led the cheer. On the line, waiting for the snap, I was so nervous I felt like I was about to throw up. Sarah would be the receiver for this play. She was fast, but inexperienced, and had a habit of messing up plays under pressure. Dan wouldn't be expecting me to throw to her. The element of surprise was the only thing we had going for us.

Our center snapped the ball. I caught it and looked for Sarah. She ran straight out and cut toward post. I passed the ball off to where she should be just before the other team grabbed my flag. As I let loose, I strained to see whether Sarah ran the play right and cut the right direction. It was like a slow-motion scene in a sports movie when Sarah caught the ball completely in the open and sprinted across the goal line.

The next thing I knew, I was being hugged by all the girls. We screamed and bounced and chanted.

Zach worked his way through the mass of girls surrounding me and hugged me, picking me up off the ground and swinging me around. "Great job, QB1!"

With all the heat I felt in the moment, it took every ounce of restraint I had not to kiss him, fiercely. I craved the freedom to share my joy openly with him. I craved him.

Sarah beamed ear to ear. She was going to be impossible to live with after this. At that moment, I felt glad, like really glad to be a Double Deltsie. Happy and proud. I had real friends and a place to belong.

Dakota was suddenly beside us. "Hey, offensive coach, give the head coach a chance to congratulate his girl."

Zach and I exchanged an intimate glance full of our reluctance to let go of each other. He wanted to kiss me as badly as I wanted to kiss him.

"Catch!" Without warning, he tossed me to Dakota.

I screamed, playfully, flirtatiously, as Dakota caught me. He kissed me, full out, full tongue, before I could protest. I cupped his cheeks in my hands, pretending to be in love with him. Did he have to kiss me so authentically, with real tongue?

The girls cheered. And I thought again, *This is all wrong.*

Zach pulled Sarah into a hug, laughing as he congratulated her. Appearances mattered. I wondered if anyone but me noticed the difference in the way he held us. Hoping they did and hoping they didn't at the same time. Jealousy is an irrational bitch. The ugly green monster climbed on my back. I wanted the world to know Zach was my guy. *Mine.*

Dakota set me down. "Party at the Tau Psis!" he yelled as the Tau Psis streamed onto the field.

We screamed and cheered our way down Greek Row to the frat. We were the champions! And proud of it. The game was over. We owned the homecoming trophy.

The guys scooped Sarah and me up, carrying us on their shoulders like we were victorious warriors. When we arrived, the house shook with music. And the kegs were being tapped.

Dak poured Sarah, Zach, and me beers and made a toast. "Raise your glasses, everyone. To the best damn flag football team on campus! Love my powder puff girls!" He hugged me and kissed the top of my head.

I took a sip of beer. Dakota, and most of the guys around me, chugged theirs and began refilling red plastic cups.

Dakota continued making a short speech. "Everyone should be proud of their effort. A special shout-out to Sarah and my gorgeous girl Alexis, the heroes of the game." He bruised my lips with a kiss, like he owned me. Going too far again in this quest for authenticity. Trying too hard.

Sometimes I got the feeling Dakota was taking this charade too far to get back at Zach.

"And everyone who executed the *Friday Night Lights* Special to perfection," Dakota continued. "Coach Taylor would be proud. If he were real. So I'm going to have to be damn proud in his place." He lifted his glass and chugged down his second beer. At this rate, he was going to be hammered before the speeches were over.

Zach was still on his first beer.

"To our coaches—Dakota and Zach!" I yelled, lifting my glass.

More cheers. More drinking.

"To Dak—one hell of a leader and coach." Zach looked Dakota in the eye. A moment of understanding passed between them.

I swallowed a lump in my throat and chased it with a gulp of beer. When the toasts and the speeches ended, the party went into full swing. I hung out with Dakota, his arm slung over my shoulder as Zach, Seth, Paul and Dillon hung out in their own little clique off to the side, out of the main action. Because of Zach's role in the win and Dak's patronage, the Tau Psis may have tolerated them for the night. But they weren't brothers. They were still inferior.

The frat guys grabbed a football and Dakota and pulled him away from me onto the lawn to show off their football moves. By that time, Dakota and the guys were stinking drunk. They stumbled as they ran, tripped, and laughed like everything was hilarious.

I stood on the front porch, watching them swagger like drunken peacocks. Hot stuff.

Zach came up alongside me. Without looking, I knew it was him by the way my body tingled with desire. I was hot for him, and only him. I wanted to celebrate with Zach. Not Dakota. Not the Tau Psis.

"I was just heading out," he said. "Before I go, I wanted to congratulate you again. Great game tonight, pledge."

I turned to look at him. His eyes sparkled with heat.

"I'm going with you," I said.

"What?" He looked like he was trying not to grin.

I leaned up and whispered in his ear. "No one will miss me if I disappear for a while. I'm desperate to be with you...and celebrate."

I smiled like a flirt, a smile that reached my eyes and couldn't contain my desire. I wanted intimacy in every way. I wanted his thoughts on the intimate details of the game and the beauties of our strategy. I wanted to feel him next to me and in me. I wanted every part of him. "Meet me in the alley."

"Up against the rough brick of a wall again?" His whisper was hoarse and excited.

It revved me up even more. "Just meet me."

I watched as Zach said goodbye to a drunken, cocky, loud-mouthed Dakota. "Take care, number two," he said at the top of his lungs to Zach, like he was showing his supremacy. Like he couldn't help himself.

Remembering what I'd heard about the party where they'd fought, I held my breath as I waited for Zach's response.

"Good job, head coach." Zach slapped him on the back. "You earned the win."

I let my breath out. Everything was going to be okay.

A decent interval after Zach left, I slipped out unnoticed. Dakota was so wasted, and full of himself, that I highly doubted he would miss me all night. On my way out, I saw Sarah necking with one of the Tau Psis. And Katie sneak back to a room with another.

I slipped into the alley. Zach waited for me in the shadows. I threw myself into his arms and kissed him, breathless with desire for him as I took his hand. "Come on. I have a plan. The house will be empty. Everyone's here celebrating. If we run, I can be back before anyone notices I'm gone."

Zach ran his hand down my arm. "Your room or mine?"

"Neither. Too risky." I ran my hand through his hair. "Sarah and Katie's. They're both occupied, if you know what I mean." I skimmed my fingers over his cheek. "No one will charge into her room looking for her or me. She always leaves it unlocked. She won't mind if I use it."

Zach took my hand and started running, dragging me along. "What are you waiting for, pledge?"

We ran the entire way and slipped into the house through the houseboys' basement entrance. I was right. The house was deserted. Breathing hard and laughing, we sneaked to the second floor. Sarah and Katie's room was unlocked, just as I knew it would be.

We slid inside and closed the door, jumping and laughing at the sound of it clicking closed.

He pulled me into his arms. "Fantastic game, pledge. I was proud of you out there." He kissed my neck.

I was high with adrenaline from the win and the thrill of getting caught. Breathless from the run. Dirty from the exertion of the game. And totally desperate, wet, and ready for him.

"Thanks, coach. Now stop talking and show me how much." I grabbed his sweatshirt and T-shirt in one handful and pulled them up, going on my toes to lift them over his head.

He helped me out, pulling them off and tossing them aside as I ran my fingers over the hard planes of his chest. I licked his erect nipples, circling them with my tongue before latching on to suck them.

He gasped and held me against him. "You make me so hot and horny, pledge." He slid my boy shorts off while I unzipped his jeans and stepped out of my shorts and panties.

I had a sweatshirt on over my sports bra and boy shorts uniform. He pulled it off over my head and reached for my sports bra.

"Forget the bra. Just do me." I breathed the words into his ear, scooped my sweatshirt up, and tossed it on Sarah's bed.

He walked me back toward the bed, kissing my neck, whispering in my ear. "Your hair smells like grass and damp dirt. Your neck tastes salty. The smell of football is sexy as hell on you." He licked my neck. "I've never done a champion quarterback before."

I shivered. "Just score, will you."

"Anything you say. I'm going to make you sweat even more." He pushed me onto the bed.

I fell back onto my sweatshirt, on my back, wrapped my legs around him, and pulled him inside me.

"I love you," I whispered, still breathless, and rocked against him.

"I love you, too, QB." He held my gaze, poised at my opening.

"Don't tease me. Make a winning drive, QB1," I whispered back, egging him on. "And make it hard."

He drove in. I gasped and rocked back into him, locking my legs around him, pulling him in.

The twin bed rocked against the wall with each drive. Faster and faster. Harder and harder. The house was empty. Everyone would think either Sarah or Katie were entertaining. What did we care if anyone heard?

I was close, so close. "First and ten, do it again." I dug my fingers into his bare back.

He thrust so deeply, I gasped with the pleasure of it. "Score, score, score!"

The flimsy twin bed squeaked and groaned. One more thrust...

I inhaled, waiting for the waves to break through the incredible tightness building in me, longing for release. "Zach, Zach, Zach!"

This was true bliss.

The door burst open. "What the fuck is going on in here?"

CHAPTER TWENTY

Alexis

I screamed. "Get out!"

Dakota and Morgan stood in the doorway, with their arms supporting a stinking drunk Sarah.

Zach pulled out and reached for his jeans, shielding me as much as he could from their view. I wrapped my sweatshirt around my waist and reached for my boy shorts.

"I knew it!" Morgan screamed, slurring her words as her face contorted with jealous rage. "Douchebag! I'll make sure you're kicked out of the house now. You can't make a fool out of me."

Dakota's eyes were glassy. He was totally bombed and slow to understand. He looked stunned, like he was caught in the headlights and at a loss what to do and how to react. How angry should a betrayed decoy boy-friend get?

I hadn't even known Kelly was in the house until she came running and brushed past Dakota and Morgan. "What's going on here?"

Morgan swayed on her feet, obviously drunk, too. Just not as drunk as Sarah. Her eyes were bloodshot, highlighting the fury burning in them.

"I feel sick," Sarah said, and threw up all over the front of herself and on the floor.

Morgan ignored the stench and the mess. She stepped forward around it and stabbed her finger into Zach's chest. "How dare you! You refuse me for two years and ruin everything by screwing a pledge?" She tried to dodge around him and lunge for me.

Zach caught her by the arms. "I'm sorry, Morgs. This isn't about you."

"You have to go. I won't stand for the humiliation." She shook free of Zach's grasp. "You both have to go. Houseboys can't fuck the girls in the house. It's against the rules. Isn't that the excuse you've always given me?"

I was embarrassed for her.

Kelly looked uncomfortable, too. "Morgan, calm down. Let me handle this."

Dakota looked down like he just realized Sarah had vomited on his shoes. He turned green.

I thought for a minute he was going to upchuck, too. He stared at Zach. "You fucked up again, buddy."

I made a split-second decision. This was my fault. I wasn't going to give Dakota and me away as decoy phonies. I had to play along. "I'm sorry! I'm sorry, Dakota. This is all my fault."

He handed Sarah off to Kelly and turned.

"Don't leave," I said.

He walked away.

"Kick them out!" Morgan screamed in her drunken slur. "Both of them."

The stench in the room was overwhelming. Kelly looked pained and uncertain. "Zach, I think it's best if you go now. You'll have to clear out. About your job—"

"I'll be out by morning."

"No!" I screamed. "It's not his fault. It's mine. I went after him. I suggested this. It's all my fault. Kick me out, but don't fire Zach."

Zach ran his fingers through my hair. "It's okay, pledge. It will be okay."

I grabbed his arm, but he shook it off and brushed past Morgan and Kelly and out of the room.

I took off after him. Morgan blocked my way. She was red in the face as she grabbed my arm. "Bitch! I will see you punished. You'll never be Greek again." Her breath stank of stale beer.

That and the smell of the vomit made me gag. "Shut up! Just shut up!"

"Back off, Morgan." Kelly guided Sarah gingerly around the mess on the floor toward the bed. "We'll decide what to do about Alexis later. She's entitled to a fair hearing."

"Don't kick Zach out." Sarah's plea startled me. "Please. He's one of us." She fell back on the bed.

I shook free of Morgan's grip and ran after Zach. I was too late. He wasn't in the hall. When I ran downstairs, the front door was open. I checked his room. He was gone.

I texted him. *Don't leave me. We'll work it out. I need you. I love you.*

He texted back. *I love you, too. I just need to be alone right now and think.*

My mouth went dry as I remembered what he'd told me about the day in the woods. I'd just taken his new family and support system from him. What had I done?

Zach

I walked around campus, trying to get a grip and figure out what to do about this fucked-up situation. All of a sudden, Dak was the injured party here. I was the bad guy. Just when it looked like we were working things out. *Shit.*

As the cold air cleared my head, I knew I had to talk to Dak. I didn't know what the hell I was going to say to him. I had to say something. In person. Had to know whether we should come clean about the shitty decoy thing or let him be the injured party. Dak was all about his image. We'd just crapped all over it.

I headed for the Tau Psi house. The party was still going strong when I arrived. I stood in the back alley behind the house, steeling my courage. I would be lucky if the Tau Psis didn't beat the shit out of me before I even found Dak.

A girl staggered out the back door of the house, into the alley and the row of parked cars. The lighting was dim. As she passed beneath the streetlight, I recognized Morgan. What was she doing here? Why had she gone back to the party?

She walked unevenly, clearly plastered and barely able to walk. Just out of the circle of light, she collapsed in a heap behind a row of parked cars.

Shit. She wasn't my favorite person right now. But I couldn't leave her passed out in the cold in the alley. How many times had I rescued her ass after a drunken binge at a frat party?

Before I could move, Dak and a group of guys tumbled out of the house and piled into Dak's car, oblivious to Morgan. Dak slid into the driver's seat. The brake lights came on.

My pulse sped up. The car was parked with its nose to the building. There was only one direction Dak could go—backward. Over Morgan, who was directly in the path of his car. Collapsed in a heap in the dark where he couldn't see her.

I waved at him and yelled at him to stop. He didn't see or hear me. The car lights came on. The engine revved. The brake lights went off.

I was close enough. I didn't think. I raced to her, lunged for her, and grabbed Morgan beneath the arms. I swung her out of the way, tossing her clear of the car. I stood and raced to move out of the way.

"Zach! No!" I heard Alexis' scream just as Dak's car slammed into me, knocking the air out of me.

I hit the trunk. The force threw me backward. For a second I felt like I was flying. My head hit the asphalt pavement. I was on the ground, unable to move, smell-

ing exhaust and staring calmly at the wheels of Dak's
car as it backed toward me.

A crazy thought hit me: *This doesn't hurt at all.*

I saw my baby sister, all grown up and beautiful.
She smiled at me and I knew she'd forgiven me a long
time ago.

"I don't want to die," I told her.

More than ever, I wanted to live. Alexis made me
want to live.

Alexis

I ran to the car, waving and screaming. I pounded
on the door like a madwoman, begging Dakota to stop.
Trying to blot out images of Zach's head crushed beneath the tires. Dakota hit the brakes inches before
running over Zach.

Dakota opened his door. "What the fuck!"

"You're stinking drunk. You just hit Zach. Didn't
you see him? Shut the engine off."

Dakota turned the ignition off, jumped out of the
car, and staggered to the back, swearing.

I pulled my phone out of my pocket and fell to my
knees beside Zach, putting my hand on his chest. "He's
breathing."

Dakota fell on his knees beside me, shaking so badly
he could barely speak. "I've killed my best friend."

"He's alive. You haven't killed him!" Like saying it
could make it true. Tears spilled down my cheeks. My
fingers shook so badly I misdialed 911 twice before I
got it right.

The others guys had piled out of the car now and stood in a circle around us. A couple of them were on the phone to 911, too.

I tried to talk to the 911 dispatcher, but I was so upset I could barely make sense of their questions. One of the guys gently took the phone from me and took over, giving details and directions.

I heard him speaking, but it didn't make sense. It blurred into the background noise. Everything else became hazy as my focus narrowed to Zach and only Zach.

Blood ran out the back of Zach's head. I reached to cradle Zach's head in my lap.

One of the Tau Psis stopped me. I hadn't even been aware he was there. "What if his neck is hurt? What if you damage something by moving him? Wait for the paramedics."

"He's bleeding," I cried.

I took my sweatshirt off and put it over Zach, not feeling the cold as I pleaded with him. "Don't leave me. You promised. You promised you wouldn't." I begged Zach. I pleaded and bargained with God, promising him anything if he would just let Zach live and be himself again.

I didn't hear the sirens or see the flashing lights until they appeared at the end of the alley. Everything happened at once.

Morgan was still passed out. I had forgotten about her until a team of paramedics began examining her.

I felt a hand on my shoulder. "We'll take over from here."

Someone helped me up.

"Don't let him die! Don't let him die." I sobbed and sobbed.

Someone put his arm around me. "They'll take care of him. Let them do their job. Talk to me—what happened here?"

It took me a second to realize the guy was a cop.

I couldn't. I just couldn't. I shook my head, unable to speak. The cop put his arms around me as I soaked the front of his uniform with my tears.

I heard the paramedics talk as they loaded Morgan into an ambulance. They said something about pumping her stomach.

I hung on to the cop until I realized the paramedics were loading Zach in an ambulance, too. I tried to break away. He held me firm as I begged the medics. "He's my boyfriend. I have to go with him. Please."

"I'll drive you to the hospital." The cop led me toward a squad car.

I looked around for Dakota. He was handcuffed. They were loading him into a squad car. "No! Let him go. It was an accident. Please. Zach's his best friend."

The cop held me back. "They'll sort it out. Come on. Let's get to the hospital."

It seemed like the nightmare would never end. On the way to the hospital, I begged, pleaded, cried, and explained what had happened. How no one could have seen Morgan on the ground if they came out of the house and jumped in the car without going behind it. How Zach was trying to save her. I blubbered unintelligible stuff about Dakota.

The cop took my official statement while I waited in the hospital lobby. "One of the kids at the party said you're the driver's girlfriend? You told me the victim is your boyfriend."

"It's complicated," I said. "I'm friends with both of them." That, at least, was not a lie.

After I gave my story to the cops, I called my parents.

Mom picked up. "Alexis?" She sounded worried. And why shouldn't she be? I was calling her in the middle of the night. I knew I was going to scare her, but I needed to talk to her.

I started sobbing. "There's been an accident. Dakota ran over Zach."

Mom gasped. "Oh my God. Zach the houseboy? Is Dakota all right?"

In a way, her reaction was natural. Like everyone else, she thought I was with Dakota. But it made me mad all the same. "No, he's *not* all right. The cops hauled him off. But he'll figure a way out of the trouble." I paused as my anger built. "Aren't you going to ask about Zach? He's the one in emergency fighting for his life." I took a deep breath. "He's the one I love, Mom. The houseboy." There. It was out. And it felt good.

"But I thought...what happened with Dakota? You can still make it right with him."

I sighed, too frazzled and stressed to get into it now. "Don't. Just don't. I can't explain right now. I'm in love with Zach and always have been. You suspected when you visited. Now you know for sure. I was just with Dakota because everyone wanted me to be. Be as mad as you like. It won't change anything. I'm not going back to Dakota. I'm not giving Zach up." Why hadn't I had the courage to do this before?

"Baby, I'm sorry," Mom said.

I didn't know if she meant about Zach and Dakota, or about me being in love with Zach.

She popped back into mom mode. "What can I do? What do you need? I can hop on a plane and be there with you—"

"No." As much as I wanted to curl up and just be her little girl, I didn't need her with me being judgmental about Zach. Or trying to talk me out of him again. "Thanks, Mom. I can handle it."

"If you need me—"

"I'll call," I said.

"We'll talk about all this and sort things out later." She used that firm, motherly voice. The one that warned that she was going to lecture me and try to get me to comply with her wishes. Only now was not the right time. Not with what had happened. Not when I was so upset. "After things settle down."

In my opinion, there was nothing to talk about.

Before I could reply, Kelly, Em, and a bunch of other girls from the house burst through the emergency room doors.

Kelly spotted me. "Where is he? How's Zach? Heard anything about Morgan?"

Em rushed to me and threw her arms around me. She pulled the phone out of my hand and answered my mom's questions before hanging up. "You're in love with Zach, not Dakota, aren't you? I should have guessed. Why didn't you tell me?" Her eyes sparkled with understanding.

But I had no words.

She nodded like she understood and mercifully changed the subject. "Your mom sounded upset. Is it because of Zach?"

"It's because of everything." I couldn't talk about it. I broke up.

Em pulled me close and literally let me cry on her shoulder. She didn't ask questions or make judgments. She just let me bawl my eyes out and talk when I felt like it. Eventually, I would tell her everything. But right now, I just couldn't.

Em sat with me through the long night with her arm around me, handing me tissues and giving me hugs. Kelly was great. She begged nurses for news and got coffee.

It was touch and go. Zach had a head injury. His brain was swelling. They pumped Morgan's stomach and treated her for alcohol poisoning.

They moved Zach to ICU and let me sit with him for only a couple of minutes. Hooked up to the machines, he was pale, still, and looked like death. The sight of how bad he was scared me. I whispered in his ear, "Hang on and fight, Zach. You can't leave me now. Don't die on me. Please."

They had to pry me away from his bed.

No one tried to talk me into leaving the hospital. Everyone had heard by then about Dakota and Morgan walking in on us. Everyone but Em thought I was cheating on Dakota with Zach. I let them believe it. At that point, I didn't care what anyone thought.

Early in the morning, just before dawn, a striking woman burst into the waiting room. "Where's my son? My boy's been hurt. Oh, God, someone ran over my boy! Not again. Not *again*." Tears streamed down her white face.

A man had his arm around her. They both looked worried and terrible. They must have been driving all night. They obviously hadn't told her who'd been behind the wheel.

When I looked into her eyes, I saw Zach's. *He looks like her.* The realization hit me with the force of a physical blow. He looked like this woman who didn't love him. I hated her and felt sorry for her at the same time.

The nurse showed her and the apparent stepdad to Zach's room. It wasn't fair. I loved him and they wouldn't let me stay. She treated him like crap, like a throwaway, and got to sit with him.

Finally, a doctor came out. When we cornered him, he assured us Zach's condition was stable before he hurried away.

"That's a crap term, not a medical condition. Doctors use it for the press and outsiders as a way of getting off the hook without violating the patient's privacy," Em said. She had a lot of doctors in her family. "What does stable really mean? He isn't getting worse, that's what it means. That's all."

"I'm staying until they let me see him." There was no way I was leaving. I curled up on the hard chair in

the waiting room. Em curled up in the chair next to
me. I didn't remember falling asleep. I woke, startled,
to a gentle touch on my shoulder.

"Alexis?"

I looked up into the sympathetic eyes of the man
from last night, Zach's stepdad.

"I'm Terry. Terry Collins. Zach's stepdad."

I nodded and sat up, suddenly wide awake. "Zach—"

"He's fine. He's awake. The doctors say he's going to
be okay. He has a moderate head injury with some mild
swelling, but no cranial damage. They put him on diu-
retics to take the swelling down. The meds seem to be
working."

The news was so good, I could barely believe him.
"He's really going to be okay?" I wanted to collapse
with relief.

Beside me, Em popped awake. "What's happened?
What's going on?"

"Zach's awake!" I smiled at her with tears in my
eyes.

Terry smiled reassuringly at both of us. "He's
bruised, but nothing appears broken. He was very
lucky. The doctor stitched up his head. We're transferring him to a Seattle hospital to be evaluated by a neu-
rosurgeon. As a precaution. They're arranging for an
ambulance to transport him. They'll be moving him as
soon as the paperwork is done. He's asking for you.
He'd like to see you before he leaves."

"Go!" Em gave me a little shove. "I'll wait for you
here."

I combed my hair with my fingers as Terry showed me to Zach's room. I was a mess. I still had Zach's blood on my rumpled clothes. My mascara had run. My makeup was smudged. But none of that mattered. Nothing mattered but Zach. The head of his bed was elevated. He was sitting up, leaning back against it.

"Alexis!" His eyes lit up.

I raced to him and took his hand with tears standing in my eyes. I would have kissed him or hugged him, but frankly, I was afraid of hurting him. Of doing something I wasn't supposed to. Of giving him germs or something. I'd been taught a lesson in how fragile life was. I was still skittish.

His mom sat beside him on the far side of the bed, openly studying me.

I didn't know whether she liked what she saw or not. On the outside, I looked terrible. On the inside, I was soaring. I really didn't care what I looked like or whether she liked me or not.

"Mom, this is the girl I've told you about, Alexis."

She nodded. "Dawn Collins." She stood, still appraising me. Openly curious.

Zach nodded toward the door.

She took her cue. "I'll leave you two alone. Don't wear him out. He has a long trip ahead of him."

She stared right at me with a fierce, maternal look in her eyes that shocked me. Did she actually care about Zach? She chose now to go all mama bear on me? She left with a final backward glance at her son.

I stood beside Zach's bed, smiling at him, aching to touch him, still afraid to.

"Aren't you going to kiss me?" He tugged my hand, trying to pull me toward him.

"Are you strong enough?" I said.

"Are you going to kiss me with a passion that kills?" He smiled and tried to laugh, but winced in pain instead.

"Hardly. I'll be gentle." I kissed him. *Lightly.* And took his mom's chair, still warm from her body heat, beside his bed. I grabbed his hand again and squeezed. "You promised me you wouldn't do this. You promised you wouldn't sacrifice yourself."

"I wasn't trying to die this time, pledge." He spoke slowly and deliberately, as if he had to concentrate on every word. He was still pale. As he looked at me, it was evident his eyes had trouble focusing.

"I didn't think. Just reacted." He flashed a half-grin that any other day would pass for a half-assed attempt. But today, given the effort it took, it was as brilliant as any he'd ever given me.

His poor face was bruised. His head was shaved and bandaged where they'd stitched it. There were bags beneath his eyes. Scrapes and cuts on his face, arms, and hands. An IV in his arm. He'd never looked more wonderful to me.

I leaned close to him. "Is it over now? Have you finally paid the price? I can't believe you were willing to sacrifice your life. *For Morgan*, of all people."

"Worth it." He squeezed my hand. "How is she?"

"They pumped her stomach." I took a deep breath. "She's fine."

"AndDak?" He slurred the two words together. "He was arrested?"

I nodded. "At the scene."

Zach leaned back and closed his eyes, as if the effort of talking was wearing him out. "Drunk or not, not his fault. I'll tell the cops. He didn't see her. Couldn't. Not the way she was lying." His Adam's apple bobbed as he swallowed. "He would have killed her."

"Zach." I rubbed his arm. "Don't think about it."

"Glad he won't have that guilt." He opened his eyes. "It's over now, Alexis. From the minute I fell in love with you. You give me a reason to live."

Tears welled in my eyes. "I love you, too." I kissed him again, gently.

"I'm not made of glass." He gave me a weak grin. "Give me a real kiss."

I leaned down and kissed him again. "I love you *so* much."

He ran his fingers through my hair. "I have to go home. The doctors and my parents are transferring me to a hospital in Seattle. They've ordered an ambulance for me."

"Yeah. Terry told me." I stroked Zach's cheek.

"Dad's going to meet us in Seattle." He paused. "Sorry. It's like thinking through a fog. Seattle, I think that's what Mom said." He licked his dry lips.

"Water?" I poured him a glass and held it for him while he sipped from a straw.

"After they check me out, I'll have to recover at home," he said. "For a month? Something about head injuries and complications peaking at four weeks. I've had concussions before. I can handle it." He was tiring fast now. "My parents are fighting over who gets to have me while I recover. I become a hero and suddenly everyone wants me. It's crap."

"Zach—"

"It's like living in a parallel universe." He sighed. "I think we're going to be okay. We might even get along eventually."

"Are you dropping out?" I could barely ask.

"Dropping out? No way." He squeezed my hand. "I'll be out on medical leave until I've recovered. And they're sure I don't have any lasting effects."

I didn't want to, but I had to ask. "Will you come back to the house?"

"I think I'm kicked out, don't you?" He tried to smile again and winced.

"I'm sorry. We probably both are." I cared more about that than I ever thought possible. I didn't want to lose the sorority sisters I'd finally found.

He shrugged. "You'll be fine. The girls are more forgiving than you think. But they'll have to do something. You might get off with a warning."

"Maybe." I tried to sound upbeat. Being kicked out was still nothing in comparison to what had happened.

"It will work it out. Trust me. Mom and Dad are so shaken up right now, I could talk them into anything. Guilt is a bitch. I'm going to ask them for an apartment." He laughed and winced. "Shit, Alexis, I'm going to miss you. But I'll be back. As soon as I can. I promise."

CHAPTER TWENTY-ONE

Zach

Post-concussive syndrome, PCS, I had it in spades. Headaches. Dizziness. Fatigue. Irritability. Something the doctors called emotional lability, which meant I laughed and cried unexpectedly at inappropriate times. I couldn't concentrate. My memory was off. I couldn't remember the accident. At Mom's house, my twin brothers drove me crazy. I couldn't stand all their noise, noise, noise!

The doctors told me to stay off alcohol, that I probably had reduced tolerance to it.

Alexis called every day. We talked for hours, which kept me fairly sane. She wanted to come to Seattle and see me. I didn't want her seeing me like this or walking into the shit I was dealing with.

Mom put up with all my crap without complaining *much*. She and Terry and Dad argued about what was best for me. Dad wanted me to stay with him, where it was quiet. Mom fought him.

The first Saturday I was home, Terry took the twins out to give me some peace and quiet. Mom stayed with me, working in her office while I watched movies. I heard her talking to someone.

She came out a few minutes later, upset. "That was your dad. He wants you to come stay with him."

I laughed. Almost hysterically. And then I was crying, out-and-out sobbing my eyes out. Damn emotional lability.

"Zach?" Mom sat on the sofa next to me.

"Does he really want me?" I looked her in the eye. "Or are you just saying that so you can get rid of me? Is he fighting it? Making excuses for why he can't take me? Like he has my whole life?"

"You think I don't want you?" She looked almost startled. And guilty. Horribly guilty.

"I don't think. I *know*. You haven't wanted me since I ran over Lily. And you know the hell of it? I don't re-member it. Just like I don't remember Dak running over me. I don't remember *her*, Mom." I started crying again.

Mom got tears in her eyes. She put her arm around my shoulder. "I do. I remember every beautiful thing about her."

I looked at Mom. "You never talk about her. You don't have any pictures of her around."

She wiped a tear away. "It's too damned painful. For all of us. Oh, Zach, my boy, we thought it would be easier on you not to have a reminder of her around, because of what happened."

I wasn't buying her story. "But you blamed me. You blamed me for everything—"

"No!" She squeezed me harder and pulled me into a full hug, as she cried. "I blamed *me*. Don't you understand? *I* was in charge. I should have been there. I should have stopped you."

She took a ragged breath. "I blamed *me*."

We were both crying. She stroked my hair, giving me affection she'd never shown me before.

"I was twenty-five years old." She sounded stunned by how young she'd been. "Not that much older than you are now. Just a kid myself." She dabbed her eyes. "I didn't know how to handle things. I *couldn't* handle it. The pain was too great. I loved your dad, loved him with everything I had. We'd been together since high school. Shane was the love of my life. But *he* blamed me, accused me of being an unfit mother. And I believed him.

"And I blamed him back out of self-defense. Called him terrible things. Told him he was the bad parent. I blamed Shane for encouraging your fascination with driving. For letting you sit in his lap while he drove. For sitting with you in the car and letting you pretend to drive. For showing you how to put the car in gear.

"When Lily died, I lost the man I loved, too. I lost my rock. I lost *everything*."

I held Mom tightly, as if she was a lifeline, trying not to laugh inappropriately. This was definitely the wrong time—even with emotional lability, I seemed to know that. "You bounced me back and forth. *Neither* of you wanted me."

She sighed. "Neither of us could handle being parents. Neither of us felt adequate. I'm not proud of it, but we used you to hurt each other." She sobbed again. "We messed you up."

At least she didn't deny the obvious. They *had* bounced me back and forth. I gave her some credit for making a small admission of guilt.

"I'm not *so* screwed up," I said.

"No? Maybe not *so* much. No thanks to us." She tried to smile.

"You're fine with the twins. You love them." I couldn't let her completely off the hook.

"They were my fresh start." She stroked my hair.

I looked up at her through tears in my eyes. "Why didn't you get us help? *I* needed help. *We* needed help."

"Zach." Her voice broke. "You were only three. I had no idea you needed help. I had no idea *how* to get you help. I was too deep in hurt myself." She took a deep breath. "I'll get us help now. Family counseling to see if we can start building functional, healthy relationships with each other.

"I'll get us *all* help. You, me, Terry, the twins. I couldn't stand to lose you, any of you. I couldn't live through losing another child. This accident has brought me clarity. Made me see how selfish I've been. I love you, Zach."

"Dad, too? I have a lot to say to him. I'd like to hear his side."

Mom hugged me tightly. "I'm going to call him. Right now. And insist. We'll all get help. We'll be a family again. We *will.*"

If Morgan hadn't been a jealous bitch. If she hadn't gotten drunk. If Dak hadn't gotten drunk, too. If he hadn't run over me, I would have lost my family forever. Mom got us all into family counseling the following week. Even Dad. We had a long road ahead, but this was a start.

Slowly, over the weeks, my PCS symptoms lessened and gradually disappeared. I was lucky. PCS could last months or even years. I made another decision. I wasn't ready to get married yet. But I *was* ready to give Alexis a symbol of my commitment to her.

Alexis

Zach was coming back! Coming back to me. October had crawled into November. Time crept by excruciatingly slowly without him. The month he'd been gone felt like a year. A year of gossip, rumors, and accusations.

He was coming back to his own apartment. We could be together. Despite all the bad stuff, like the rumors about me and Dakota. Like being in deep trouble with my parents. Like having to make nice with Morgan. Everything was working out. Because I loved Zach, he was all that mattered.

After Zach left, I was called before a secret, closed-door meeting of the five-member standards board.

Victoria, the no-nonsense VP of the standards board was surprisingly gentle with me as she handed down my punishment. "We've all messed up and lost our heart to the wrong guy. I'm living proof of that." She gave me a gentle, encouraging smile. "Zach is hard to resist. Most of us have crushed on him a time or two." She choked up. "We love that guy."

She cleared her throat. "We love you, too. We want you to stay in the house. That said, forbidden love has consequences. In this case, we have to fine you for breaking house rules." She paused. "As Double Deltsies, we don't use punitive measures and fear for control. We like to think of discipline as corrective action with the goal of house harmony. You and Morgan have to find a way to get along. Understand?"

I did. But they'd given me an impossible task. Morgan hated me.

The powers that be also voted to make Zach a big brother, even though it was really rare for a Geed to be given the honor. The house voted to give him a special award for saving Morgan's life. They even offered to let him keep his job. He refused it, saying he wanted to date me without causing problems and he'd rather be a big brother than a houseboy now.

My parents were slowly coming to terms with me dating the houseboy. They were a little mollified when they found out how successful his parents were.

Zach didn't want to press charges against Dakota. But the cops had picked him up drunk. It wasn't Zach's decision. He swore out a statement in Dakota's defense.

Dakota and I had a decoy breakup. The Tau Psis would have ostracized me, except for Dakota. He stuck up for me and opened up to me like the true friends we were. No one could understand our friendship after all that had happened.

Zach texted me that he was on the outskirts of town. It was a cool, sunny November day. I put on a jacket and went outside to sit on the steps and wait for him.

When I saw his car turn up the street, my heart practically leaped out of my chest. The girls had left an open parking spot for him out front. I ran to him, bouncing I was so excited, as I waited for him to park.

He jumped out of the car and pulled me into his arms.

"You look good!" I said. He looked whole again. "I missed you so much!"

"You look totally hot." He kissed me. And kissed me. And kissed me as my sorority sisters gathered on the front steps of the house.

They held back like they were waiting for something.

Zach's eyes danced as he pulled something out of his pocket. "You've heard the rumors?"

I frowned, puzzled. "What rumors?"

"That I've been shopping for a promise ring." He opened a wooden jewelry box. A promise ring with a tiny diamond sparkled in the November sunshine. "So?"

"Yes! Yes!"

He took my hand and slid the ring on. I threw my arms around his neck and kissed him. As my sorority sisters swarmed around us, welcoming him back and congratulating us, Dakota drove up and jumped out of his car.

He joined the group and put his arm around Zach. "Welcome back, QB1!"

In that sparkling moment, everything was perfect.

Are you the kind of person who sits through all the credits at the movies, waiting and hoping for that surprise little scene at the end? Even though you might be the last person left in the theater and the staff is busily sweeping up popcorn around you? That scene is called a stinger. You don't always get one. When you do, score! It might be a funny scene or an outtake. Maybe it wraps up a small dangling thread. Or sets up a sequel. My husband *loves* them.

This book is technically a standalone, cliffhanger-free book. But it does have a stinger. If you love stingers, it's your lucky day! If you don't, read the next page at your own peril.

Gina

STINGER

Zach

There was still one thing I hadn't told Dak. One thing I'd done to him that he didn't know about. That made me disgusted with myself. I'd slept with Jordan. For revenge. Way before I met Alexis. The summer between high school and college. While Dak was still dating Jordan.

Then they broke up. I was relieved. Case closed. They weren't right for each other. Everyone could see that. Except them. Crap. Why did they have to get back together?

While I was home recovering, Jordan visited me and begged me not to tell Dak about it. Ever.

So maybe I shouldn't. But as I'd learned, it's hard to keep a secret forever.

Gina Robinson is the award-winning author of the contemporary new adult romances *Reckless Longing, Reckless Secrets,* and *Reckless Together* and the Agent Ex series of humorous romantic suspense novels. She's currently working on the next installment of the Switched at Marriage Series.

Connect with Gina Online:

My Website: http://www.ginarobinson.com/
Twitter: @ginamrobinson
Facebook: www.facebook.com/GinaRobinsonAuthor

www.ingramcontent.com/pod-product-compliance
Lightning Source LLC
Chambersburg PA
CBHW072126250626
47159CB00007B/2585